# Table of

Fake Ex-Wife to ...................................................................... 1
Chapter 1 ................................................................................. 3
Chapter 2 ............................................................................... 13
Chapter 3 ............................................................................... 23
Chapter 4 ............................................................................... 33
Chapter 5 ............................................................................... 43
Chapter 6 ............................................................................... 55
Chapter 7 ............................................................................... 63
Chapter 8 ............................................................................... 71
Chapter 9 ............................................................................... 79
Chapter 10 ............................................................................. 91
Chapter 11 ............................................................................. 99
Chapter 12 ........................................................................... 109
Chapter 13 ........................................................................... 119
Chapter 14 ........................................................................... 127
Chapter 15 ........................................................................... 133
Chapter 16 ........................................................................... 141
Chapter 17 ........................................................................... 151
Chapter 18 ........................................................................... 159
Chapter 19 ........................................................................... 167
Chapter 20 ........................................................................... 175
Chapter 21 ........................................................................... 183
Chapter 22 ........................................................................... 193
Chapter 23 ........................................................................... 203
Chapter 24 ........................................................................... 213
Chapter 25 ........................................................................... 221
Chapter 26 ........................................................................... 231
Chapter 27 ........................................................................... 241
Chapter 28 ........................................................................... 249
Chapter 29 ........................................................................... 257
Chapter 30 ........................................................................... 267

Chapter 31 ................................................................. 275
Chapter 32 ................................................................. 283
Epilogue ..................................................................... 291

# Fake Ex-Wife to Mr. Grumpy

Kathilee Riley

Published by Kathilee Riley, 2021.

# Fake Ex-Wife to Mr. Grumpy: Accidental Daddy Pregnancy

Enemies to Lovers, Surprise Baby Romance

Steamy Forbidden Novels
*Kathilee Riley*

Copyright © 2022
by Kathilee Riley
ALL RIGHTS RESERVED. No part of this publication may be reproduced, stored in a retrieval system, or transmitted, in any form or by any means, electronic, mechanical, photocopying, recording, or otherwise, without the prior written permission of Kathilee Riley.

Published
by Kathilee Riley

# Chapter 1

### Brooke

Adulthood is like looking both ways before you cross the street, but still getting hit by a huge semi, anyway. I'm having flashbacks of my teenage years, when all I wanted was to launch out on my own. Regret is like bile in my stomach right now. I'd give anything to be a kid again.

But that's a fantasy.

I'm a single mom with a seven-year-old and an advertising business. I can't run away from my responsibilities.

"I can save this. I'm not going to lose," I whisper, trying to breathe deeply without welcoming the lingering dust in the vents into my lungs. "This isn't my first time at the rodeo. I've survived this before, and I'll it again."

Despite my optimism, the bills still tremble in my hands, most of them stamped with PAST DUE in giant red letters. There's a positive side to this somewhere. Maybe this new wave of problems means I can handle more than I think I can. Because that's how things work, right? More shit gets added to our plates so we can find out how strong we are.

It's the timing of everything getting under my skin, that's all. My son, Ben grows like a weed and eats for two, which means my domestic bills are sky-high and will continue to climb as long as he's living under my roof. Add to the overhead costs for my small advertising business that are often more than I earn, and I'm about to lose my mind.

Having my own business was a great idea in theory. Now, I sometimes wonder if I made the right decision to leave my nine-to-five. I loved my job as a marketing rep, but I hated the toxic environment. Besides, I'm talented at what I do, so why should I use my skills to make someone else rich?

I sigh, dropping the stack of bills on the desk. "This is why. Kudos to me for taking the hardest possible path."

So what do I need to pay to make sure my house of cards stays stable? I've already taken the lowest rent office possible, but I'm two months behind on my business loan and if I don't make at least one month's payment, I'll lose my business. Which means I need more than the mom-and-pop stores that are on my client list.

I can't raise the prices for them, especially when they tip me in homemade goodies that my son loves. Oh no. Either way, something has to give.

Glancing at the old clock on the wall, I see it's already two-thirty. I have to run to the bank, make a payment on the loan then pick Ben up from school. I take a slow breath. I can do this. I know I can. I've dealt with worse.

With the new surge of positivity running through my veins, I hit the bank, make a payment on the loan which will give me another month to figure out a way to earn more profit, and cut my eyes at the drop in my checking account. There's no use dwelling on the problem. I'll find the right solution somehow.

The afternoon traffic slows me to a crawl; I turn up the radio, singing along to my favorite pop band to pass the time and keep my spirits up. Since Ben's father left, I tried my best to keep a smile for my son. It's not always easy, but I want to keep him sheltered for as long as I can.

I pull up to his school and expected, I'm one of the last parents to arrive. He's nowhere near our pickup stop and I suspect he got tired of waiting and went by the playground. True to form, he's there rocking on the swing. My heart sinks when I realize he's not alone.

Two bigger kids stand nearby, their mean expressions directed at him. I don't know what they're saying, but it's enough to make Ben's face red. As I get closer, the bigger kid stoops down and scoop a handful of pebbles. The smaller kid giggles as he hurls them at Ben. He ignores them, his gaze focused straight ahead. My heart swells with pride for that kind of strength.

But pride gives way to fury when the smaller kid moves forward to shove him roughly.

"Hey!" I scream, anger surging through me. "Leave him alone!"

The kids take off, laughing. Ben's face is even redder than before. He leaps from the swing before I reach him and walks past me with his head down. When we get to the car, he jerks open the door to sit in the front seat. His eyebrows bunch together, the way it does when he's pissed off.

"How was school, honey?"

"Fine." He looks out the window, like he always does after pick-up.

I sigh. "Ben, you can talk to me about anything, got it?"

"I know, mom," he mumbles.

"Do you want to talk about what those boys did just now?"

He shakes his head.

"Have they ever hurt you in anyway?"

Again, he shakes his head.

I want to push for more details, especially since it's not the first time they've bullied him like this. Making a mental note to talk to his principal, I pull away from the curb. Silence settles between us as I maneuver the car into the traffic that's getting thicker by the second. I hate rush hour traffic because of how demanding it is on the gas in my car. I can't afford to top up more than once a week.

"So... what did you learn in class today?" I ask Ben.

He shrugs.

# 6

I should know more of what's going on in my seven-year-old's mind, but he's a closed book right after school. Last time I asked him about it, he said he was processing what he learned. Like a computer.

I rub his messy blonde hair.

"We can get your hair cut soon; however you want."

"Even a mohawk?" he asks, the silent haze evaporating.

"A little one. You can only get the giant fan with dyed tips in high school," I tease.

He laughs and ends up telling me all about his day, how he learned plenty about volcanos and they're going through a book he doesn't like in his English class — then he stops. I glance at him and see a frustrated look in his eyes.

It's new ... well, maybe not new, but he never had that serious edge until he and I had a talk about his Dad not coming back home. I thought Greg was the one. He swept me off my feet during our freshman year in college, and we were at the altar with a baby on the way by the time I hit twenty. It was our happily ever after. I was sure of it. The way he doted on our wonderful son, how attentive he was with me, even when he was tired from work. I felt lucky, even when the issues began, because I knew we'd get through it. I could count on him. There was no way we would fail, I found love on my first try.

Wrong.

Two years ago, out of the blue, Greg decided this wasn't *his* happily ever after.

So he'd left, sending divorce papers exactly seven weeks later, and promising to take care of Ben. Still in shock, I'd signed the papers, unwilling to dive into a long divorce battle when he was surrendering custody to me. Despite his promise to be there for his son, we haven't seen Greg since the divorce. No calls. No texts. Only one card a year for Ben, on his birthday. Always on time, always short, and always with twenty-five dollars. Nothing more. Ben didn't even like the cards. He stared at the envelope every time, sighing like the weight of the world was on his shoulders before opening it.

I ruffle Ben's hair again. "What do you want for dinner? Pizza? Chicken nuggets? Spaghetti?"

"I like pizza," he says, hauling his backpack over his shoulder as we walk inside the small house I got to keep after the divorce.

We work on his homework together, eat pizza together, then he's through a shower and out like a light. A good kid who deserves the best. I'll always have a smile for him. I'll always make sure he knows how much he means to me. I'll always make sure he knows that life can be hard, but it's a choice to cave under the pressure. Pressure he shouldn't have to feel.

After I check on him a second time, I pull out the cookie dough ice cream and turn on a stand-up comedy show. There's nothing that a little humor and sweet treat can't fix. I let myself enjoy the hour-and-a-half-long special before getting in bed myself.

I need my brain at full capacity and I'm excited to escape into my dreams for a bit, but I can't sleep. I keep seeing those darn bills. Letting loose a deep sigh, I roll on my back and slide my arm under my head, thinking of when my problems first began. Thinking of who's at fault for making me struggle to stay in the black each month. In my mind's eye, I see him; tall, dark and confident, and I'm itching to slap that cocky smirk off his face.

Adrian Thorpe. A for asshole. T for thorn in my side.

My business had been doing well until he took over Horizon Communications, an advertising company he's turned into an industry giant within a few years. Now he has a ton of little outposts that all feed his company and he snaps up the clients and clears out small businesses like me. He's got the money, he's got the reputation, and he's steadily stealing my clients.

Every time we face off over clients, he comes out on top. It's either that panty-dropping smile or his ability to undercut my prices, but he's been snaking them away and ending up on top every single time.

Like he gets the luckiest rolls on the Monopoly board and even if he does hit someone else's property, he's got enough saved to do more than pay the fine – he can buy the place and make more.

Maybe I should see if I can get a glimpse of his business model. I can't cut prices, but I offer plenty of experience, plenty of kindness, and direct customer service without all the litigation and red tape. If I can find what separates us – other than the amount of money in his pockets and the price tag on his suits – I can come out on top. For once.

With no urge to sleep, I get out of bed and reach for my laptop. Coming out on top means spending time researching his company, finding out how his team approach clients, how they rope people away from little firms like mine, and take notes. I browse through the company pages for a while, coming to a pause when I see a photo of Adrian himself.

He's in his signature pose: arms crossed, with his hip resting on his desk, with a bookshelf and an amazing view of the city in the background. His steely-gray eyes are so intense, I find myself drawn in. Confidence is laced in every feature – his perfectly straight nose, his high cheek bones, his sharply cut and perfectly shaved jaw.

Adrian Thorpe is a caricature of perfection. Smile that doesn't show his teeth, so he looks approachable and relaxed despite the muscles that are obviously layered under his suit. His thick black hair perfectly organized, tie pin in place, cuff links showing, not even one bead of lint on his jacket.

If I didn't know better, I'd say some editor airbrushed him too. But I've seen the man in person, and he looks this perfect all the time.

I narrow my eyes at his photo. "I'd love to see you after a night of drinking when you're a rumpled mess."

He'd still be attractive. Ugh. I hate that he's so perfect. Yet, I can't deny that he fascinates me. He's a man who commits one hundred percent to his business while the press eagerly swirls around wondering who the next woman on his arm will be. No close friends, just employees who buzz about him like eager little bees hoping to get one second of notice.

And yet, this grumpy man has an empire built from dollars and demands while I have ... debt.

A mountain of debt that only grows under me.

I have friends, I have true joy in my life, I have skills and talent and promise, but all of it means nothing when I can't make ends meet and can't live the life I want.

Right now, I can't even afford to send Ben to the summer camp that's coming up in a few weeks, the one he's been so excited about. The thought sends my heart crashing to the floor of my stomach.

"Don't beat yourself up, Brooke. Go to sleep," I tell myself.

I shut my laptop, roll over again and stare at the clock, calculating how much sleep time I have left. Five hours. Four if you consider the fact that I'm still wide awake. I'm still restless because there's no solution to the problems I'm facing right now. I need to find a way out of this mess. Soon.

Maybe I can make plans to visit my best friend Stacy this weekend, or my parents. They might have some advice other than 'cut your losses and close down' or 'get a second job', neither of which are an option with Ben.

I want to give my son everything I had while growing up—and so much more. I want him to have every possible advantage in life. He should be able to explore every opportunity and really discover who he is without the burden of growing up too fast.

My breakthrough is coming. I don't know how, or when, but it's coming. All I need to do is keep working my ass off. Something will give soon enough.

IT'S SEVEN IN THE MORNING, and I'm feeling the effects of losing sleep last night. My eyes burn as I race through the house, gathering Ben's things for school. For some reason, Ben loves how hectic it is reach morning. He enjoys watching me throw together breakfast, race to get dressed and ready, how I narrate putting his lunch together with songs while he eats. I usually love that he enjoys 'rush hour' as I call it, but this morning not so much. Lack of sleep, my piling bills, Adrian 'Asshole' Thorpe are among the reasons I'm grumpy as hell. Still, I force a smile on my face and humor Ben. He remains upbeat until we get to school, and I see the two kids from yesterday smirking at us.

"Tell me the truth, Ben. Are they giving you problems?" I ask seriously. On top of everything else, I don't want to keep worrying about him.

"No, they're not. They're just ... sad." He shrugs. "For some reason they don't like my smile."

I gently turn his chin to face me. "You're sweet, honey, but if they try to hurt you again..."

His bright eyes are on me, eating up my words. I never rehearsed this conversation. If he runs to get help, they'll probably come back and bully him for that. If he tries to fight them—well, I've never seen my son fight.

"Don't give them the opportunity to get the best of you. Take the high ground," I suggest. "If it gets really bad, talk to a teacher."

He considers that and nods. "Have a good day, Mom."

"You too, Ben."

There's something nasty crawling over my spine telling me that neither of us is going to come home as happy as we want to, but life can be filled with surprises and if that means I get one new client and

Ben gets through another day without learning how cruel kids can be, it's a winner in my book.

When I get to my office, I note which bills I paid yesterday, and remove them from the pile of overdue letters. Then I get to work designing new Ads for the bakery in town, the new ceramics shop that launched a few weeks ago, and for my oldest client, a fast-food chain, I put together a whole ad package. Everything from booklets to billboards, bus ads, and opening signs along with the online marketing I love best.

I know how to cut down the prices, how to draw up something that translates into a memorable five second clip that will play on social media and create enough buzz to turn browsers into paying customers.

After spending seven hours working, I check my social media inboxes for any information on new clients, then my email, ending with the mailbox on my phone. Each time my cheeks cramp more trying to keep my smile in place. Disappointment courses through me when I find there's no new request for my services. It's pretty clear that I need to advertise for myself at this point because I'm getting nowhere fast.

Pushing the heel of my hand to my forehead, my strawberry blonde hair curtains my face as I give myself exactly five minutes to feel every bit of frustration, panic, and upset in me before rewarding myself with a snack and a good day with my son.

My mini-meltdown gets interrupted after two minutes by a phone call. Whispering a prayer, I quickly lift the cradle, a smile on my lips. "Goldfish Advertising, this is Brooke Dean, how may I help you?"

"Ma'am, we're calling from Brandy Elementary. Your son, Benjamin, has been in a fight and is waiting in the principal's office."

My heart deflates. Assuring the school secretary I'll be there in half an hour, I rub my temple, willing the incoming headache to go away. *It's just a hurdle, not a problem*, I tell myself before grabbing my things and running out the door.

# Chapter 2

### Adrian

I relax in the plush, high-back chair in the boardroom, my gaze moving around the room, directly meeting the eyes of my team. My accountant, Ariel blushes and looks away. I know what's on her mind. She had too much to drink during our office party a week ago, and I offered to take her home. In return, she offered to strip for me. Despite my protest, she took her clothes off, anyway. I beat a hasty retreat, hoping she was too drunk to remember it all the next morning. She wasn't. Now, she blushes whenever we are in the room together.

Now is not the time for that kind of thinking, though. This is a professional environment. Those thoughts will definitely get her in trouble if she doesn't curtail her emotions.

"Our client retention as of this quarter?" I ask clearly, my deep voice bouncing around the room.

The shuffling of papers greets me until my assistant Liz folds her hands. "Eighty-seven percent retention with a new client gain of five percent compared to last quarter."

"Thank you Ms. Masters." I nod to her.

"What is our profit versus last quarter?"

"We're up by twenty percent compared to this time last year and seven point five compared to last quarter," my finance manager Danny says, already bored no less than five minutes in.

"And our expansion?"

"Currently on pause."

My eyes flick to Mr. Amber, our regional manager. He must still be sporting that bruised ego from last month's meeting when I reminded him that jokes have no place in a meeting when money is being discussed. Business, unlike pleasure, has clear goals to be accomplished, an obvious margin of success, and laughing is out of line as far as I'm concerned. I've invested all of myself for the last three years and in those three years, this company, the managers, the shareholders, and the employees have profited from my business model.

"Why?" I demand.

"There are a limited number of businesses in the world and some already have advertising that works for them," he says, not backing down.

"And yet, what results have our clients seen since we've been involved? Peter?" I say, continuing to look at Mr. Amber.

"At the minimal side, a ten percent increase in revenue. On our top side, a fifty-two percent increase in revenue and customer growth," Peter replies obediently.

"I think those numbers speak for exactly how much we can help these other businesses. Too many are set in their ways and locked into complacency thinking that as long as they're doing well enough, they don't have a reason to do more."

Pushing to my feet, I set my hands on the table, knowing I have the full attention of everyone in the room. I own it, just like I own their asses – whether successful or failing.

"This company, before I stepped in, was a modest advertising firm that always made ends meet with profits left over. For the last three years, we have been number one. We've become a billion-dollar company and have shattered record after record with each passing year. That is what happens when there is someone pushing for more and not settling for the bare minimum."

Silence answers me.

I arch an eyebrow. "Would you rather potential clients settle for the bare minimum, Mr. Amber?"

"No. I'm just stating that expansion has risk. If we push too far and spread ourselves too thin, we may have problems."

"Then I think some of this wonderful profit margin can contribute to hiring the best and brightest to join our team, don't you think? And it can also go towards opening a new location in Seattle where we can handle both coasts and clear another barrier to success."

With that, he sits back and lets me outline the details for our expansion. Once the meeting is done, I dismiss everyone in the room. Ariel, however, lags behind to show me our latest reports, standing much closer than necessary. I'm twice her age, but I know when a woman wants me. I don't miss the flush on her cheeks and the way she twirls her hair around her fingers. It's obvious her blushes aren't from embarrassment of the night she took her clothes off, but the effects of a stupid crush on me.

"Ariel, the reports are perfect," I say sharply. "Thank you. Enjoy your weekend."

She opens her mouth to say something, but I'm already walking out of the conference room. I've learned my lesson about mixing business and pleasure. Letting Ariel in my bed would mean one of two options: she wants more, realizes she can't have it and throws a fit, potentially harming the synergy in the office, or she will let it distract her in the workplace and she'll spread rumors which will have others thinking I'm that easy to manipulate.

No matter how sweet and eager she is, it's a no. She should know, like any other woman who approaches me, I prefer to enjoy my time with a woman, then leave before any attachments can happen. It's safer that way for everyone involved.

Even if the lag between women leaves me feeling ... unfulfilled with too much time on my hands. But that's what working out at the gym and hanging at bars are for, anyway. Which is my normal weekend when there isn't something work related to attend to.

On Friday after work, I hit the gym, jogging from my house to get to the fitness center where I work out as long as possible, and on Saturday, after checking my unopened emails and making a few calls to my weekend team, I take a break on the couch in my living room that's barely used since I moved in three years ago. If someone should step in my apartment right now, they'd think I'd just moved in. It's sparse. There aren't any photos on the wall, no beautiful plant tucked in the corner, nothing that identifies me. It's just a modular couch, a pexi-glass center table and a huge, flat screen TV against the wall. I'd meant to hire an interior designer, but still haven't gotten around to it.

There's no reason to rush, anyway. No friends coming by to watch the game. No girlfriend cooking in the kitchen, asking me to come dance with her. Nothing but peace ... peace that I don't want today. I want distraction. I want fun. I want something to take my mind off this gap until I'm back in the office, doing what I do best.

"Fuck it," I huff, dragging on a casual button up and slacks.

I head to my favorite bar and Danielle, the owner and bartender, greets me with a once over and a frown.

"What?" I snap, hating the brief scrutiny. Danielle's eyes are the kind that seems to look right through me.

"For a big shot, you look like shit," she comments.

"Thanks."

"Maybe not shit," she amends while pouring me a whiskey sour. "More like fake."

"Fake?" I snort. "That's ridiculous."

"Come on, you seriously look like a ken doll. Perfect outfit, perfect face, hair all ... done. Look around, Adrian. You stand out like sore thumb."

I glance around the room, which is almost filled, pretty usual on a night like this. Patrons are all dressed similarly, jeans, t-shirt, crop tops for the ladies. All except for a tall, leggy blonde, whose green, glittery dress hugs all her delicious curves. She flicks her sapphire eyes up at me and smiles. I pretend I don't see her. I take the drink from Danielle. "Would you rather I look like a slob?"

"No." She flirts with another patron and gets their drink before returning to me. "I'm just saying, you might have a better chance of leaving with a girl and coming back with the same girl if you weren't so determined to hide all your flaws."

"Am I paying for a drink or a therapy session?"

She considers that and shrugs. "Aren't all bartenders therapists? We just deal with the less messy issues."

From the corner of my eye, the leggy blonde raises her hand and another drink appears in front of me. I hesitate. She's over eager, direct, definitely attractive enough that she could have just about any guy in here, but she's zero-ed in on me.

"Who's that girl?" I ask Danielle.

"Don't know. It's her first time in here. Not as big on talking as you are. But it's because you're sweet on me."

"I wonder why." I take another long drink.

"Because I get you drunk and don't want anything but your money, obviously." She glances at the girl again. "Going to throw out a fishing line? I bet she's the first bite."

I ignore her comment and finish my first drink quickly. The leggy blonde gets up as I accept the second drink, raising it to her across the bar. She takes the vacant seat by my side and I notice two things at once. She's sleek and beautiful, and she absolutely knows it.

She looks me over and laughs softly. "I can't try my usual moves on you."

"No?"

"You have this been-there-done-that, already-bought-the-T-shirt air about you. Like you wouldn't bat an eyelash if I dropped to my knees right now and sucked your cock."

I pause, my glass raised halfway to my lips as I stare at her, surprised. She smirks and orders another vodka soda. Danielle gives me a smile that says 'good luck'.

"I'm Adrian."

"Celine." She puts her hand in mine. "We're clearly the only two people here willing to get all dressed up to drink."

"Apparently, it's going out of fashion."

"You're not." She braces herself on my thigh. "You are the first person to catch my attention all week and I'm not an easy one to catch."

"Who says I'm the one who caught you?" I ask before taking a drink.

She bites her bottom lip, mischief and hunger glittering in her eyes. "Do you want to? I don't mind a game of chase as long as it ends the right way."

"What's the right way, then? I don't like disappointing beautiful women," I murmur, stroking along her jaw.

She leans forward, her hand sliding up my thigh, as if she's determined to feel my cock before she's willing to commit. "It has to end with you celebrating your win in bed … with me."

Direct is the best term for her. I'm not sure how much I like it. I prefer a coy woman who lets me have the lead. But after two more drinks, I can't deny that she's fine as fuck and my cock is more than happy to take over for the night.

Her mouth on mine in the elevator to my penthouse makes a better case than her words. She loops her arms around my neck and licks into my mouth hungrily, moaning softly when my tongue strokes hers. She tugs at my shirt, trying to get me undressed before we're even inside.

I pick her up, making her squeal and giggle as her shoes clunk to the floor, and toss her down in bed. "You didn't even run."

"Looks like I didn't need to." She pulls her dress over her head and leans back while licking her bottom lip.

Celine definitely knows what she wants and isn't afraid to get it. I can admire that. Not to mention she's gorgeous. A lithe body dressed in the most expensive lingerie I've ever seen. I rip it off her and flip her over, kissing along the back of her neck.

"Adrian," she moans as I rub over her pussy. "Please. No teasing. I need you to fuck me now."

"So demanding," I growl against her throat.

She pants and tries to touch me, but I order her to grab the sheets. "If you let go, I'll stop."

"I like orders," she pants.

I'm sure she'd agree to anything if she got a good, hard screwing as reward. I oblige and grab a condom, roll it on and keep rubbing my cock against her. She whimpers, begs, moans, all for me, but she never takes her hands from the sheets.

Thrusting into her, she makes a high pitched sound and rolls her body back against me. I hold her in place, keeping her wrists where I want them. I fuck her hard, pounding into her as she tries to talk dirty to me.

I let her talk, not bothering to answer when I can fuck her instead. She doesn't need my words. She's wet enough already.

She comes twice, her entire body tightening until I finally finish with her the third time. She slumps forward and makes a pleased sound in her throat. Rolling over, she eyes me while throwing her leg over my hip. "There goes round one."

"I have an early morning tomorrow," I say while untangling myself and leaving the bed.

She pouts. "Are you kicking me out? I thought we'd order some food, make love again, fall asleep together, then I could make breakfast for us."

I gape at her. This is not how one-night-stands work. We fuck—no making love— then she leaves. I'm nice enough to pay for the cab. That's the end of it. Maybe she'll get the picture with some space. After leaving her curled up in the middle of my bed, I get through a shower, hoping she'll get dressed and let herself out. It's not the first time a woman has wanted to linger after sex, but like the others, she'll read between the lines.

But when I come out, she's still there, still naked, now sitting on the edge of my bed, her long legs parted, showing me how ready she still is. A sneaky smile makes her eyes twinkle as she gets to her feet, reaching for my towel. I grab her wrist and push her hand away.

"Come on. You know how much fun I can be. Don't you want more?" she says with a pout.

"Get dressed. I'm calling you a cab," I say, reaching for my phone.

She grabs the phone from my hand and shakes her head. "Playing hard to get, are we?" she asks. "Isn't it a little too late for that?"

"Celine, it's time to go," I grit through my teeth.

Clicking her tongue, she trails her fingers down my chest, pressing herself against me. "Say it like you mean it," she whispers, reaching down to grab my cock.

I don't appreciate the deviation. I've made it clear she needs to leave, so why the fuck is she clinging to me? And why the fuck is my cock getting hard again?

"I'm serious, Celine. It's time to go."

"I don't want to go. Tonight was so good, wasn't it? Don't you want more of me? To get to know me? To fuck me again?" She licks her lips, fondling me again. "There's no denying it, Adrian."

Something tells me that saying no isn't my best option. There's something off about her. At least, that what my instincts are screaming right now. The wild look in her eyes is also a bad sign.

A rough sigh escapes my lips as she strokes down my chest. "Be honest, baby. You don't want me to leave, do you? You want me all to yourself, tonight and the rest of the weekend."

Fucking hell. At this point, I'll say anything to get her out of my apartment. "How about we take a rain check? We'll meet up again. Tonight, I do have to get to bed. I'll pay for your cab."

She breaks into a wide smile. "Promise?"

"Yes, I'll pay."

"No, that we'll meet up again. I'm not going anywhere without your number in my phone," she says seriously. "I've never had a night like this and I'm not going to miss out on you."

Jesus. What the hell did I get myself into?

I take her number instead, and she doesn't put her clothes on until I promise to call and set up a real date. Getting her to the door is another battle. She keeps trying to kiss me, to claw at me, to tease me and work her way back into my bed.

"Come on, once is nice, but twice is better." She bites her bottom lip.

Has she always sounded like a mewling cat?

I give her a patient smile. "It would be, but duty calls and I'm a slave to industry."

"But you're the boss. You can do whatever you like," she says, earning a raised brow from me. We didn't discuss our personal lives tonight.

"How do you know that?" I ask.

"Everyone knows who you are, Adrian Thorpe," she says with a smirk, clearly pleased with herself for surprising me.

My stomach churns. I try to keep my tone light as I usher her through the front door. "I'll call you."

"When?"

"Soon."

"And when is soon?" She puts a hand on her hip. "I hope you're not trying to give me the slip, Adrian. Celine Monroe always gets what she wants."

Am I going to have to carry her down to the cab and literally shove her in? "I will call you by Monday," I offer.

She jerks me down a little to kiss my cheek, whisper in my ear, "Next time you can use me however you want. Fuck all my holes over and over again. Then I'll taste myself on you before you come down my throat. I'll lick every inch of your body, and I mean it. Nothing's off limits for me. I'll show you all the things I'll do that no other woman would dream of."

Oh, fuck my life.

I manage to keep my face even considering those implications are beyond anything I'd enjoy. She walks out with a little bounce to her step. I shut the door and shake my head.

"There's always one bout of crazy a quarter." I brush off before deleting her number from my phone.

# Chapter 3

### Brooke

I wipe down the kitchen counter and glance at my son who's still moping in his chair. He still has a bruised eye from the fight, but the bloody nose healed up quickly. I open my mouth to say something to lift his spirits, but the buzzer for the dryer goes off and I work on doing laundry.

I should know what to say to him. He didn't start the fight. Those two horrid boys need to get involved in some kind of contact sport, so they have a way to get their anger out. Only my son got in trouble. Only my son got yelled at. Only my son was called a 'troubled kid'.

Ben is *not* troubled. He's dealing. He hasn't had a single issue since his dad left or even before then. Sure, he's a little quieter now, but that happens with kids. It's not like he's running around vandalizing walls and punching kids.

I fold one of his shirts and look at the blood spots still staining it. I'll have to get him a new one. It was his favorite. I set it to the side and load the washer. I'm moving the dried clothes to the basket when my phone rings.

Pulling it from my hip, I answer in the most chipper voice I can manage. "Goldfish Advertising, this is Brook Dean. How can I help you?"

"Ms. Dean. This is Mr. Hanson."

"Oh, Mr. Hanson. How did you like the material I sent over?" Mr. Hanson is the managing director of the fast-food chain who recently acquired my services. With the money earned from this gig,

I'll cover most of my past due debts. All I need is an approval from their end.

There's a slight hesitation on Mr. Hanson's end. "Yes, I did, Ms. Dean," he finally says.

"Great. I really think social media marketing will appeal to a wider audience."

"I appreciate that, but I ... I have to ask that we end our working relationship at this point." He keeps hesitating. "I'm sorry, Brooke. You've been wonderful, but I, regretfully, have to back out of this deal."

"What?" My stomach dips, and I grip the edge of the laundry basket. "Is there any kind of feedback you can leave? Did I do something wrong? Is Mrs. Hanson okay?" His wife has been going through chemo after being diagnosed with breast cancer last year.

Mr. Hanson clears his throat. "It's nothing on the personal side of things. Darla is doing well."

I sigh. "I'm glad to hear that. She's a fighter. If it's the cost—"

"In the effort of staying honest, I have gotten a more creative offer from Horizon. It will benefit the business on a greater scale."

The laundry basket falls from my hand. "I see," I whisper. The tears form in my eyes, and I furiously wipe them away.

"You run a wonderful service, Brooke. You are a true gem, but I can't let my own feelings factor into what's best for my business. Should anything change, you are my go-to girl."

"Thank you, Mr. Hanson. Give Darla my best." I force a smile to keep the liveliness in my voice. "I appreciate your honesty."

"Listen, I have a few colleagues who need advertising with budgets that work better for your business than Horizon. I'll refer you to them. You'll do right by them, I'm sure."

"Thank you." His promise should lighten my mood, but it doesn't. Promises don't pay the bills. I'm right back at square one.

Bidding him goodbye, I hang up. I finish moving the wet clothes to the dryer, turn it on, then stare at the clothes I still need to fold. I take a slow breath, but it's not enough. Fury courses through me. I'm mad enough to punch the wall, wishing it was Adrian Thorpe's face.

Wincing from the pain, I sink down against the dryer. I wrap my arms over my knees and cry, trying to keep quiet so Ben doesn't get distracted from his cartoons. I'm tired of losing. Sick of worrying about my bills, about my son's welfare. If things don't turn around soon, how will I take care of Ben?

As if my thoughts had conjured him, the pitter-patting of his feet grow louder, bringing him to me. I sniff and wipe my nose as he appears in the doorway. He sits next to me at once, locking his arm with mine. "You're really good at your job, Mommy."

"Thanks, Ben."

"I've seen your pictures. And you're so nice. People really like you." He rests his head against my shoulder. "Grandma says the harder a person works, the further they get. Sometimes life is hard though."

"Yeah." I rub his head. "Life is hard."

"But you work even harder and you never give up. Even if people are mean or if they say no." He slips under my arm and hugs me. "I'm proud of you, Mommy. You help people and you're going to get rewards from it."

I kiss the top of his head and hold him tightly, feeling a rush a pride. "When did you get to be so smart?"

He laughs. "I pay attention in school."

My son's a miracle. He's always been especially in tune with people's emotions, but there's this look in his eyes that make him look older than he is. Like he's lived a hundred lifetimes but doesn't always have the words to say what's on his mind. I brush my fingers through his hair and lift his chin.

"I love you to the moon and back, got it?"

"I love you too, Mommy."

"We're both in messes right now, aren't we? You at school and me at work."

"I like coming home to you though. We have fun. We get good food and play. That's worth a mess, right?"

"Right," I say, wiping at my eyes. "But we do need to talk about what happened at school, little man. What happened to your face? Was it those two big kids I saw?"

"Yeah," Ben mumbles, his face falling.

I pull him off the floor with me and guide him to the kitchen so we can cook together. He leans against the counter while I get the ingredients out for dinner.

"They said that Dad left us because he didn't like us," he murmurs suddenly, and I pause to look at him. "Because I was too boring and wimpy. They called you names."

I sigh. "Did you fight them?"

"Yeah." He nods, not ashamed. "Grandpa said I'm the man of the house and I have to be strong. But I don't know how to hit."

"Benjamin."

"Then they hit me. And kicked me. Mr. Ashley saw us and said I started it, and no one listened to me. Zack and Dylan said I was lying, and they were trying to be nice and I punched them," Ben grumbles.

Sighing, I pour the packet of pasta into the pot. "I don't want you coming home hurt, Ben. It makes me feel like I'm doing a bad job because I can't protect you."

"It's okay. You're not a superhero, Mommy. You make really good food though. I like when we have cupcakes," he says, grinning and flashing the hole his tooth is still trying to grow into. "Plus, I gotta get strong. That means losing sometimes."

"I might have to make you the brains of the operation. You just keep getting smarter." I poke his side, watching him squeal. "Just promise me, no more fights?"

"Even if they're being mean?"

"Yes. Mean people have to deal with themselves. We don't have to deal with them though. We get to forget about them as soon as we walk past them. And they're still stuck with their personalities and karma." I kiss his cheek.

"How do you know?"

"I've known a lot of mean people," I reply, shrugging. And I think of the Ad convention coming up next weekend that'll be filled with people, good and bad. It could save me too. I just have to make sure I dedicate my week to preparing for it.

"You do?" Ben asks.

I blink as I realize I didn't finish my thought. I nod at Ben, giving the chili another stir. He grabs some more cheese and puts it in. I rub his shoulder. "And I've known really good people. The good people always end up happier because they don't let the bad people keep them down for long. Okay?"

"Who's a good person?"

"You are. And Aunt Stacy, Grandma and Grandpa. You know Mr. Booker too, and his wife, who always give us cookies?" I beam. "There are a lot of good people in the world and you'll know they're good because they make your heart better. They make you smile until your cheeks hurt. They make you strong by supporting you."

He considers that.

"That's how you make me feel."

He beams. "You make me strong too, Mommy. Like I can take on the Decepticons and all the villains."

I pat his head and kiss his nose. "See, isn't that better than thinking about those mean boys or letting them make you feel bad?"

"Yes."

"And you don't have to defend me, honey. I do that all by myself. Don't let anyone ever let you feel like you aren't good enough at what you do. You're learning and growing. Whatever they say is a reflection on who they are."

He nods with understanding, his expression a litter brighter than before.

We eat dinner together while watching his favorite show – Transformers – then run around and play tag before relaxing with ice cream and a Disney musical. He pulls out the book we've been reading together and motions to the next chapter.

"Can we keep going?"

"Of course."

We read together, taking turns with each paragraph and writing down words he doesn't know until he's yawning and only has a few sprinkles left in his bowl. I pick him up, carry him to bed, turn on the nightlight before he can remind me and look at the stars and planets that show across his ceiling.

"You have the coolest room, little man."

"I have the coolest mom," he says. "I love you."

I tuck him in and kiss his forehead. "I love you too."

"To the moon and back?"

"To Jupiter and back."

He giggles and nods, soon settling into deep sleep.

Sleep comes easier tonight. Maybe it's the breakthrough I had with Ben, or the internal confidence that our lives will soon change for better. I don't know how or when, but I'm positive it will.

---

THERE'S SOMETHING ABOUT Sunday that makes it my favorite day of the week. It's not the fact that it's a day off from work—as a mom, there's no day off, especially with a seven-year-old who's filled with so much energy. I love hanging out with Ben, playing at the park, visiting Mr. and Mrs. Booker at their bakery for those tasty, discounted pastries, and riding our bikes around the neighborhood to burn off the calories. Then we'd get home and crash until it was time for dinner.

Today, however, we're doing things differently. The Ad convention is next weekend and I need to get prepared. After settling Ben down with a snack and a movie, I get some work done, make some business cards that I can print myself, so the ink doesn't go to waste.

The doorbell rings as the last card slides from the printer, and I approach the front door with a smile. Without checking the peephole I know it's Stacy, my best friend of twelve years, coming over with Thai food for dinner.

"You're a godsend, girl," I breathe with gratitude, taking the bag and kissing her cheek. "I've been so buried under work, I didn't have time to cook."

"Don't mention it, girl," she replies. "I've got you. Always."

There's no doubt in my mind she means every word. She's been holding me down since day one, especially after Greg left me. There were days when I wanted to hide under the covers, and she wouldn't let me. I'm glad she pushed me to get back on my feet. I don't know what I'd do without her.

A loud squeal brings me back, and I move away from Stacy just in time as Ben barrels into her. She lifts him on her side with a loud grunt, her thick, back-length dreadlocks swinging like a chandelier.

"Aunty Stacy!" Ben exclaims.

"My sweet potato!" Stacy returns, giving him a squeeze. "Did you grow a little taller overnight?"

"Yup! I did!" Ben replies, looking pleased with her comment.

She lets him down and he bounces around her, eagerly telling her about his week and talking almost nonstop until he has food in his mouth. For the next hour, he's the center of attention as he continues to tell Stacy about a new game that will be launched next week.

Finally, he slows down, and when he starts rubbing his eyes, I hustle him off to take a shower then tuck him into bed. Stacy gives me a knowing look as I drop beside her on the couch with a huge sigh.

"It's going to be okay, Brooke."

"Yeah..." I drag my fingers through my hair, dropping my head on the back of the couch. "I know."

She rubs my shoulder. "I can't believe Hanson dropped you for that shitty company, though. He'll regret it soon enough. Horizon can't possibly offer the personal touch you do."

"No, but they still have the edge. They offer more creative packages, have an entire team to manage the workload, and can afford to be more flexible with pricing," I point out. "But the Ad Convention is coming up next weekend. Ben can spend time with my parents and if I snag two big fish, I'll be okay."

"Okay isn't where you want to be, babe," Stacy says, pouring us both a glass of wine. "I love you, I do, and I believe in you, but okay means your office overhead gets covered with enough left over to pay the home bills. You want to be 'good' at bare minimum. Then you start saving for his college fund."

"Ben is going to be the top of his class, I know it. Colleges will be fighting to have him." I beam with pride. "He's going places."

"There's no doubt in my mind, Brooke." She lightly touches my shoulder. "How about I take some of your cards with me to work. I have plenty of coworkers who are trying to start side businesses and can't get themselves out there. It won't be huge projects, but it will help and word spreads."

"You're not actually telling me exposure works, right?" I arch an eyebrow.

"Obviously, they're going to pay you. I'd be offended and shame them if they push for a discount. I know how much we make." She tosses her locks over her shoulder.

"Alright. I'll give you some cards tomorrow. I appreciate it," I say with a smile. "I'll make you a shirt or something."

She laughs and we keep going back and forth about life until I'm better. Really and truly better. My best friend believes in me and she's a realist. My son has faith in me and he's not a dummy. I have to follow my own advice. Let problems and unexpected issues roll off my back like I'm a duck and keep moving forward rather than wallowing.

I'll be a successful business owner. I'll fall in love with the right person who can be a good husband and a good father. I'll support my son. The future is bright as long as I let it be, as long as I focus on my goals and shut out the rest of the noise.

Stacy hugs me as she leaves and taps my cheek. "You make my days better, Brooke. You know that? Your son wouldn't be half as amazing without you and a lot of people love you. Your time will come. I'm sure of it."

"You didn't go to a tarot reader or something, did you?"

"Nope. This is all me. Real as it gets. Trust your gut, woman. You're amazing. Own it," Stacy insists, sashaying to her car and getting in without a single worry for me or anything else.

I take a deep breath and focus on her words. I have to own who I am. I'm not going to sacrifice my sweetness or friendliness for some horrible cutthroat attitude to move forward in life. It would be a horrible lesson for Ben and it's not who I am. And I am more than good enough. So I'll work on perfecting what I can and attack the convention with positivity.

A smile opens more doors than a frown, after all. I'll prove it next weekend.

# Chapter 4

### Adrian

I hate meeting new people, but it's a necessary evil. I send out the best from my sales team to make friends while two hold down our stand. Wandering through the huge auditorium, I remember names long enough for a conversation, charm potential clients, especially women, and speak with rivals like they're equals, offering some advice that may help them hold their own.

They can't blame me if they fail. Only themselves, even if they don't want to admit it. Still, I hate all the handshakes, hate pretending to care about what they have to say. I care about the bottom line, nothing else. It bugs me that I'll be absent from the office for a full weekend.

Taking a deep breath, I prepare myself for another round of mix and mingling. I glance at the clock. One more hour, and I'm out of here.

My cell phone rings as the rep from a small cosmetic company approaches me. Arranging a smile, I stick up my index finger and she slows down with an understanding nod. Pulling the phone from my pocket, I resist the urge to roll my eyes as I see Celine's name on the screen. Silencing the phone, I tuck it back in my pocket. It's been three weeks since our one-night stand. Three weeks of regret. If only I could go back in time, back to that night at the bar...

That damned Celine is more than I bargained for. I should have listened to my gut and rejected her drink instead of taking the easy lay. I should have known my empty promise would have come back to bite me in the ass.

I deleted her number from my phone the same night she left my apartment, assuming my ghosting would make her forget me. It didn't. I'm still trying to find out how she got my personal number, but she's been calling non-stop since then. At first, I tried to be polite, to let her down gently, but for some reason, me answering the phone encouraged her. When she started showing up uninvited at my home and office, I decided to look her up and find the best way to cut ties.

Unfortunately, I found a bunch of articles that left me tugging my hair with regret. I should have been more careful. She's an out-of-control televangelist's daughter who's been kicked out of bars, has been the center of several broken marriages, and has made more apologies than any person her age should need to.

When I saw the sixteen Facebook statuses about her 'relationship' with me, I'd called her father. I told him in no uncertain terms that I was going to get the law involved if she didn't stop harassing me. The bastard had the gall to laugh. Even worse, he suggested I marry her, that she'd be a good wife.

"She needs someone with a firm hand to guide her," he said.

"She's an adult, not a child," I replied. "Besides, I'm not interested."

"I'll make it worth your while," he promised. "Name your price."

I scoff. "You're joking, right? Are you seriously selling your own daughter?"

"It's not selling if you're both in love, Adrian."

"I just told you; I'm not interested in Celine," I said through clenched teeth. This man is as crazy as his daughter.

"You'll change your mind when I tell you how much she's worth," he countered.

"Listen, Bishop Munroe, tell your daughter to stop calling me or I'll file a restraining order."

He sighed. "Fine, I'll handle it, but are you sure about this? How about I give you a few days to think about it? Celine is a little… wild, but she has a good heart. She needs a decent man in her life."

Code for him trying to pawn her off on me so he could get some peace. I'm not interested in that kind of game. "I'm sure."

A sudden squeeze on my shoulder brings me back to the present. I blink, turning to look down at Liz who's staring strangely at me.

"Are you okay, Mr. Thorpe?" she asks me.

I nod. "Miss Masters. How is the day going?" I glance around for the cosmetics rep, satisfied when I see her talking to a member from my team.

"We have six potential clients and I got news that we have secured a building for the expansion in Seattle. So far, all is going well," Liz replies, her expression tentative.

"And the issue I asked you to handle for me?"

She winces, and the hesitation is more pronounced. "It's difficult to prove harassment on an office line, but I'm working on it. So far, we haven't gotten any calls from Ms. Munroe this weekend, so I suppose that's the best we can hope for. The police advise that trying to dissuade her may be the best for a quick solution."

"Talking with her is impossible," I state clearly. "She refuses to walk away."

Her eyes shift to something behind me and she swallows. "Yes… I understand what you mean." She sticks out her chin. "Celine's here."

The hell? I scan the crowd and see her standing with a group of investors, sticking out like a sore thumb in a bright red pantsuit. God damn it. This fucking…. How can she not recognize a no when she's been slapped with different versions of it over and over again? It was last Wednesday that I let her down—again—after she followed me to my favorite cafe. I had just settled down with my coffee and my iPad, going through my work email when she showed up, dressed to the nines, but in a way that highlighted every asset she has. Without waiting for an invitation, she sat down and announced she'd planned a vacation for us and wanted my input as her boyfriend.

"We're not dating, Celine," I muttered, not wanting the other diners to hear. Thinking back, I probably should have. A little public embarrassment might be what she needs.

She shimmied her shoulders, her face filled with glee. "Aren't we? This feels like a date to me."

I leaned forward, giving her a direct stare. "We had a wonderful night together, but that's it. I don't have the time to commit to a relationship. I'm sorry if I led you on."

She'd waved her hand and continued talking as if I said nothing at all. After the café, she got even more aggressive. I found her in the lobby of my apartment last Saturday, wearing nothing but a trench coat. Not wanting to draw attention, I discreetly ushered her out. This morning, she sent a link to a list of wedding venues. One round of sex and the girl thinks we're engaged? It's inane. Stupid, beyond stupid.

And I'm over it. I dart around the auditorium, trying to avoid her. Liz helps me by distracting Celine twice. I don't appreciate her fucking with my business or getting in the way of me doing work.

Gino, a past client flags me down and introduces me to his colleague Marcus, a man who's got a profitable video game business but without the advertising he needs. We talk for a while, I give him my card, and we end up discussing packages available. The moment gets ruined when an arm slips into mine. I don't need to look. Celine's perfume floods my senses, filling me with dread.

"You're so sexy when you're hard at work," Celine purrs, stroking my jacket. She gives my potential client a disarming smile "You should absolutely hire my boyfriend's firm. He's the best."

Jesus Christ.

"Is that a fact?" Marcus asks.

"It is. There's a reason Horizon Communications has been dominating the industry for so long." She rubs my chest. "This man right here. Besides, he's so damn cute, how can you say no? I mean, look at him." She pats my cheek while ignoring my barely hidden glare. "This is the face of a man who knows how to make your company successful."

I force a smile. "Thank you, Celine, but totally unnecessary."

"Anything for my future husband, she presses against my side. "We're going to have the best wedding ever. Right, baby?"

Marcus gives me a smirk and raises my card. "I'll call you to finish this conversation, Adrian."

I try to plead with him with my eyes, but he walks away, checking out other booths. If this woman just cost me a good client, I'm going to do worse than make a scene. I pry my arm from her, but she keeps grinning.

"Did you miss me, baby?"

With my eyes on the crowd, I nudge her to a corner of the room and shoot her a sharp glare. "What the fuck are you doing?"

She stares up at me, confused for some reason. "I've missed you, baby. You're not being a good boyfriend. I'm all for the chase, but I don't like not getting a reward. I hate that you keep pushing me away." She puts her hand on her hip, her lower lip extending in a pout that would've been sexy if she were any other woman.

"We've had this conversation, Celine. We are not in a relationship. Get that through your head."

"You're so silly." Her expression clears and she goes on about how I'm the one, and how she's a perfect match for me.

I'm about to tear my hair out when a beautiful, curvy blonde moves into my line of sight. Brooke Dean. We've run into each other a few times over the years, since we both work in the same industry, but those meetings have never been pleasant. The woman hates me for reasons unknown. Frankly, I'm too busy to find out why, but I'm still curious. Her hateful demeanor seems to only be reserved for me. Looking at her now, she seems quite pleasant, laughing with the head of a rival firm.

She glances in my direction and the smile disappears, quickly replaced by a frown. I return one of my own and she cuts her eyes at me, returning to the conversation.

"Are you even listening to me?" Celine asks, but I ignore her, my eyes still on Brooke.

From what I hear, she's been having a tough time. I've had new clients regretfully say they'd left her firm because she didn't have the same options, but that she's absolutely lovely and it's a shame she doesn't have a team, that she's pure sunshine and happiness and the sweetest person they've ever met.

My most recent acquisition – Mr. Hanson said I should hire her. That she'd be an amazing part of the team and a real asset. It's something I've never considered. She's a rival. But right now, with her strawberry hair pulled half up, her khaki skirt and her navy button-up showing off her curves along with that glare ... she looks like heaven itself.

She glances my way again, her scowl even darker than before. Why do I get the feeling she'd bash my head in the wall if she got the chance? Goosebumps fill my arms. That woman can be scary if she needs to be.

Scary... Mhm.

"Adrian," Celine says, grabbing my arm.

Please, keep glaring like that, Ms. Dean. I need you.

I pull out of Celine's arm again and point at Brooke. "You see her?"

"Who, the frumpy woman glaring at us?" Celine snorts. "She's just jealous of our love, baby."

"She's my ex-wife. Our marriage ended pretty intensely and she's still crazy over me. In the bad way. Slashing tires, breaking windows, threats. She's pretty messed up over the breakup and she'll go after any woman I'm seen with."

Celine leans her head to the side. "Then why isn't she coming over here?"

"We're in a crowded auditorium, Celine. She won't make a scene. But I can't rule out the parking lot. I don't want her to try attacking when you leave."

She shrugs. "I'm not scared of her. Besides, you'll protect me."

"Honey." I hate the word. "This is me trying to protect you. What kind of man would I be if I let you get hurt?"

Her eyes go all starry and she rubs herself on me like a needy cat, clinging to me with her damn manicured claws as she smudges her blush all over my shirt. "I knew you loved me. I can handle that brat."

"That's what my last girlfriend said."

Her thin eyebrows lift. "What do you mean?"

"She beat my last girlfriend to a pulp after keying her car and slashing her tires."

Celine swallows, wariness filling her face. "Really?"

"Really. She makes herself look sane around people, but trust me, she's the kind of crazy that scares *me*, and I'm not easily scared."

But I can tell Celine is still on the fence. I clear my throat. I have to sell this, have to make sure it works properly so I can get this spoiled psycho off my arm and out of my life. I adjust my tie. "I better go talk to her to keep you safe."

"Are you sure? Maybe we should head to your apartment and forget all about her. She can't follow us there, can she?"

"Let me do this," I say, patting her head since that's the most I can make myself commit to. Especially since I'm already about to swallow my pride when it comes to a wanna-be rival. I head across the room as Brooke walks away.

Perfect.

I hurry behind her. For such a short woman, her legs are quite limber. She gets to the elevator before I catch up to her. After pressing the button, the doors open for her at once. Shit. Rushing forward, I stick my hand inside and haul her out. She gasps and shoves against me.

"Are you crazy! Get your hands off me, asshole!"

Damn. The venom in her voice leaves me speechless for a beat. What the hell did I do to her?

Whatever it is, I'll find out soon enough. I'll do my best to fix it, too. Right now, I'm focused on getting this annoying problem off my hands.

"I need you," I say, and her head jerks back, surprise filling her face. "Your help, that's what I need," I clarify.

She folds her arms on her chest, the action forcing me to drop my gaze to her cleavage. The shirt covers most of her, but with the top button being undone, it gives me a glimpse of her voluptuous breasts.

"My eyes are up here, you pervert," she snaps.

I meet her furious glare with a somber expression. I'm not in the position to be anything but humble right now.

"What do you need me for?"

"Pretend to be my ex-wife for the day. Dial up the crazy, scream at me all you want, vent every frustration out of your system. You can even slap me, I don't care," I say in a rush.

She blinks those dark eyes at me, looks over my face for a beat shorter than normal, then shakes her head. "After everything you've done to tank my business, you're still trying to run it in the ground, aren't you?"

"What have I done to tank your business?"

She pokes my chest. "You stole my clients."

"I didn't steal your clients. They came to me. Why would I destroy your business when I'm already doing well?"

She shrugs. "Beats me. I can't explain the motives of a power-hungry dick."

From the corner of my eye, I catch Celine watching us. I take Brooke's arm and she pulls away, then shoves at my chest. Perfect. It would have been even more perfect if she'd slapped my face.

"If you touch me again, I swear to God, I'll cut your balls off," she snaps, pointing in my face. Now, leave me the hell alone."

Edging around me, I manage to catch her again, pulling her around a corner into a hallway. "Ms. Dean. I need you to discourage a woman who's stalking me. If you play it up, she'll leave me alone for good. It's just for one day."

"An important day. Do you see all the potential clients around? I can't afford that kind of drama."

"Then outside!" I lose a tiny measure of control, my voice rising. Brooke shoots me a, oh-no-you-didn't glare and I spread my arms to block her from leaving. "I'll get her to come outside. You can do whatever it takes to scare her away. Please."

I realize I just said please, a word I haven't uttered in years and to this woman who already wants to slap me for stealing so many clients away. Oh well. Can't be helped. Time is of the essence. I can't wait around for her to decide then tell me to fuck off, banishing me back to Celine's clutches.

Fuck my pride for the moment. I need this noose around my neck gone.

"No." She flicks me off and tries to leave again.

I push her back against the wall, blocking her exit with my arm. She glances from my arm, to me, and folds her arms over her chest. "You caging me in isn't going to change my answer. Mr. Thorpe. You have women on the payroll, get one to help you."

*Too late*, I think. Liz would have done it without question. Would have been perfect, but all I could see was Brooke glaring at me and I acted without thinking. Shame on me, but I *need* this right now.

"Name your price," I challenge. "Everyone has one. What's yours? Money? A whole department working under you at my agency? What?"

She takes a slow breath and I expect another fuck off, but I realize she's thinking. Her eyes flick up and she actually mouths something to herself as she considers what I'm saying and considers her options. I look around to make sure that Celine hasn't managed to find us, but damn, this is cutting it close and I need her to think faster. A hell of a lot faster if this is going to happen today, like I need it to.

One more moment with Celine trailing after me, calling me, showing up where I least expect her is going to make me go gray, is going to ruin my sleep, is going to steadily break me down until things start to slip.

One day from Ms. Dean will fix it all which means she literally has my balls in her hand. I grit my teeth. "I need an answer, Ms. Dean. Quickly."

# Chapter 5

### Brooke

Here I was, about to leave this mess of an attempt early since no one even took a card after talking with me, but now Mr. Thorpe – billionaire without a single issue – is begging for my help. Actually, I think I could tell him to beg and he would.

It's a nice change. Just like making him wait. Even though I'm more inclined to help whatever poor girl got involved with him, I could use this opportunity to help my company and, more importantly, I can get some innocent little thing to move on and away from this womanizing S.O.B.

"Name your price," he murmurs, his husky tone washing over me, distracting me. I ignore the swirl of desire in my stomach. I'm not attracted to him. *I'm not.*

"Everyone has one, Ms. Dean. What's yours? Money? A whole department working under you at my agency? What?"

It takes a second for the rest of his words to sink in. I shake my head, making space for my common sense. Yes, I have a price. A huge one. *Let's see how well you handle this request.* I fold my arms on my chest, narrowing my eyes at him. "I want in on the advertising contract you've got with Uncle Sal's B-B-Q."

"What?" He stares at me for a long moment. "That's impossible."

"Impossible, Mr. Thorpe? Or is your problem not as serious as you let on?" I arch an eyebrow. "I can still walk away. Can you?"

He hisses a low string of curses between his lips that nearly makes me blush, words that would get his mouth washed out with soap in my home. He opens those steely eyes and fixes them on me. Despite how much I want to hate him, that look reaches down to my soul and spreads electricity across my system.

The photos online don't do him justice. None of them really captured the power of his gorgeous body. I see that now. But he's breathless, bothered, a little ruffled, and it makes him so ... real. So ... I kick myself in the butt internally for thinking about anything but this deal.

When he still doesn't reply, I attempt to get past him. His powerful body blocks my way. "Yes or no, Mr. Thorpe? I don't have time to waste."

"Yes." He nearly cuts me off.

"I want it in writing," I clarify. "Your lawyers could get you out of a verbal agreement."

Groaning, he watches as I pull a notebook from my handbag. He scrawls across it, rips the paper out and hands it to me. I take a picture and read it out loud for both of us.

"I, Adrian W. Thorpe, agree to a true 50-50 partnership with Ms. Brooke Dean of Goldfish Advertising in the contract of Uncle Sal's B-B-Q chain in perpetuity of the contract held by Horizon Communications."

Then his signature. Perfect. I take a slow breath before signing as well. "Make sure the legal team gets this."

He stuffs it in his pocket. "Now, are we going to do this?"

"Sure, but ... If she's really determined, you realize it will take more than one day, right?"

"How about we cross that bridge if we get there?"

Adrian shifts aside, making my exit clear, and the electricity between us fizzles out. When he adjusts his suit and motions for me to leave, like it's a business meeting, there goes the rest of that warmth. He's the kind of man that likes to be in control of everything and can't have a single thing fall away without his say so.

Unyielding, cold, cutthroat. The kind of entrepreneur I refuse to be and normally the kind I'd refuse to work with. But this deal is going to help me stay afloat. It will give me at least a year where I can work on getting new clients, maybe even poach some of his. Who knows? I can even hire another person on my team.

Adrian's footsteps sound behind me, making me aware that he's still with me. For a big guy, he sure moves lightly. We approach the end of the hallway and he moves closer, flooding me with his scent. It makes me want to slow down, to have his arms around me so I can lose myself in him, even for a minute.

Ugh. I must be high. Or drunk. Or I really need to get laid.

Yup. That's it. I need to put myself out there again, meet a great guy and screw this insane longing from my head.

As we approach the area where the elevators are, I stop and turn to Adrian. "Okay. When are we having this showdown you hired me to do?"

Adrian glances behind me and groans. "Now," he hisses. "Pretend you're mad at me."

Oh, this requires no acting on my part, Mr. Thorpe. I've been mad at you for so long.

From the corner of my eye, I spot a tall, stunning blonde coming toward us. She's perfect. Definitely his type. Definitely crazy-looking, too. It's right there in her big, blue eyes.

"Miss Dean," he hisses again.

Falling into character, I twist and give him a slap on his cheek. His eyes widen and he moves his hand to the injured spot. Yup, he didn't see that coming. I'm also glad the lobby isn't crowded right now.

"How dare you ignore me for some other bitch, Adrian? I don't care what the stupid law says. You'll always be my husband. We are attached for life, you hear me?"

"I told you, Brooke. We're done. I'm free to date anyone I want. Get that through your head."

"We'll never be done. Until death do us part, remember? If you ever try to move on, I'll make you and that bitch's life a living hell."

The elevator doors open and Adrian steps in, surprising me. *Where the hell is he going?* Staying in character, I follow him. "Don't you walk away from me, Adrian! I'm not done with you!"

I keep shouting at him, waving my arms around until the doors close. A smirk teases his lips. "You are actually better than I thought."

"For some reason, I don't think that's a compliment," I reply.

"It is."

"In other words, I make a pretty convincing deranged ex, is that it?"

He rubs his jaw, covering his mouth for a second, but I still catch the glint in his eyes. I guess business sharks aren't allowed to smile. What a shame. I bet he has a nice one.

No! I need to banish those thoughts right here and now. Even if he's tall, gorgeous, muscular, and has a deep velvety voice that's like a caress, he is absolutely not the kind of man I want in my life.

I want someone reliable, someone who wants and enjoys commitment, someone who I can build with, can trust my son with, who can be the example instead a flashing neon sign of where to go wrong.

"Is that it?" I ask Adrian as the doors open to the ground floor. "It's seems like a short job for such huge payout. Not that I'm complaining," I hastily add.

"Not exactly," he replies. "I'd bet my last dollar she's on her way down now."

"So, I'm just going to keep yelling at you for having another woman in your life?"

"Keep being possessive. You can slap me, kick my car tires, scream and curse. Just leave my balls alone and don't bruise my face," he says.

I blink at him. "That's a really low bar."

"I don't have a script ready, apologies," he says, no humor, nothing but a simple statement.

When we get outside, I shove him. He nods once. "Go, she's watching."

"You are the worst kind of human!" I yell, shoving him again. "A true piece of work."

"I'm allowed to have a life, Brooke."

"Really? Really? After you wasted all my years, after I handled all your problems, used my time and love to nurse you into the man you are today, some other woman gets to have you? How the hell is that fair?" I demand.

"It's over. You have to let it go. Let me go."

Growling, I kick his shin.

"There is no reason to get aggressive," he hisses.

"There is plenty of reason to be aggressive!" I screech. "You got the best years of my life and what did I get? Huh? A divorce that destroyed me? Insults and no friends left after I spent forever defending you and your stupid choices!"

My eyes haze over as I think of Greg. "Not even anything to numb the pain! Just you leaving us! Promising me happily ever after, a good life, joy and safety and everything else, just to take it away without a reason or an excuse and give it to someone else?"

"Brooke," Adrian whispers, his voice softening and confusion filling his face.

"I don't think so. You don't get to be happy when I have to work for every little goddamn thing I have. You don't get to move on to someone else and give them the best of you when I got the worst. I will ruin any relationship and make sure every woman you think about moving on with sees the very worst in you – the real you. Not this perfect fucking picture!"

He grabs my shoulders. "Hey."

"You promised me everything!" I feel the tears coming. "So why does some other women get to have it? Because you think she's shiny and new? You'll toss her to the side like me and if you don't, I'll make sure that she sees you for who you are before you can rip her heart and throw away the pieces you selfish, deadbeat, son-of-a-bitch!"

I punch his stomach, the action not fazing him one bit, but it makes me better, anyway. I haven't experienced this much anger in years. It was always sadness. It was always pain, never this white hot, destructive energy that ripped through me.

"She left. Calm down." He takes my arms, but his grip is soft.

I struggle from his hold, but he lifts my chin. Seeing his face erases my memories of Greg. I blink a few times and exhale shakily.

"You pack a pretty solid punch, Ms. Dean."

"Sorry."

"Don't worry about it. That worked perfectly."

"If she wants you, she'll be back." I breathe, pushing my hair back from my face, rubbing the tension from my neck.

"Are you okay?"

I push his hand away. "I'm fine."

"You don't seem like it."

"I said I'm fine," I snap. "Why do you care, anyway?"

"Ms. Dean—"

"We're colleagues, not friends. You don't need to pretend you're concerned about me."

"I am concerned. Is this how passionate you are about everything? I can't have someone so volatile on my team."

I roll my eyes. "Of course. You only care about the bottom line, don't you? We're not on a team, Adrian—I'm sorry—Mr. Thorpe. We can handle business over email and make sure the client gets the best. I have no illusions. We're too different to work long term. We'd fight for real if we were locked in a room together for even an hour. Don't worry."

Without waiting for his response, I storm to my car, willing myself to calm with thoughts of seeing Ben soon. I dab at my eyes and straighten my shoulders. I won a war today and got what was left from the divorce out of my system. That's what's important, not Adrian's emotionless response. I'm doing better than I was four hours ago.

"Brooke."

I whip around and find Adrian right behind me, so close our bodies almost touch. I nearly drop my keys. "What do you want?"

"I'm protecting my investment. That was real rage, not fake. Something I should know about?" He arches an eyebrow.

If he was anyone else, I'd believe he actually cared. A part of me wants to believe he'd be willing to have a conversation, to step in, maybe even to take care of me ... but that's the hopeless romantic talking, not my normally sensible self. And that romantic mindset is clearly still struggling over losing Greg despite how long it was.

So I'm not going to give Adrian, who doesn't care, who isn't anything but polish an inch when it comes to my life.

"Ask any divorced woman and you'll get a story. It's fine. I'll be back to my sunny self soon enough. Now, if that's all, I have to go. I have a date planned."

He frowns. "Oh? On the same day as a conference? That's rather irresponsible. I only work with partners who take their business seriously, Ms. Dean."

"Stop fishing for reasons to back out of the deal. My son comes first, always."

His face softens. "You have a son." I wasn't a question, but I nod anyway.

"Sorry that we can't be all as business focused as you," I huff. "I have an actual life that's not built on pretend games and one-night-stands. You'll have my full attention at work and that's all you need to worry about."

He offers me his hand. "Good. I look forward to our partnership."

I shake his hand. "Don't forget to get that piece of paper to your team. I want everything documented."

Smirking, Adrian squeezes my hand a little. "I will see you on Monday, Ms. Dean. I'm looking forward to it."

Our hands stay like that for a moment. He's so big, so warm, and he seems genuine about looking forward to working with me, which isn't what I'd expect. A man like him usually has no faith in women, especially in the workplace, right?

No. I'm not going to read into this. I'm not going to examine the angles until I can turn him into someone with a good heart and decent intentions. So I drag my hand from his.

I nod. "Enjoy the rest of the conference, Mr. Thorpe."

"Enjoy your date, Ms. Dean."

I feel his eyes on me as I get in my car, but I force myself not to look at him. The flutters in my stomach are still there, triggering thoughts that makes me want to press my thighs together. I turn up the radio enough to drown them out, but they keep swirling, rippling around me like they're not sure what to settle on. My emotions are in a tailspin. I'm happy that I got the deal with Adrian. I'm terrified of the anger that ripped out of me, the real dreadful things that I pushed down for so long.

And I'm confused at my reaction to Adrian and his to me.

Why do I want to believe there might actually be something of a decent man in there? Especially when I know his reputation and his image. No. Logically, I know better. He just used me to get rid a clingy girlfriend by lying instead of taking the direct path. That's a billboard for commitment problems.

How can he be so committed to clients and not be committed in his personal life?

No. No. These are questions I don't need to ask. What I need to do, is get home to my son and my parents, join in on dinner and forget about everything but the positive. So I spend the drive singing to the radio and relishing in the huge win I just got.

I'll be able to pay every past due bill and get in the black for the first time in months. I'm looking forward to enjoying the fruits of my labor. I don't know; buy some decent clothes for Ben, treat myself to a manicure... we deserve this break. I hope there's plenty more to come.

Mom rushes out of their bungalow as I pull up to the driveway, her red hair a wild frizzy mess. She has paint all over her clothes which means my son is covered in paint too. But I love the mess and the huge smile on her face. This is what coming home should be like.

"Any luck today?" she asks me before I turn the engine off. I understand the anxiety. She knows how much I've been banking on today being a success.

"Even better than I expected," I reply, and her face lights up. "I'll tell you all about it inside."

Ben barrels into me as I enter the foyer. I scoop him up and kiss his cheek as he hugs me. "Did you do a good job today, Mom?"

"I did a *great* job." I show him the gold star sticker he gave me this morning with his photo of me having plenty of people offering me money. "This was my good luck charm. Thank you for making it for me."

He hugs me again. "You're welcome, Mom."

My dad comes down the stairs as Ben drags me to the dinner table. "Did you tackle the world today? Destroy the competition?"

"I got a huge deal, one I'm positive will lead to more," I reply, sitting down to join in on dinner. "Wow, this looks great. My day was boring compared to this meal alone. I want to hear all about your day!"

My son dives in, eagerly talking about how he and grandma painted the back porch in a mural of plants. Dad tells me that he's never seen a better drawing of a lizard and that my Ben is a great artist who should be paid for his work.

My mom helps me with dishes after dinner and rubs my back between drying dishes. "How are things going, really? You seem a little reserved for someone who had such a huge breakthrough today."

Typical Mom. She always sees right through me. "With this new client, I'll be all caught up by the end of the month. But I may have taken a deal with the devil."

Her brows lift. "Who's the devil?"

"Horizon Communications." No need to mention Adrian's name. It will only raise more questions from Mom, ones I won't want to answer.

"That company who's been stealing your clients? Are you sure, Brooke? They are sharks, honey. They'll eat you alive."

I shake my head. "Not this time, Mom. I know what they are capable of, but I'm not going in blind. This deal will be worth the trouble."

"Depends on the deal," she murmurs. "Just don't forget about work life balance, okay honey? Making money is great, but making memories is better. It does more for happiness than any wallet size can."

"I know, Mom," I assure, my gaze shifting over to where Dad and Ben are playing Jenga. I beam as Ben manages to get another block out without toppling the tower. "A job is a job. Life is what happens around that. I wouldn't give up my time with Ben for anything."

"You're a good mom. I just worry." She sighs. "It's hard being a single mom, but remember, we're always here to help. We love having Ben around." She pinches my cheek. "We'd love more excuses to have *you* around."

"We could start doing dinner once a week, but definitely not on Thursdays. Ben has tutoring for English and Math and it's hard to get everything in order. He wants to start soccer too, and go to camp."

"He wants to do everything, like another spunky kid I remember having." She hugs me. "No one is ever prepared for life, honey. I'm glad you're still you."

My smile softens as we join in on game night, switching to checkers, then go-fish and Uno, playing until my dad has to pull out his glasses to focus on the numbers. Ben helps eagerly, promising not to cheat.

Soon, I notice my parents are exhausted. I take Ben's hand and ask if he'd hate going home with me instead of spending the night. He shakes his head, excited to practice reading together and for the pancake party I promised him in the morning.

Work can wait until Monday. Right now, I need a chance to enjoy the little things, the things that actually make life worth it.

Out of everything that happened today, I realized exactly how important the little moments are. If I don't treasure them, I'll become as jaded and narrow minded as Adrian. And I'm sure, absolutely sure, that I want to be nothing like him.

Once we get the meeting done, we can work from our separate offices and spare each other insufferable time together. We'll survive, and Ben and me ... we'll be better than we've been in years.

## Chapter 6

### Adrian

It seems my fake ex-wife has had some effect, after all. Since Brooke's 'meltdown' a few days ago, I'd only gotten one text message from Celine, saying she needed to really think about things before moving forward with me after seeing how possessive my ex is. She's not sure if she can handle my baggage. I'm glad I chose Brooke. Liz would have had trouble raising her voice at me.

Brooke was perfect. Though, I'm still mildly concerned about that amount of anger in a woman so many consider a ray of sunshine. However, she got the job done and nothing else matters.

There's a thought that's been lingering in my head. I don't remember the last time a woman wasn't flattered by my attention or the last time a business associate didn't eagerly bend over to keep my favor. She's something else entirely, someone I may have to keep an eye on ... but potentially someone I could respect.

As I usually do on Mondays, I have my walk-through in each department of my company, verifying employees are working and not wasting company time with personal affairs, then I return to my office for follow-up meetings with my new clients. I had to inform Salvador from Sal's B-B-Q that his contract is being split with a brand new think tank and of course, by the end of the conversation he was thrilled. Why wouldn't he be? No one has a bad thing to say about the intriguing Brooke Dean.

"Mr. Thorpe." Liz stops me on my way from the coffee machine, the office phone pressed to her chest. "There is a woman at the front and security is requesting clearance."

"Name?"

Liz puts her ear to the phone, asks the same question, then looks to me. "Brooke Dean? She said you'd be expecting her. Did you pick up another stalker this weekend?" she adds with a smirk.

"Not at all. She's my new partner on Sal's BBQ account. Which reminds me, I need his file."

She eyes me carefully, like she's not sure she can trust me and says something to the security officer before hanging up and handing me Sal's file. She follows me into my office, sits and crosses her legs, tablet ready for notes.

"Has the legal department made you aware of the change to this account?" I ask.

"No." She pushes her dark hair back. "Please, share."

"Brooke Dean and I are splitting the workload fifty-fifty. I will get the necessary bank details so we can include her, as she and our agency will be splitting the profits evenly."

Liz arches an eyebrow. I wait for her to say something and she does the same. I appreciate Liz greatly. She shows a dedication and control that few in our industry have. She is all about work and couldn't care less about my looks. I'm not her type, something she made clear when I propositioned her after having too much to drink one evening. Granted, that was my first week on the job, back before my 'no fraternizing with the staff' rule. I'm glad she turned me down, because I needed her on my team. I need her even more now.

Although, she can be maddeningly persistent when it comes to business agreements she doesn't approve of. The silent treatment is one of her tactics. She continues to watch me, not moving, not blinking, until I sigh.

"Do you have a comment, Ms. Masters?"

"Mr. Thorpe, do you really think you needed to offer a fifty-fifty contract without review by the heads of departments?"

"I did."

"Would you care to explain?"

"Miss Dean provided me a unique service and, based on necessity to our business continuing to move forward smoothly, she was able to name her price. Mr. Amber should be happy she didn't ask for her own department here or he'd be on the street today," I say as I start up my computer. "Any follow up questions?"

"Does this concern the unfortunate girl who has been trying to secure you as her husband?"

"It does."

"I see." Liz goes back to the normal morning check list. "Ms. Dean will be coming up shortly and I will be sure to take your ... contract." She holds it up with obvious disapproval, "to the legal department so we can move forward as you promised."

"I appreciate your diligence."

"Of course you do." She stands. "If you need anything else—"

"I could use a shoulder rub," I tease without a smirk, just to see what she'll do.

She taps a few things on her tablet. "I've booked you a massage tomorrow night. Enjoy."

With that she walks out. Liz, again, is a gift. If all my employees were as disciplined as she is, I wouldn't have a single problem. Shame. Perhaps I should hold them all to her standards and incentivize it with a raise. Or perhaps we should have some staffing changes again. Fall in line or fall out of business.

A good motto.

I glance at the time and see it's already 8:45. Brooke is either not used to early mornings or she has different hours than I'm used to. The usual workday starts at eight and I'll have to make sure she's aware of that going forward. Among other things.

Liz guides her into my office, but I see Liz pause as she opens the glass door. Brooke finishes saying something, and Liz actually smiles, and not the professional "a client may see me" smile. No, this one is full; her eyes squinting, teeth showing, in a soft happiness I haven't seen on her.

I can still hear Liz's soft giggle when Brooke comes in. Her hair is in a full bun on the top of her head and rather than a suit, she's wearing a deep blue button-up shirt with a white skirt that hugs her hips and brushes the top of her knees, complete with black flats. Interesting decision.

"Ms. Dean."

"Mr. Thorpe." She offers me a muffin. "Good morning."

I stare at the muffin on my desk for a beat too long since she laughs. "I promise, it's not poisoned. It's from a local bakery I work with. An apology for my meltdown on Saturday."

"What is there to apologize for? You completed your end of the deal." I set the muffin at the far side of the desk. "Now I'm completing mine. Did you bring your banking information so we can get you entered into the system as a consultant?"

She digs through her purse for a moment, commenting on how she can 'never find anything', then provides me a voided check. Disorganized. That's a strike against her. I scan it into the system, make sure Liz gets it, and shred the check before moving on.

I show her the file and she eagerly takes it, reading and taking notes on a piece of paper. I start to talk, but she holds her hand up. "One thing at a time please. I'm behind and I'd like a chance to form my own opinions before you share yours."

"I don't see the point in that. I'll make copies of the file, though it will not leave this building and you can review it after I explain the plan we have in place."

She puts her leg over her knee and I see her foot bouncing, but she doesn't raise her head. She takes notes, but I continue anyway. "Since Sal's B-B-Q is a very well known name, I don't think we need billboards, but there are some booklets coming out about the city where we can include a few pictures of the food and dining area as well as a review or two. We can also put some adds on YouTube and cable TV so that way we have full saturation of ...."

She hasn't looked up once.

"Miss Dean are you listening to me?"

"You have a pleasant voice," she murmurs before shutting the folder and flashing a smile that makes me feel ... something I don't want to acknowledge. She's wearing a genuine smile, but it bothers me because I *know* she hasn't been listening. "Now, what were you saying?"

"I don't make a habit of repeating myself," I mumble.

"I warned you," she replies, none of the warmth dropping from her face. "I can't read and listen at the same time, and I'm not simply getting paid to go along with your plan."

"My plan has already been approved by the client."

"And the client will get the best. We think differently so maybe we can give them an even more 'creative' package than you usually do."

I pinch the bridge of my nose. "I should have just paid you off."

"I wouldn't have accepted. I don't like the idea of being paid for doing nothing." She makes a few notes as I consider the fact she would have turned down a lump sum of money so easily. "So, you were saying – the points you were aiming for?"

Repeating myself always makes ideas sound less viable. But I do it and watch as she takes notes. The entire time, I curse myself. If only I could have been blessed with a second Liz instead of this ... unflinchingly sweet and composed woman who pushes buttons by refusing to allow me to take the lead.

Haven't I proven that I know what I'm doing? That I'm damn good at it too? Considering Horizon has been taking her clients, we should simply go with my plan and she can do some of the work, prove herself, and we can move on. She can get the YouTube Ads going if she wants to, then we can work from our separate offices.

But that's not a damn option if she doesn't fall in line. If I can't trust her not to run off on her own agenda, then we'll be conducting all our work right here, together, where I can babysit her as needed.

She taps her pen against her lips, drawing my attention. Her dark eyes go up to the lights and I see flecks of gold there. As she thinks, I take the chance to look her over again. Brooke is a beautiful woman. Very beautiful, actually. The wisps of strawberry hair around her face, the freckles across her nose, the birthmark above her right eyebrow, gentle chin, the elegant curve of her neck to her shoulders.

She reminds me of a Hollywood actress from the forties. I bet she'd look lovely in that makeup, but she's wearing the bare minimum, if any. If she had been at the bar instead of Celine, I wouldn't have overlooked her. I doubt she would have let me take her home, but damn, I have a feeling that she would have ruined my night with conversation.

Brooke would have made me chase her.

"Have you considered having influencers go to Sal's and post on their social media feeds? A lot of people watch the short videos they post. It's more grabbing than photos and ads. It will pull in the younger crowd and spread the word further while limiting costs on our end. We can simply reimburse them for their meal, perhaps even give them a discount code."

I blink at her. I have no clue what she's talking about and it bothers me that I don't. She continues anyway. "There's also podcast and music apps that have plenty of Ads. Getting a few people to endorse the restaurant with a discount code – even if it's a free drink with a meal could be an option to appeal to people across the board."

"Interesting." I rub my jaw. Why have none of my *very* well paid employees offered ideas like these – that match with the times and seem to come so naturally to Brooke.

"Like I said, it's low cost on our part as well. If Sal is open to providing free drinks to those who mention the podcast, that would also limit his cost because drinks are the cheapest thing – by far – but the word 'free' draws people in, even if it means they buy a full meal. Then they tell their friends, or post on social media and it grows organically."

Brooke makes a note with a question mark and looks to me from under her thick lashes. "Mr. Thorpe?"

"I will look into these options," I say through my teeth. I also plan on looking into my team because no one has ever brought up these options and based on what Brooke is saying, it should be fucking common knowledge. "It seems like a potentially viable addition."

"You use a lot of words to say, 'I like your idea, Brooke,'" she teases. "You're welcome, Adrian."

"Any other questions or concerns about the file?" I ignore her comment.

"Nope. It's pretty clear cut. I'm planning on actually going to the restaurant today so I can get a good sense of the meals. And my son is a great judge of food. Another option, an old school option, is encouraging word of mouth. Maybe Sal or each manager could offer punch cards. With so many recommendations the first person gets a free item."

"You're filled with ideas."

"They've been waiting for a chance to be put to use." Her eyes go from warm to searing hot as she turns a furious gaze on me. "If someone would stop stealing my clients."

"Perhaps you should pitch better and not blame others for your failings."

"Perhaps *you* should stop undercutting prices for lackluster packages." She stands and drops the folder on my desk. "I'll take care of the ideas I've put forth after I visit Sal today."

"I didn't dismiss you," I bark. "Sit."

She takes a slow breath, turns, and folds her arms on her chest. That damn smile is still in place. "I'm not a dog, and I'm certainly not *your* dog. Speak to me like a person and I'd be more inclined to consider doing what you *ask*."

What the fuck does this girl think we're doing here? And since when does *anyone* disobey me? Brooke is going to learn it's my way or the highway really quickly if I have anything to say about it.

# Chapter 7

### Brooke

I give Adrian three seconds to revise his request, counting it down against my hip. When I fold my last finger in, I move to the door and hear a huff. "Brooke, please sit so we can continue our conversation."

"Look at that, a please. Someone aced kindergarten." I turn and sit again, crossing my legs.

He looks like he's in physical pain, and I can't say I don't enjoy it a little. His assistant had warned me he's demanding and expects things done his way, a warning I appreciated, but it's not the kind of work relationship I tolerate. I don't expect him to commit to our partnership given his very public trend with women, but I expect respect.

"I would like to make something clear as we jump into this partnership," I say, folding my hands over my knee. When he motions for me to continue, I take a slow breath. "We are equals here. We both have something to bring to the table. I won't bark orders at you, and I won't accept any orders barked at me."

Adrian stands and sits on his desk, getting close enough that my hand brushes his thigh. Just a simple brush and I can tell how firm it is. I imagine that's how firm he is all over. His broad shoulders, flat stomach... my eyes drop lower, and my cheeks heat. Huffing a soft breath, I return my attention to his face.

Focus, Brooke. Focus.

"We are doing each other favors, Brooke, nothing more," he continues, clearly unaware of my distraction.

His voice is that same warm velvet and there's something calculated in his eyes. He presses both hands to the desk and grips, making the cut muscle of his arms stand out more. He looks me over with enough time that it's like a caress.

Still, his jaw is tight. "Remember who has the billion dollar company."

"Remember who has the reputation for commitment and kindness." I stand again and tap his chest. Yes, it's firm. And delicious, and ... no. Adrian is the kind of guy girls fall for when they give an inch. I won't. "I'm going to do my in-person research. We can have another meeting over phone or email tomorrow."

He tries again to catch me, but I know better. Those crooning words are nicer than the over-exaggerated sentences where he can sit on the fence, but he'll do whatever he wants to get what he wants – obedience, compliance, or a woman.

At least he only wants me to be compliant.

I count myself lucky. On my way out, I wave to Liz and she blinks a few times in surprise before nodding to me. "It was a pleasure, Ms. Dean."

"Please, call me Brooke."

She smiles gently and her stern face softens. She's gorgeous. Shame she's stuck in this office. She could make Adrian a lot more money with that smile and her intelligence. A fight for another day.

After going by the office and making sure my clients are set, sending out some more of my own advertising, and making a file for Sal's B-B-Q, I feel better. Time away from Adrian is going to make all the difference. It's how I'm going to keep my head on straight and avoid him.

"I don't want an easy lay," I tell myself. "I don't want another Greg."

It's true. It's honest. But Greg barely holds a candle to Adrian in the looks department, or the raw sex-appeal. However, Greg was able to commit for almost seven years and I have a feeling that holding Adrian in place for seven days would be an enormous feat.

Brushing that thought to the side, I look at the time and decide I don't need a lunch break if I visit my newest client.

I head over to Sal's first restaurant. The big, bubbly owner is even nicer in person. After taking me on a tour of the restaurant and running through the menu, he sits and talk with me while I dig into his most popular meal. It's delicious; true comfort food that makes me feel amazing without having a ball of grease weighing me down. It's absolutely messy and the two of us laugh over the fact I need a bib, but he actually talks with me.

"Honestly, technology is my biggest issue. I can't wrap my head around the fancy software and gadgets. Throw me into a kitchen and I'll work my magic, give me one of those smart phones and I have to ask my daughter how to check my email."

"How old is your daughter?"

"Twenty-three." He shows me the wallpaper on his phone. It's a photo of him and a beautiful, dark-haired girl standing on her toes to kiss his cheek. "Her mom and I divorced, but she's my whole world. She recently graduated from business school and is hard at work to help me expand the company. Without her, I'd just have this one shop."

Smiling, I show him a picture of my son. "I understand completely. Everything I do is to support my Ben. He's such a good kid and I want to give him the brightest possible future, the best possible life."

We continue talking about our kids and by the time I leave, I've already outlined me and Adrian's plan for getting him more exposure online. He loves it and promises to give me a discount whenever I bring my son in. I offer him a handshake, but he goes for the hug. His big body dwarfs me, making me safe, and I can't stop myself from welcoming it.

"You're a wonderful man, Sal. Your customers are lucky. You should raffle off a hug every month."

He does a full belly laugh and holds me up another ten minutes with conversation, then he walks me out, adamant at making sure I get to my car safely. "I was worried when Mr. Thorpe said he was testing out a new think-tank with my business, but now I'm glad he did."

"You are?"

"You've got that old touch, Brooke. You make me feel like I'm more than some check to cash. I'm a person. You're the first person from any Ad agency to actually come in and try my food and talk to me. It's nice."

"It's been nice for me too," I assure, checking the time. "Well, I have a meal to bring to a very lucky boy."

"Don't let me hold you up!"

The smile stays on my face all the way on my drive to pick up Ben. He immediately sniffs the air as he gets in the car. "You brought food?"

"I met with a client today and the food was so good, I bought some for you." I motion to my shirt. "I made a mess."

He scarfs the whole thing down before we get home, trying to tell me about his day while his mouth is full of the pulled pork sandwich. After cleaning up, we dive into homework. As we're going over multiplication, my phone rings.

I pick it up without thinking. "Brooke Dean's Goldfish Advertising, how can I help you?"

"Miss Dean. It's after seven and you answered your phone. I'm impressed," Adrian says.

"To what do I owe the pleasure of a phone call?" I say, before correcting Ben on some math. "Write it out, little man. Remember how?"

Ben nods and does it next to the problem before correcting his answer. I ruffle his hair. "Good job. That's the best way to check your work until you memorize them."

"Am I interrupting?" Adrian continues.

"Just homework time. What's up?"

"You spent a long time with Sal today," he replies.

"Yes, I did. He's wonderful man. It will be a pleasure working with him."

"He called to let me know how much he appreciated meeting with you," Adrian says, voice unreadable. "He also said that you suggested introducing his daughter to the social media marketing you brought to my attention."

"And?" I tap the remaining question of the four times table for Ben to do before we move on to five since it will be easier.

"He's very pleased. Well done," Adrian says.

"Glad to hear it."

"But, Brooke..." His voice now carries and edge that makes me frown.

"Yes?"

"You messed up by not running your suggestion by me. Don't overstep again or there will be consequences." With that he hangs up.

I stare at the phone open-mouthed, not sure if I am more shocked or pissed off. Such nerve! We're partners. I'm not his goddamn employee. I don't need his approval for anything.

Right?

Ugh. I don't know how partnerships work, so even if I'm wrong, he could have been gentler with his response to me. Rolling my eyes, I put the issue behind me—for now, and instead focus entirely on Ben until he's in bed. I treat myself to ice cream and standup comedy, laughing at Gabriel Iglesias' 'Fluffy' persona. My phone buzzes and I see a text from Adrian. He expects me to be in his office by eight in the morning.

Scoffing, I text back that I'll be there at nine.

8am, Ms. Dean, and I'm serious, he replies.

I don't think so, Mr. Thorpe, I counter.

I straighten my spine when the phone starts ringing, a smirk on my face as I press the answer button.

"Yes?"

"Ms. Dean. You are hell-bent on annoying me, aren't you?"

"I have a son. School drop off is at eight. I can't drop him any earlier," I say simply. "Phone calls work just as well as being in front of you."

With the bonus of him not being able to eye me like he'd rather be doing scandalous things than talking business. But that's my carnal side talking again, right?

"Fine. I'll be at *your* office at nine. I look forward to seeing your business in the flesh."

The color drains from my face. "What?" My office isn't exactly visit-worthy. It's badly in need of paint, my desk and chair have seen better days, and the AC vents are so old and dusty, it's a miracle I don't have lung issues by now.

"Is there something you're hiding from me, Brooke?"

He says my name like a purr, and it sinks under my skin and jumpstarts my cob-web covered heart. I swallow those emotions and shake my head. "No. I'm not hiding anything. But I don't understand why we can't meet over the phone."

"I'd like to dig deeper into your ideas considering you've already pitched them to our client. We also need to schedule time to record the ads and meet with Sal *together* so it's clear that this is balanced effort."

"Sounds good, but we can do that at your office."

"Yes, if you're here by eight. Otherwise, I'll be coming at your office by nine."

This is obviously a power struggle; one's he's determined to win. I back down. I'm too exhausted to fight. "Nine it is," I say.

"Good," he replies, sounding pleased. A sudden shrilling cuts into the brief silence.

"You're still at the office aren't you?" I ask.

He takes his time answering. "I don't see how that's relevant."

"Adrian, there's more to life than work. After our meeting tomorrow, I won't be answering my phone outside of business hours because I don't live to work."

"Lack of dedication?"

"It's knowing that a job is a means to an end. I don't want to wake up from work when my son is in college and wish I would have spent more time with him, or my friends, or my family."

He doesn't answer and I pull my phone from my ear to make sure he's still on the line. I clear my voice. "Are we done?"

"Until tomorrow."

I hang up and set the half-eaten bowl of ice cream to the side. I pull a blanket over my legs and pick at it. The T.V. fades to white noise. Even though I don't want to think of Adrian, and I don't want him taking up room in my mind, I can't help but wondering if he has family or friends outside of work.

Maybe that's why he dedicates everything he has to the business. Maybe that's why I can't beat him when it comes to clients no matter my appeal. A job will always be a job and not my life. My parents set the bar for that and I enjoy getting to do things that I *want* to do after work.

Perhaps Adrian needs to be reminded of what life has to offer and he'll realize what he's missing out on. He can see the joy of family, of commitment, of actually being present instead of trying to get another million dollars in the bank account he'll never use for travel or fun.

Maybe I can learn from him and he can learn from me. I nod to myself, toss my bowl in the sink, promising myself to do dishes tomorrow, pick up a few things, then check on Ben. He lays in bed, in a position that would absolutely murder my back, but I lean against the door frame and smile.

Already seven. I swear, just yesterday he was taking his first steps, staring at his feet with intense determination as he crossed the few feet to me. And now, all troubled about school, working on math, taking steps into a world of his own with every passing day. Moving away from me and into his own self.

"No matter what Adrian wants, you'll come first, Ben," I promise, crossing the room to kiss his forehead. "I love you to the moon and back."

Absolutely nothing Adrian throws at me can compare to the love I have for my son, or my determination to be there for him, to show him the best and make sure he gets it. He deserves more than empty promises and seeing me spin in circles over someone who's temporary.

"We're going to make it," I whisper, giving him another kiss before heading to bed.

# Chapter 8

### Adrian

The clock on the wall of my living room says nine-thirty, but my body feels like it's after midnight. I get through a hot shower, my aching muscles screaming with each movement. Brooke may be right; it's probably time to slow down a bit. Still, I don't like her poking holes in my life or pointing things out. It's maddening especially when she wears that damn gorgeous smile while she does it. Why can't she fall in line or fall at my feet like every other woman in my life?

Well, *almost* every other woman in my life.

My first foster mother hadn't fallen all over herself to love on the little eight year old thrown into her house. She'd used me for the paycheck. Just like the family after her. The third family isn't worth mentioning, but my last foster mother … she'd been too much. Too intense, too clingy.

Always wanting to control me, to be overly involved, to insert herself everywhere. I hated it. Thank God for her husband who understood and gave me the space I needed. He'd raised me to be smart, to put my value in the things that wouldn't run away or use me. The things I could have a direct impact on with the right action.

With Brooke, I'm reminded of everything I don't have, especially in that fucking phone call earlier. Listening to her help her son with math and congratulate him on getting it right, it stirred something in me. Yet, I don't understand her placing him before her job. I get that if he was sick or something, she'd need time, and sure she can't book a weekend trip out of the blue or stay out until ten p.m. every night, but she needs some fucking balance and dedication.

No wonder she's been stuck.

I'm not the broken one. She is.

I did my research. She was with her ex for seven years, married for five, a clean divorce from the outside, no custody battle – he just gave up rights to his son. She hasn't had a serious relationship since. It's been two years, but she's probably not getting laid. Although, she did mention going on a date.

I don't know. I'd only been half paying attention, thinking she'd simmer down after a weekend of getting laid and come into work eyeing me like candy or the enemy, but bowing to my will either way. Now she's the one making a stand, twisting me up, and I don't know if I love it or hate it.

"Sleep," I order myself. "Stop thinking about her."

But I can't, and my thoughts aren't exactly pure because I keep thinking that if I can tame her in bed, I could tame her in the office. We only have one contract together; would it be the worst thing in the world if I fucked her? Would it be terrible if I fucked her for a week straight, made her sweet and submissive so I can have my own way?

Yes, it would be terrible. It would never end well.

Besides, Brooke doesn't seem the type to engage in a fling. She's beautiful, smart, but boring. Maybe even a prude. For all I know she's the 'wait until marriage' type. I could respect that discipline.

I should. I will. There's a reason I don't mix business with pleasure, and I'll keep that reminder at the back of my head whenever we meet.

Pushing the filthy thoughts aside, I brush my teeth, do my normal nightly skin care, and get to bed with a podcast playing, soon falling asleep with the image on Brooke's warm smile on my mind.

I TWIST IN THE MIRROR in my office, smoothing the front of my shirt. It's not my usual practice to leave home without a tie or jacket, but I'll be overdressed if I show up like that to Brooke's office. I even leave the top button undone, telling myself it's not for Brooke. I want to do something different.

My heart's racing, and I don't know why. It's a simple meeting with my partner, nothing else. Sure, she's hot as fuck, and I'm still battling with the urge to seduce her, but she's not the first beautiful woman to catch my eye. I'm certain she won't be the last, either.

I pull up to the address she gave me, and I check the details twice. It's a commercial complex, but the building seems in great need of repair. Passing by each office, I see more evidence of wear and tear. I'm sure Brooke's office isn't in a better state. It's approximately 8:45 when the elevator opens on Brooke's floor. To my surprise, she's already there, wearing slacks and a white dress top. Her hair is down today, cascading in lovely rolls that brush her face and are begging to be pushed behind her ear. She nibbles her thumb nail as she studies something on her computer intently.

"Ms. Dean."

Her head shoots up. "Hey." She checks the time. "You're early."

"If you're not early you're late."

"If you're too early, you're a burden," she mumbles, as if it's the normal way to answer that statement.

I look around. The office is less than I expected and so dark. There's a printer that looks like it belongs in a house instead of an office, only her laptop, and a plush-looking chair in front of her desk. Small, dimly lit, with a roughness to the air that makes me worry about my lungs.

"It's not a penthouse, plus my clients never come here. I meet them at their businesses," she says, eyes not on me.

"You're focused today, especially for someone who's not an early bird."

"Contrary to what you might think, Mr. Thorpe, I take my job seriously," she replies. She types something into the computer, moves the mouse, then folds her hands under her chin, her elbows on the desk. "Have you had breakfast?"

"Yes." I sit and marvel in how perfect this chair feels. I could spend all day here and be comfortable the entire time. "Are you ready to discuss our social media strategy for Sal?"

"Of course."

We go over the details and rather than picking apart everything, I'm surprised that she's adding on to what I'm saying, not arguing. How I missed that the first time, I have no idea. The longer we talk, the more qualities she reveals.

She's studious, clearly puts her research and her conversations to work, making every plan specific to the client. She references some of her past clients and where things were successful, then backs what she says with other references. I might respect her business sense and her intuition when it comes to dealing with me and the client. It's new. Hell, if I'd had an inkling that she was this capable, I would have snapped her up a long time ago.

Only in the business sense. That's it. Even if her dilated eyes, the excitement making her glow, and the quick, yet thought out answers make her impossibly more attractive. Is she this creative in bed?

"Adrian?"

I blink, her confused face coming into focus. "It's a good plan, Brooke. I can't disagree." Even though I want to.

She flashes a heart stopping grin that I swear I feel. Now it's obvious why her clients call her sunshine. She's radiant and warmth rolls off of her like a summer day. Is that why I swear I smell a garden here?

"I'm glad to hear it. Should we go talk to Sal?"

Her stomach growls. I almost smile as she pats her belly. "The food was amazing last time, by the way. Have you eaten there?'

"No," I reply.

"My son approves and he's a picky eater. I don't think I've ever seen him eat anything that fast." She picks up her purse and keys.

"Now?"

"Of course now." She motions me towards the elevator. "You should definitely see him at work and we should tell him the plan. He's been excited. I even got an email today."

I'm not surprised at all. Just like I'm not surprised that she tries to insist on driving. She loses that battle with a huff and her arms crossed under her breasts, pushing them up until I can see her cleavage. If I was a lesser man, that would have swayed me.

In the car, she turns on the radio and turns it up, singing along to a pop song from the nineties. I glance at her at red lights as she wiggles in the seat, dancing horribly. When she hits a note perfectly, I can't stop my smile.

She meets my eyes and shoves me. "Come on, you have to know the words to this song. It's a classic."

"Not my taste."

"Then you're missing out." She continues singing, like she's serenading me alone.

I can't remember the last time a woman was like this around me. The women I've been with, who have lasted longer than a week, were always very self-aware. They were careful, quiet, always went with the flow and never disturbed the peace.

The song ends, and she doesn't miss a beat, just keeps nodding until the next one begins. "Have you ever been to a concert, Adrian?" she suddenly asks.

"Of course, I have," I reply, affronted. "Do I look like someone living under a rock?"

She giggles. "When was the last time you attended one?"

"Mhmm... I can't remember. I think it's when an old friend dragged me along to see a stoner band. Sublime, I think they're called.."

"Great band. I love doing karaoke to their songs." She rolls down the window, not caring that her hair whips around her face. "What does a man like you do for fun?"

"I work. Keep myself in shape, maintain my house, and get eight hours of sleep a night," I list.

She keeps watching me. After one full minute, she adjusts so she's facing me in her seat. I fight the urge to tell her sit properly. She's an adult. If she wants to be unsafe that's on her.

"That's not *fun*. Come on, you have so much money. You have to travel or enjoy an expensive restaurant or do something with all that other than pay for nice suits."

"I'll get to retire in a little over ten years and never have to worry. I'll get to do everything without compromise."

"Not a bad plan. Delayed gratification."

"It makes it all the sweeter."

She laughs and nods. "That's what I tell my son when he starts craving the weekend on a Tuesday."

I chuckle. "Instant gratification breeds greed and entitlement. It's good for a kid not to get everything they want."

"Sometimes." She goes quiet after that.

I want to dig into the silence, but I shouldn't. So I don't. We meet with Sal and he's twice as bubbly as I remember him. He dotes on Brooke, calling her sweetie and honey until she gently asks him to use her name. And he doesn't mess up again.

Still, they laugh, have a good time. I almost miss her dropping information about business. She does it so slyly and naturally. Like it's a fun conversation, but not the focus. I order something and stare at it, sure I'm going to make a mess.

"Dig in, Mr. Thorpe. We can get you a bib if you're worried."

I snort. A bib? As an adult? Absolutely not. But I don't like having messy hands. "May I have a fork?"

Brooke hands me one and doesn't judge how I eat as we go over the important details of the package we're offering him. By the end of the meal, he's delighted, saying this is even better than the original one we offered. And I'm actually blown away by the food. It's delicious, even if I normally can't stand barbeque.

Just before we leave, Brooke slaps her forehead. "I almost forgot to order another pulled pork sandwich. My son wolfed it down when I brought it home. I swear, he even licked the sauce off his shirt."

Eww.

Sal beams. "Kids are the best critics, always painfully honest – never sparing feelings."

"He said to give you a gold star."

Sal beams.

On the drive back to her office building, I glance over at Brooke. "You're smarter than you let on."

"You're catching on finally," she teases. "People are more receptive when they feel like everything is about them, like they're being praised for the business they've poured their lives into. And how can we give them the best service if we haven't been a customer?"

"I haven't thought of things like that in a long time."

"Because you're stuck in your tower like Rapunzel running contracts and focusing on numbers." She actually taps my nose at a stop light. "You need to loosen up, Adrian. Let your hair down."

"Are you planning to come save me from my tower?" I ask.

She nearly chokes on her laughter. "Yes. I will, if that's what it takes for this partnership to work. And look at how you've improved, not barking orders at all."

"Just wait until we meet again on Thursday," I warn, trying to get my heart to still. The idea of a woman not only wanting to, but eagerly saving me from a tower surrounded by red tape in procedure is more than sexy, it's ... endearing. But that kind of thinking isn't allowed with Brooke.

I have to put a pin in it now.

"We'll see, won't we? Maybe I'll bribe your kind side with breakfast."

"Oh, my kind side is bribe-able?"

"I'll find out when I actually see it." She sticks out her tongue, then pokes her hand out the window, catching the wind. "I forgot how nice it is to be a passenger in a car."

And I forgot how nice it is to actually enjoy my job. A smile tugs at the corner of my mouth. "All those references I've gotten about you aren't wrong."

"Is that a compliment?" She gasps and puts a hand to her heart. "From *the* Adrian Thorpe?"

He snorts. "Don't get too excited."

"Too late, I'm already planning our wedding."

Her response breaks me. I laugh, cancelling the flutters that are like little butterflies on my chest and turn up the music. Brooke giggles and leans back in the chair, looking perfectly at ease, perfectly delightful, and too damn beautiful to be real.

And just like that, she finds the first chink in my armor.

Fuck.

# Chapter 9

### Brooke

After spending nearly all day with Adrian yesterday, today seems boring in comparison. Which is stupid. Adrian's personality is as warm as a block of ice, and he's no fun to be around. I keep reminding myself of that as I meet with a new potential client who Sal referred to me, create a new banner for old client, and respond to a few emails in my inbox. In every free moment, my mind turns to Adrian.

That killer smile in the car, the real one, not the one for show, was beautiful. Disarming entirely. And it made me hot all over, made me all gooey and ready to swoon. Until I reminded myself who he is.

The serial bachelor. The man who takes what he can get and leaves without a trace or a single concern. That is Adrian Thorpe. Yesterday was a fluke. His compliments, him actually telling me about his life.

Tomorrow, he'll be his normal moody self and that will be the end of it. I'll be reminded again of why our partnership is only about business, not pleasure, and nothing will happen between us. Adrian is only loyal to himself, not to his workers, not to his women, and definitely not to me – since I fall somewhere in between.

I'm not going to overstate my own importance or let myself think of him as more than a business partner. I'll control my emotions and do my best to keep him out of my dreams so I can't get into trouble even on the subconscious level.

But I catch my refection in the elevator mirror while riding up to his office after noon, and I realize exactly how much work I put into myself today. I'm wearing a cute blue dress that's perfectly professional, but definitely shows off my legs. I put on lipstick, even if it's not bright red, added some volume to my eyelashes and color to my cheeks, and I wear my hair in a half updo.

I even committed to heels. They're short, but it's a change.

One he doesn't deserve. I don't dress up for men I don't like. And I don't like Adrian. I don't. I have to keep beating that into my head until I get my heart to register it as a fact.

"You look really nice today, Brooke," Liz comments as I exit the elevator on their floor.

I give her a grateful smile. "Thanks. So do you. How have you been?"

She groans. "My boyfriend has me running in circles. We've been together for four years and we're not moving forward. We should at least be talking about moving in together."

"Absolutely," I agree.

"But really, I think I need to get out of the house more. I work, grocery shop, hit the gym, go on dates, but I don't really have fun, or go to bars like I used to." She rubs the back of her neck. "Feels like the type of things single people do."

"Do you want to hang with my best friend and I on Saturday? We're going out to celebrate my partnership with Adrian, and I bet you and Stacy would get along since you're so much alike."

Liz gapes at me. "You're inviting me out on a girls' night?"

"I mean, if you'd rather not, then—"

"No!" she said hurriedly. "I'd love to! I'm not used to this. I haven't had friends in ages."

We exchange numbers and she leads me to Adrian's office with a smile, which disappears the second she walks in. It's like she's a robot that got turned on. Work mode: activated.

Adrian is sitting behind his desk, the signature frown even darker than before. He's obviously not pleased with whatever he's staring at on the computer screen. But even with the scowl, he still looks heart-stoppingly gorgeous. I shift my eyes to the center of the desk. It's like I'm being pulled under when I stare at him.

"Mr. Thorpe. Brooke is here for your one o' clock. Also, please don't forget the board meeting at four today. Also, you have three missed calls from Miss Monroe."

Adrian's head shoots up and gapes at Liz. "Celine?"

"Damn it." He rubs his temple. "I thought we'd gotten rid of her for good."

"She wants you to know she can handle your ex-wife. She's not ready to let you go." Liz shrugs, looking to me. "Recurring problem."

"I told him one incident wouldn't scare her away," I say with a smirk.

"Men." Liz says and walks out.

Adrian's jaw drops as she walks out and he points at me. "You are a bad influence on her."

"I warned you when you were plotting," I remind, ignoring his comment. "Based on what you told me, she won't disappear that easily. Now, what are we meeting about, other than the poor girl who wants your love?"

He snorts. "So much for a jealous ex-wife."

"I'm so sorry. Would you like me to throw another fit and get another fifty-fifty contract?" I offer.

Adrian measures me for a moment, as if he's not sure I'm serious. "You're good at what you do ... at least with Sal's contract."

"A better compliment than last time. Wow." I grin.

We start to get into the plan of action, but my personal phone rings. Adrian glowers at me coldly, those steel eyes threatening to leave me with frostbite, but I see it's Ben's school. I pick up and leave Adrian's office to talk in the hall.

"Hello?"

"Miss Dean, your son has been in another fight," the principal's sharp, disapproving voice lashes my ear. You need to pick him up right away. He's suspended for a week."

"Suspended? Principal Sinclair, that's totally unfair." Frustrated, I stomp my foot.

"Is it? I think not. This is becoming a pattern that needs to be addressed. I suggest therapy," she replies, a slight coolness in her tone.

"He doesn't need therapy. It's a *problem* that those other two boys have with my son. There's no way none of your staff has missed the active bullying I've seen when I pick him up from school," I counter.

"Ma'am—"

"Let me get this clear – you have a zero tolerance policy for bullying, but when two *large* boys say my son overpowered them both, you accept that? I bet they love getting away with it."

"Say whatever you want, Ms. Dean. He's still suspended."

"He is *not!*" I argue. "I'll be there in fifteen minutes to speak with you."

"This is not a negotiation."

"You're going to make it a negotiation and you're going to call his teacher into the office, or I am going to reach out to the superintendent. I will be *that* parent and trust me when I tell you, I have plenty of time to be a thorn in your side."

"Perhaps that's time you should spend speaking to your son about what's appropriate ways to deal with stress and an absent parent." Her tone is so haughty and rude and I can picture her flipping her hair.

I lower my voice to a hiss. "There's something you clearly don't understand Principal Sinclair. My son has *never* suffered from his father leaving. If anything, he's gotten more focused." I hear a gasp around me, but don't care. "Secondly, I can be a bitch if I want to be and I don't have to follow your rules when I'm a parent. If I have to get others involved, I won't be the one who's looking for a job. Especially if I happen to speak to some of the other parents who are very concerned about the bullying going on in your school."

She holds her tongue and says she'll see me soon.

I look up and see the blonde from the convention—Adrian's stalker. She stands by the elevator, gaping at me. "You have a kid?"

"Yup. And right now, my kid needs the functional parent—me," I grumble. It's times like these I wish Greg hadn't left me with the responsibility of raising a child on my own. His input is so needed right now.

The blonde crosses her arms, frowning. "Adrian didn't tell me he had a kid."

I pause, realizing her mistake. Should I set her straight, or help Adrian out? He'll owe me plenty if I go along with this.

"Yes," I reply after deciding. "Adrian and I have a son, and I'll do anything to get my family back." I move closer, arranging my face into a threatening glare. "Anything."

She glances at Adrian's office then back at me. "You don't scare me, you crazy bitch. Adrian wants me. Get over it."

"Did he tell you about the last woman he tried to date? She's seeing a therapist because of me. I destroyed her. Trust me, I'll do the same to you. Stay away from Adrian."

Again, she glances at Adrian's office door, a resigned look filling her face. "You can't make a man love you. Especially a man like Adrian." She eyes me up and down with scorn. "Especially looking as plain as you do. I don't know what he saw in you."

"Oh, he *sees* plenty, believe me," I reply hotly, a little stung by her remark. Then I remember the hunger in his eyes back in my office the other day. *Yup, he sees something. As dowdy as I am, I know when a man wants me.*

Celine huffs and whips around as the elevator doors open and Liz emerges. She storms past a surprised Liz into the open elevator and the doors close on her angry face.

"The hell?" Liz says to me. "How did she get past security?"

"Beats me," I reply. "But I took care of it. Adrian needs to do something about her, though. Something permanent."

"I agree. It's a pity he got involved with such a crazy bird."

"You know men. They think with their dicks, not their—"

"Head?" the deep voice interrupts me.

Horrified, I turn to meet Adrian's amused face. Well, if the slight upturn of his lips is anything to go by, anyway.

"I can assure you, Ms. Dean, I always think with my head," he says, and the lightness in his tone tells me he's definitely amused.

"Yet, you have a stalker who's still on the loose. Did you know she came to see you just now?"

The smile disappears. "She did?"

"Yes," I reply, smirking. "No worries, I took care of her." I pat his chest as I walk past him. "You owe me one, though."

"You're right. I do."

I nod, grabbing my purse. "And I'm calling on that debt right away."

"The hell you are," he protests. "There are five more line items we need to discuss."

"It's not a negotiation, sorry. That was Ben's school on the phone. He's been suspended for a fight that wasn't his fault. I need to go."

His expression switches to concern and he vigorously nods. "Of course. Go. We'll table this for tomorrow. Please let me know if there's help I can give."

I think about his response while driving to Ben's school. It was totally unexpected, very... human. Slowly, but surely, Adrian's hard exterior is being stripped away, revealing the softness beneath. A softness that makes me want to let my guard down.

Careful, Brooke. Don't fall for him, please.

Pulling up to the school, I silence my phone and head to the principal's office. Just like I asked, Ms. Carter, Ben's teacher is also present. I also notice the other two boys are missing. There's only Ben hunched over in his seat, his face drawn with defeat.

I arch an eyebrow in surprise. "I believe it's the policy to have all the parents and children present when there's a fight, isn't it?"

"It is," Ms. Carter replies, her expression slightly disapproving.

Principal Sinclair stands and adjusts her skirt while pushing her dark hair behind her ear. "This is Ben's second fight in two weeks."

"And this is the second time I'm the only parent called to pick up my child who just so happened to be the only one injured. Funny how that would happen to *the bully*."

Her cheeks heat. "Those boys have never had behavioral issues. They've never had a single issue at this school."

I look to Ms. Carter. "Has Ben had any problems in class?"

Ms. Carter shakes her head at once. "Not at all! Ben's a brilliant kid. He's been helping another student with science assignments without being asked. He's always well behaved and engaged." She looks at Ben with a affectionate smile.

Principal Sinclair huffs. "His behavior in class seems contrary to what out two victims have reported—"

"Victims?" I interrupt. "You can't be serious. Did you miss the part where they were both bigger than Ben?"

"It's their words against his, Ms. Dean," she throws back.

My poor son, still hunched over, with shame in his eyes says, "I tried, Mom. I tried to ignore them. They shoved me and tore my backpack. They threw my science book in the toilet. I didn't have a choice but to—" He breaks into a sob. "I'm sorry, Mom.

I rub his shoulders and pin the principal with a look. "Are you really going to suspend him after what he said?" I ask.

Her expression sours. She doesn't like being challenged, but that's her problem not mine. I won't let her take her issues out on my son. I'm not backing down. Sensing my determination, she settles for him being out of school until Monday.

Ben rushes to his room the second we arrive home. As I set my back down on the kitchen counter, I hear his soft cries. Heaving a sigh, I walk to his room, sitting on his bed and pulling him into my arms.

"Hey, kiddo, what is it?"

"I didn't start the fight, Mom," he sobs. "You believe me, don't you?"

"Of course, honey." I hold his shoulders so I can look at him directly. "I believe you."

He presses his face into my chest, his cries subsiding.

"It's my job to protect you, remember? I can't go around yelling at kids, but I won't let grown-ups bully you either and neither will Ms. Carter." I take his hands in mine, wiping at his cheeks. "I'll take tomorrow off and we'll get to have an extra-long weekend together."

His head jerks back, eyes brightened with glee. "Really?"

"Really. We can go to the park. We can draw together or even build some of those airplanes you got for Christmas," I offer.

"Does this mean I'm not grounded?" he asks hopefully.

"Of course not, honey. You were only defending yourself; I know that."

"So, can we finish our painting then watch TV?"

I hug him tightly. "We can do whatever you want, my sweet boy."

We finish painting the canvas he wants to gift his grandma for her birthday, then we settle into a cartoon ninja movie, and it's getting to the climax when the doorbell rings. I jump up, smoothing down my leggings and T-shirt before opening the door only to see Adrian, perfect as ever standing there. His eyebrows lift as he assesses me from head to toe.

My hair's in a braid, my thin shirt is old, and paint splattered and my leggings cling to me like a second skin. To say I'm self-conscious is putting it mildly. Why do I keep forgetting to check the peephole? I rub my forehead with a deep sigh. "Adrian, what are you doing here?"

He runs his thumb over my cheek, showing me wet paint. "Is your son okay?" he asks.

I contain my surprise, frowning at him instead. "Ben's doing fine. I doubt you drove all this way enquire about my son, though."

"Well, that and the fact you left before we could have a decent meeting," he replies.

I close the door before Ben gets curious. I don't let just *anyone* into his life. "You're here for work? Adrian, it's almost seven. I'm not discussing anything that doesn't involve pleasure right now."

Adrian smiles and his eyes simmer with heat as he replies, "Well, that can be arranged."

I feel the heat on my cheeks, and I mask it with a horrified scoff. "Get your head out of the gutter, Adrian. By pleasure, I meant activities with my son."

"Oh, that reminds me. Apparently, I'm a piece-of-shit dad who doesn't spend time with his son," he hisses, a flash of annoyance crossing his face. "Shocking news to me."

I shrug. "Sorry. That wasn't my intention, it just happened. It took care of your problem though. Celine won't bother you again."

"Ah yes. According to her text message, she's not interested in being someone's stepmom. She doesn't like sharing the spotlight, I think. If I'd known that was her kryptonite, I would have led with a single-parent backstory instead of making you out to be a crazy ex-wife," he says.

I chuckle. "I don't know. For some reason, I enjoyed being crazy for a minute."

"Besides, we wouldn't be working together, right?"

"Right."

Our eyes meet and hold. I suck in a breath, trying to force myself to look away from his penetrating stare. I feel exposed, like he's seeing my racing heart and my throbbing clit. Like he knows how much I want him right now.

The door suddenly clicks as it opens, breaking the hold Adrian has on me. "Mom?"

I glance down at Ben, but he's not looking at me. Son of a ... bulldog. Ben stares up at Adrian, his bruised cheek and split lip on display. Adrian looks down at him and I expect him to walk off. Instead he smiles.

"You okay, little man?" he asks, stooping to Ben's level.

Ben nods, touching his cheek. "Got into a fight at school."

"I see. Taking punches never gets easier."

"Mom says I'm going to go to karate class to learn how to defend myself."

"Not a bad plan," Adrian agrees. "Bullies are insecure people who can't beat your smarts."

I blink at him a few times, my lips parting. He softens all his rough edges for Ben. He isn't telling him to throw a punch and teach the kids a lesson, he isn't butting in. He's just ... talking to Ben like he's a regular person.

"Do you mind if I talk to your mom about work for a little?"

"That's up to her." Ben wrinkles his nose. "I don't have to work."

"No, but you're the man of the house right?" Adrian asks. When Ben nods, Adrian offers his hand. "I'm Adrian. I work with your mom and I'm not coming in unless you *both* say it's okay."

Ben shakes his hand. "Just don't interrupt the movie."

My son runs back to the T.V. Adrian turns to me. "I meant it when I said both of you. I want this ironed out."

"It can't wait until Monday?"

"It can't wait until tomorrow," he says firmly. "So either I'm going to the office and we're going to settle it over a video call, or you can let me in."

"You need a hobby." I sigh, but let him in. "No cursing in this house."

"Oh?" His eyes shimmer with that challenge.

"I'll wash your mouth out with soap, no matter how big you are," I threaten.

Adrian laughs, actually laughs, and my heart and stomach flip together. This is a mistake. I realize it the second I shut the door behind Adrian and welcome him in. He doesn't belong here. This is my one safe space, the one place he'd never touch, where I didn't *have* to picture him because it was impossible.

But now he's here, standing behind my couch, looking at the movie with Ben. Totally different people, but they watch the T.V. with the same unflinching focus, totally entranced. Then I see Adrian's mouth move to the words and I experience a little twinge of something.

It's not lust, but it's pretty damn close. There's something sexy about a man who can be around kids without looking at them like a problem or an intruder. There's something even sexier about Adrian Thorpe mouthing the words to a kid's movie about ninjas before my son karate chops the bear.

"Try using this part of your hand." Adrian demonstrates against the bear.

I steady myself against my door. Goodness, I think I'm going to burst watching them take on that innocent teddy bear together.

In ten minutes, Adrian has completely annihilated my misconception of him. No longer do I see him as an unfeeling, cutthroat asshole, which was my only defense. Now that it's obvious he's a human with a decent heart, how do I keep from falling for him?

## Chapter 10

### Adrian

Ben kicks the teddy bear right off the couch and I give him a high five. "Not bad."

My eyes flick over to the reason for this visit. Brooke is still leaning against the door like she's not actually part of this moment. Her eyes are soft and a little smile tugs at her lips. When she catches me watching, she bites that lush bottom lip and looks at me from under those damn long lashes.

Fucking beautiful. My stomach coils in response to that look. Ben bounces over to her as if she looks like that every day and hugs her hip. "Did you see, Mom?"

"Teddy bears around the world should cower." She ruffles his hair. "I have to talk to Adrian though. Can you handle picking up your toys in the living room?"

"I can do it faster than last time," he replies.

"I'll time you," she says, pulling out her phone. "Ready ...." Ben starts to move, but she catches his shirt. "Not until Go."

He huffs, but the second she says the word, he races around. Moving with Brooke to the kitchen, I glance over at her son as he hums to himself while working. He's so much like her. Except, I think I'd actually pay money to see Brooke clean on a timer while humming the Batman theme song.

"Sorry for the distraction," she murmurs, working on the dishes in the sink. "We can talk to Sal tomorrow, but I'll have Ben with me. He's been suspended."

"Does it have anything to do with the bruise on his face?"

She nods. "He got in a fight. Two older kids claim he's bullying them, and the principal took their side. I'm not surprised. She's had it out for me since her brother asked me out on a date and I turned him down ... exactly two weeks after the divorce." She shakes her head. "He's a nice guy, but I wasn't up for it."

"Stupid that the woman thinks that means your son's a problem," I grumble, the weight of my own memories on me.

I was always *the* problem. In the house, at school, everywhere. Unlike Ben, I decided that if they were going to label me, that's exactly what I was going to be. If kids teased me about cheap clothes, I'd fight back. If I was hit for disobedience in the home, I ran away. I was what they made me.

I don't see that in Ben really. I see a boy who's going to become a good man. One who could take over the world if he wants to. With that smile he flashes, his energy, that focus on and drive.

"Anyway," Brooke says, not flinching under the steaming hot water as she scrubs. "I've worked on some outlines for the short videos, but I really think Sal shines in his element. People love him, just like you saw. We should show him cooking, have him bonding with the diners, get some good shots and put them together into a commercial for YouTube. You mentioned the booklet and I think that would be great as well."

"Did you just compliment me?" I ask.

She sets a dish to the side. "You are a smart man, Adrian, or you wouldn't be running a billion-dollar business. Weren't those your exact words last week?"

"They were. But it's nice hearing the competition say it." I bump her hip lightly with mine.

She shakes her head, looks at the phone and raises her voice. "Seventy seconds!"

"Almost done!" Ben cries.

"So Ben will go with us to Sal's, but he's not welcome in the office," I inform her.

"Oh? Worried about your reputation, are you?" Brooke replies, putting words in my mouth.

"No, you have a firm no-cursing rule and I don't think you have the soap required to take down the whole office."

She pauses scrubbing a plate and looks up at me. "Wanna bet?"

I laugh and cover my face with my hand. She grumbles about how cursing is a pandemic as she keeps scrubbing the dishes. I think she's actually rushing through them and I'm not quite sure why. It's not because of me, is it?

"Done!" Ben runs into the room, panting.

"Are you sure?" I ask.

He thinks about it and holds up a finger before running back in. Brooke shakes her head lightly. "You're terrible. I'm sure he did a great job."

"It's always good to make them think."

"You say that like you have experience with kids."

I don't want to talk about it. I won't talk about it. I hold my head a little higher. "Preparing him for the real world is all."

"Whatever you say, boss man." She turns off the water and starts drying. Ben comes back in, panting and bracing himself on his knees. Brooke pauses and they check the living room.

I follow, even though I shouldn't. This visit is supposed to be about work, not a painful trip through my memories and measuring where they fail. Brooke looks over the clean living room, all the toys in a chest in the corner, the blankets organized across the couch and reclining chair, the table straightened, no dishes and nothing out of place.

"Good job, Ben. It looks better than I could have hoped."

"Only two minutes," he says happily. "I counted."

"I'm proud of you." She tickles him, bending over and flashing a gorgeous view of her round ass.

I shake the filthy thoughts away. Now is not the time to be thinking of sex. There's a kid standing right here, for Christ's sake.

"Give me a few minutes, Adrian. Ben needs a shower," Brooke says, and I nod in reply.

Leaning against the wall that separates the kitchen, I check out Brooke's space. It's quite small compared to my living room, but it's very homey. A cute, little center table stands between two identical, plush-looking couches, complete with wooden side tables that holds two gorgeous lamps. I glance at the photos on the wall of her, Ben, and a few people I assume are family. Happiness. That's what I see. My apartment is worth ten times this tiny bungalow, but it doesn't hold the joy I feel in this living room.

A joy that's priceless.

A joy I desperately need.

"Sorry about that," Brooke breathes, sailing into the room. "I had to ensure Ben actually takes a bath."

"I didn't mind waiting," I reply as she braces herself against the back of the couch. She's so damn relaxed, so confident in her own home, so bright and warm and fuck, I can't help wondering if she tastes as sweet as I think she will.

"Adrian?" she says, bringing me back.

I take an unwilling step towards her, trying to tell myself I don't want her. She's a single mom. She's my coworker, she's so damn different from anything I've ever wanted … but I can't resist touching her. I push her hair behind her ear and watch her eyes dilate.

"I thought we were meeting about work," she murmurs, looking away.

Do I confess my visit has nothing to do with work, but everything to do with seeing her again because I could not wait until tomorrow? Probably not.

"We were. But it seems you've taken care of more than I was aware. You should email me updates, Brooke," I say instead.

"I emailed the information to Liz and thought I copied you on it before I ..." She shakes her head. "I'm sorry, I wasn't focused. Exactly what you worried about."

"You have more on your plate than anyone who works for me."

"How do you know? I have a feeling you *never* get personal with employees. Have you ever asked about Liz's life outside work? Asked what she does on weekends?"

"No."

"How about any of your other workers? Your clients?"

I narrow my eyes. "Watch it, Brooke."

"I appreciate you trying to compliment me but doing it by putting others down isn't exactly exciting, Adrian."

I tip her chin up, surprised that she lets me. "Let me try again."

Those dark eyes widen, and I lean closer.

"I think you are a confusing mix of a person and no matter what I do, I can't figure out how you can be so genuine and sweet while still getting the job done. How you can make me furious, then prove your worth and make me want to eat my words. How you see things my people – the best paid people – miss. All while being an active mom and sexy as hell, I might add."

Her breath whooshes out of her. "Adrian ..."

I release her chin. I've said way too much especially since I've only known the woman for a week. A sexless week. That's the problem. It's been two weeks since I got laid and it's pent up lust. Nothing more.

I know better.

It's time to go, before I do something I'll regret tomorrow.

Rising from the couch, I head towards the door. "Goodnight, Brooke. I'll leave you to your son."

"Wait—"

I don't. I ignore the surprise in her voice, walk out of the house and hold the doorknob in place. It's a childish move, not letting her out, but I need her to forget everything that just fell out of my mouth. I don't talk like that. I don't give women fucking false hope. I'm not that cruel. I'm cut and dry, direct and straight forward.

And she's not going to let my slip disappear into the void like Liz would. Which means I'm going to have to deal with it.

She tugs on the door and hear her grumbling to herself. Giving up, I let it go. She yanks it open and shoots out, standing under the porch light in front of me. "What was that?"

"Lack of sex talking."

"Adrian." She takes a careful step towards me, like I'm a wild animal that doesn't trust her. "It's okay to have a heart. Most of what you said was sweet and I appreciate it."

I scoff, shaking my head. "That's not like me."

She reaches out to me and instinctively, I grab her wrist. I don't like being touched. Not really. It means I'm not in control. I wind her arm around her back, but that means we're pushed together. I feel every rise and fall of her chest against mine. Her gaze pins me, but there's no malice, she doesn't struggle to get free.

Brooke doesn't fight, but she doesn't give either and if I could figure out how her damn brain is wired, I wouldn't feel flustered. I'm sure of it.

"You have a nice smile when you show it," she murmurs. "And ..."

"And?" I ask, leaning closer. Is she going to cave? Try a move on me? Be like every other fucking person on the planet?

Nope, she pulls her other hand, the one I'm not holding up to gently brush her thumb under my bottom lip. "And you should find more reasons to smile. My friend Stacy, Liz, and I are going out Saturday."

"An invitation?"

"No." She shakes her head, confusing me again. "It's girls' night. You should get some of your friends together and go out."

"If I don't have friends."

"I'll lend you some as long as you promise to be a good boy," she whispers.

The last half of that sentence crackles with electricity. It rips across my nerves, sinks low into my stomach, hardening my cock. I crush Brooke against me so she can feel what her damn innocence is doing to me.

She gasps, tries to look down between us, blushing deeply. "Adrian, what are ..."

I lean forward, the tip of my nose brushing hers, and she softens against me. She shivers and licks across her bottom lip. I was going to tell her goodnight, but that little hint of temptation snares me.

I press my lips to hers softly, sure she'll shove me away, struggle, something, but her mouth molds to mine and I taste a hint of wine, as sweet as she is, and something else. Something immediately addictive.

My tongue strokes hers before plunging deep. She whimpers against my mouth, but her free hand tightens in my shirt as I pull her closer, her hips brushing and rubbing against mine. I change the angle and kiss her again, slow and patient.

Once kiss will be enough. I don't need to fuck her.

I don't need to put her through a one-night stand.

I don't need her.

So I start to draw back, but she nibbles my bottom lip, licks into *my* mouth, and keeps the kiss going. Freezing, I let her explore, feeling each tentative stroke, each nervous flick of her tongue. She stands on her toes, rubbing herself against me and I groan.

That seems to jumpstart her. She falls back, stumbling to her heels. Without my arm behind her, I'm sure she would have fallen. She touches her lips and focuses entirely on my shirt.

"You should go," she breathes.

"Should I?"

"My son will be out of the shower soon and we have reading to do."

"Is that what you want?" Her eyes flick to mine, hold, and I manage to steal another kiss, hungrily devouring her mouth the way I need to.

She gives in for half a minute before pushing against my chest and shaking her head. "No. You need to get laid and I need to lay off the wine."

I chuckle. "Wordplay?"

"That's what you've brought me down to." She laughs once and tugs on her arm. "Please, Adrian. We both know this won't work."

I do, but I still want more. I want to know if her skin tastes as sweet as her mouth. If her pussy is as wet. I want to make her smile again as she sings to me in the car. Hell, I want to see more of that furious momma-bear mode that I caught a glimpse of outside my office, but she's right. There's no way we'll work.

She pats my chest. "I'll see you tomorrow. Try to get laid this weekend."

"Only if you do." Although, the thought of her beneath another man isn't sitting well with me right now.

She subtly flicks me off by rolling her eye and I suppress my smile again. Even when she's back inside, my cock still strains against my pants. I shake my head. "Oh no you don't. I'm still running this show."

But it's persistent, frustrating, and doesn't want to listen.

Brooke's right. I need to get laid. Then we'll be back to normal.

# Chapter 11

### Brooke

I kissed him. Holy crap, I kissed Adrian Thorpe. He kissed me. And that wasn't just *a* kiss. It wasn't any kind of fairy-tale kiss. It was ... hot. Really hot. The kind of kiss that leads to the bedroom.

But I'll be another notch in his bedpost and while I've never shamed any woman for getting what she wants, I don't *want* that. I want stability. I want a man who loves me. A man who will stay. Charming, handsome, someone who wants marriage and kids. I want the right happily ever after, not another round of heartbreak.

"Mom?"

I look up at a freshly-showered Ben and smile. "I'm ready for reading. Are you?"

He nods, his eyes scanning the room. "Did Adrian leave?"

I brush the memory of Adrian's loaded gaze aside, giving Ben a nod. "Yes, he did, sweetie."

"Is he a friend?" Ben pushes.

"We just work together, honey," I reply. Boundaries. They're important. Giving Adrian a reason to exist without Ben getting attached. "That's all."

He shrugs, but something flashes in his eyes when he keeps looking at the door, like he's expecting Adrian to walk right back in, settle in with us, and join for the bedtime story. Never. Him being nice to Ben was more than I expected. No cursing in the house was more than I hoped.

But that sweet little fantasy is so ridiculous that he'd laugh at me then rip up our contract if I even suggested it. Hell, suggesting more than one night together would get me laughed out of his office.

So, I'll get through tomorrow and he'll prove that he's his normal self. Earlier, he was low on sex and easy to turn on. Tonight, he'll get laid, after which he'll kick himself for letting his guard down and kissing me.

As for me, I'll pretend his regret won't hurt one bit.

---

"MOM, I'M THIRSTY."

I shift my eyes from the computer screen and look over to my son sitting cross-legged on the couch. "You were thirsty ten minutes ago, Ben."

"I know, but it's hot in here," he complains.

I sigh, glancing up at the AC vent, where the buzzing has gotten louder than when we got in this morning. Making a note to call the building manager—again—I walk over to the AC and give it a hefty knock. The buzzing stops, and a rush of cold air bathes my face. This temporary fix will last two hours, tops.

I give Ben another juice box, then he trades his button-up shirt for a T-shirt. I glance down at the thick, V-neck sweater I wore today. Smart kid, even smarter than me.

He settles down and builds a Lego city on the floor while I work. I'm so caught up with designing a flyer for a new ice-cream joint, I don't notice he's standing next to me until he touches my shoulder.

"Crap, sweetie, you scared me." I press my palm against my heaving chest.

"Sorry, Mom. Are we going to the park today?"

"Absolutely. I have one meeting to go."

He deflates a little and I see his lips screw up. "Do all adults work this hard?"

"Some even more than others," I reply, thinking of Adrian. "But you'll like this meeting."

"Really?"

"Remember the food I brought you? We're going to see Sal. He's very excited to meet you and hear what you think of his food."

"Sounds awesome!" He tugs on my arm. "Can we go?"

"Not until Adrian gets here, sweetie." I check the time. He's due any minute now. My heart rate seems to realize, too, because it's picking up like crazy. A part of me can't wait to see him. The other side of me wishes he'll call to cancel. I don't want to face my feelings for him, not right now.

As if on cue, a soft knock on the front door precedes Adrian's entrance. There's no sign of the tension from last night on his face. He seems rested—translation; well-fucked. My heart dips. So, he did get laid. I'm aware he's staring at me, but I can't meet his eyes. I'm afraid he'll see the disappointment I'm feeling inside.

Adrian's shoulders turn as directs his attention to Ben. "So, you're our taste tester, right?"

"Yes," Ben replies with a vigorous nod. "I know good food."

"What do you think of Sal's?"

"Almost as good as Mom's cooking. Almost," he says seriously. "One gold star. Mom has three on her sloppy joes."

"That's pretty good marketing," Adrian says. "Are you sure your mom isn't stealing your ideas?"

Ben laughs. Adrian's eyes coasts to me, and this time, I can't look away. Those eyes are filled with too much heat for a man who got laid. It resurrects memories of the burning kiss that spread fire through every bit of my body and had my toes curling and my nipples hard.

Sucking in a breath, I force my eyes away and latch them on my son. "Are you ready, honey?"

"Yes. My tummy is empty." He pats it emphatically.

At Adrian's insistence, we drive over to the restaurant in his car, with Ben and I singing offkey all the way. Adrian's eyes flick to the rearview and his lips turn down, but he doesn't say anything. A kid can make him hold his tongue. Look at that.

Ben points at the bakery on the corner. "We should visit Mr. Booker afterwards, Mom."

"Craving desserts?" I ask him.

"Yes. But I want to see Mr. Booker too. He was sad last time when his puppy died." He traces something on the window.

"Okay, honey. We'll stop by later." Speaking of sad... "How is Mr. Hanson?" I ask Adrian.

He shrugs. "I haven't spoken to him since he signed the contract. My team handles the after sales service."

"His wife is going through chemo, you know."

Adrian glances at me. "Is that so?"

"I visited her once. Brought her some cupcakes and she was so pleased. We sat and talked for a while. Mr. Hanson was going to retire at the end of this year before she was diagnosed. They wanted to travel to Alaska and see the Caribbean."

Adrian nods, but doesn't comment. Part of me is disappointed, but the other side knows that's who Adrian is. He's very disconnected. Very emotionally unavailable. He doesn't care about people in any regard outside work. He has no room in his life for a woman like me. Last night can't happen again. He can't come over again. He can't be in my personal life, not even for a minute.

"Ben," Adrian says. "Did you meet Mrs. Hanson?"

"No."

Adrian nods.

"Do you meet a lot of people at your work? Like Mom does?" Ben asks.

"Not just like your mom. I mostly see them in the office. We discuss our business arrangement, then my team gets the work done," he replies.

Ben considers that, his eyebrows crinkling. "But if you like them, why wouldn't you go to their stores?"

I motion to my son to stop talking. At first, Adrian rolls his eyes as if it's a stupid question but his face soon softens. "I don't have the time. I have a lot of clients."

"More than a hundred?" Ben asks.

"Yes."

"But when do you have fun?"

I try to keep my lips from turning up, but can't. "Adrian hasn't had fun in a long time."

"What? No way," Ben says, his eyes wide with shock.

"Yes, way," I reply.

Ben bounces in his seat. "You should come to the park with us! Oh, Mom, could we go to the arcade? I bet he'd like that. It's my favorite place."

I chew my bottom lip. The arcade is like Chucky-Cheese but for adults. It's expensive and it's more of a birthday treat than an everyday expense. I've always wanted to take Ben there, but I could never afford it. I turn to look at him, giving him the heartiest smile I can muster. "We can do the park and maybe bowling, okay?"

I'd have to check my account balance for I make any other commitment. Something tells me I'm already towing the line.

"Okay." Ben agrees, easy as always.

My chest tightens. I hate not being able to give him everything he wants.

Adrian clears his throat. "I like games."

"Do you?" Ben asks.

"Depends on the game. I'm pretty good at skee ball."

I gape at him. Adrian Thorpe being good at skee ball? Wearing this suit in a place like that and never flashing a smile when he wins? No. It's an impossible picture. No way for it to be real. Adrian looks at me at a red light.

"What's that look for, Brooke?"

"Honestly, I think I need to see it to believe it."

"Challenge accepted," he says simply. "Once we're done at Sal's we're going to the arcade."

"Yay!" Ben cheers.

I see the slightest smile on Adrian's face, and it manages to stay as we get to Sal's. We eat and talk. Ben gives his honest answer when Sal asks about his food – of course the number one complaint is not enough sauce, which is absolutely my son.

And it means Sal makes him another sandwich with extra sauce. Ben lights up as Sal places the plate in front of him, his messy hands already. Adrian talks to Sal's daughter, and I notice he's actually talking to her, not just making a plan and monologuing.

Good for him. Mastering back and forth like a real human instead of a robot.

Sal nudges me and pulls me to the side slightly. "I think you're having a positive impact on him."

"We'll see." I shrug.

The rest of the meeting goes well. I don't expect Adrian to take us to the arcade or anywhere other than the office, but he hands his phone with the map open, to Ben.

"Do you know the name of the arcade?"

"No. I know where it is," Ben says, handing the phone back. "I can give you directions."

I keep staring at Adrian on the drive over and when we arrive at the commercial building that houses the arcade, I actually pinch myself. Adrian arches an eyebrow at me. "What was that for, Brooke?"

"Had to make sure I wasn't dreaming. *The* Adrian Thorpe, lowering himself to hang out with commoners. It's uncanny."

Adrian snorts, another unusual response. "You and Ben are hardly commoners, Brooke."

Ben runs up to us, hustling for ticket money. Before I can dip in my purse for the last remaining cash I have, Adrian hands Ben a hundred dollar bill. Open-mouthed, I watch as he follows Ben to the ticket stand. Besides the three-piece suit he's wearing, Adrian doesn't seem out of place. In fact, he looks totally relaxed, like he wants to be here.

I move closer to him while Ben throws himself at a Fruit Ninja game, shaking my head. "Why are you doing this?"

"Someone keeps telling me to have fun." He looks around. "Who knows fun better than kids?"

I want to bring up the kiss from last night, but I don't. Instead, I watch in something close to awe as Ben and Adrian talk and spend time together. Ben keeps roping me back in, but Adrian proves he's not full of crap when he makes a new high score on the skee ball machine.

Ben starts to get frustrated with it, but Adrian helps him adjust the angle. He's so patient with Ben and so focused and sweet, it goes right to my heart. When Ben runs off to the next game and Adrian spots me staring at him, he closes the space between us.

My throat bobs as I swallow. He wipes under my bottom lip and my brow furrows. "What are you—"

"You're practically drooling, Brooke. Is it because of the kiss?"

"What kiss?" I ask, trying to cool my blush, surprised that he brought it up. "I told you goodnight and went back inside."

"Is that how you remember it?" he asks, amused.

"That's what happened." Because if I think about him kissing me again, my knees might give out and he's not the kind of man I should swoon for. "Were you fantasizing about something else?"

He leans forward and whispers in my ear. "I don't fantasize about kissing, kitten. You wouldn't be able to handle my fantasies."

My pussy tightens with need. If I rock my hips, I would feel how wet I am. "Adrian—"

"That's how I know that kiss is real." He purrs before kissing the spot below my ear. "It was innocent."

Fuck.

It's not fair that I'm that easy to turn on. Adrian exhales over my skin and goosebumps pop up. I force myself to think. "Nothing you do is innocent, Adrian."

"Better remember that when you want to tease me." His fingers brush my hip. "Including wearing those leggings that cling to you like a second skin."

With that, he follows Ben, like he didn't just set my body on fire. He's like a damn cat. He makes it seem like his actions are never on purpose. But those words ... those were on purpose.

I follow them around and once I stop expecting Adrian to corner me again, I let myself have fun. Adrian is actually enjoying himself, too, laughing with Ben like he's known my kid forever. In fact, to a stranger, they could be father and son.

Ignoring the pang in my chest, I sit in a booth and watch them play a dancing game that makes Ben laugh like never before. I love that he's happy. I hate that the source isn't a temporary one. For Adrian, this is a deviation from his normal routine, nothing more. I don't want Ben getting attached.

It's a quiet ride back to the office, with Ben passed out on the back seat. Tears threaten to fill my eyes when Adrian carries him from the car and lays him on the couch, then brushes back the hair from his forehead. Ben stirs a little, contentment filling his face.

Adrian backs away, his tender expression giving way to a wicked look. Without warning, he comes at me, blocking me from my door. "So, Brooke, am I real person now?"

I shrug. "Maybe. I can't tell if you're pretending or not."

His fingers nearly brush my hand, but he doesn't touch me. The frustration that winds through me is absolutely not allowed. I'm not allowed to want him. He won't catch me if I fall for him. I'm sure of it.

But oh, I wish he would.

Because I'm falling.... Hard.

Goddamnit.

Adrian is a gorgeous man, dedicated, determined, ambitious, and admittedly, he's really good with Ben. I'm not surprised of my feelings for him. But I'm not giving in to it. I can't.

"Adrian ..." I swallow and meet his eyes. "Thank you for today. I really appreciate it and I know Ben did too."

"You're welcome. He said we should hang out every weekend," he murmurs. "He did also mention I might be more fun than you."

"You let him loose in an expensive arcade. Of course you'd be more fun."

"I'm teasing you, Brooke." He tips my chin up. "Ben loves you. He kept talking about playing in sprinklers and having a water gun fight."

"You're letting a kid manipulate you. I'm wondering if you're as big and bad as you seem."

"Want to find out?" That hungry look in his gray eyes makes me hot all over. I'm wet. From that look, from his teasing. He pins me to the wall without touching me. "Be careful when you play with me, Brooke. Like you said, I'm not innocent."

No he's not. Adrian winks and heads to his car, leaving me hot, bothered, and nearly ready to make a second deal with this devil – one that would give me a whole lot more pleasure.

# Chapter 12

### Adrian

When I get back to the office to check my emails, I realize I'd just spent the entire day with Brooke and her son. When was the last time I spent a weekday out of the office? Even worse, when was I willing to put work to the side for a woman?

It's the kid.

It fucking has to be. There's something about him that makes me want to let loose. My problems seem a million miles away when I'm around him. Maybe it was his innocence. He's not yet soiled by this cruel world. Pulling on his energy has been good to me.

Although, if I'm being honest, he's not the only source of my exhilaration. Seeing the awe on Brooke's face gave me such a high, I never want to come down. I like being the reason for that smile on her face. I want to make her smile like that all the time.

No.

I shake my head at myself. What is wrong with me? When was the last time I entertained thoughts like these?

Never. And I want to keep it that way.

Damn it. I shouldn't have followed my impulse. After leaving Sal's, I should have kept up with my schedule and returned to work.

I run my fingers through my hair. No. I can't live with regret, especially when I had a good time. Teaching the kid how to play the games and kick ass while riling Brooke up one comment at a time was a thrill. Almost as good as getting a new acquisition.

It I've won something, especially given how turned on Brooke was when I left her office. I'll let her stew. Mostly because if I fuck her, she'll expect commitment. I can't blame her. I haven't been upfront or clear.

If only we'd met under different circumstances. If only I hadn't met her son or spent time with him. I'd give anything to throw her into bed and fuck her until my name is the only thing she knows for an hour before setting her free to find a man to live up to the bar I set in bed.

Fuck, I shouldn't have kissed her.

Shaking my head, I throw myself into work until Liz knocks on my door. At my call, she enters, looking me over and arching an eyebrow. "Your hair is out of place, Mr. Thorpe."

I run my fingers through it, brushing the stray locks from my face. Liz turns to leave after she drops the folder on my desk, but she doubles back and looks me over. "Where were you all day?"

"Working with a client."

"And that took all day?" She knows something. She's trying to corner me, I'm sure of it. When I don't answer, she continues. "It's not terrible to have fun, sir. In fact, there have been some studies that say that it improves workplace productivity."

"Discipline does that," I say, pulling the folder. "Ah, I was hoping Marcus wouldn't get scared away by Celine." Her behavior at the convention left me wondering if the businessman had decided to work with another rival instead.

"Apparently not." She goes to retrieve her tablet and we discuss the new client until seven o'clock rolls around. Liz finally stands and lets her hair down. "I like Brooke, by the way. She breathes positivity into the office."

"She's a distraction."

"For who?" Liz asks.

I hold my tongue. She's fishing. Subtly, that's for sure, but she's definitely trying to get me to say something. Brooke is beautiful and so damn sweet that I can't help wanting more than a working relationship. Because I want to know if she curses when she's fucking. I want to know what she looks like as she comes. I want her to moan my name rather than say it.

Shaking my head, I pat my hair back into place again. "Enjoy your weekend, Liz."

"Try to have some fun."

"I plan to."

Because I need to get laid. Badly, if today is any indication. Once I get some semi-decent sex, I'll be able to move on. Brooke's appeal will fizzle away, and she'll go back to the unorganized woman who doesn't like taking direction unless she's the one calling the shots.

Too much like me.

That's all. So I'll go to the bar tomorrow, pick up a girl, have some fun, and call it good.

I'll pull away from her life, stop with the damn home visits and go have a talk with her son's principal if she tries to suspend him again. Ben is just ... just like I was as a kid. Wanting to do everything, turn over every stone, experience as much as possible.

I'd rather not think of him anymore. Especially considering he has Brooke as a mom. A real mom, someone I never had. Beyond being hot, she dedicates herself to him so completely when she's home. She indulges him when possible, makes sure he has fun. I'm sure he thinks she's the best person in the world and honestly, he's lucky to have her.

Too many people, myself included, lost the lottery on good parents.

Shaking the memories away, I throw myself into work, drafting a contract for Marcus's gaming company, then force myself to head home, hit the gym for two hours to exhaust me, jerk off to soften the tension that's been building over the last two days.

When I lay back, I shake my head and dig the heel of my hands into my eyes.

"Stop thinking about it."

But I can't. The memories swirl around me. The sad faces of the case worker every time she'd have to track me down after I ran off. The frustration etched into her features when she was trying to rehome me, not that she ever let me see it when I was paying attention. But I knew I wasn't wanted.

I was 'too much'. I was problematic. I was a bad kid. Getting in fights, stealing to pay for food when my foster mother locked the pantry and fridge. I learned quickly that trust is a word, not a feeling. It's a manipulation tactic. When someone trusts you, they ignore their logic, which means you can turn it on them.

Letting anything escape my control would ruin me then, and it will ruin me now. Even with Brooke. She's sweet, but that could all be a cover. A cover for her kid and her business. Who knows what's actually lurking in her head or in her heart?

---

SERIOUSLY, I NEED A life.

It's seven pm on a Saturday night, and for the first time in my life, I'm bored. I've already spent most of the day at the office, following up on several reports that were due, then threw myself into an hour and a half workout at the gym. I have an easy life. One I like. I don't need 'fun' or anything to distract me from work, but after yesterday, I'm restless. I get through a shower and consider what else there is to do other than hitting the bar for a one-night stand.

Although, sex sounds better than anything right now. Yet, I can't muster the urge to even try getting laid tonight.

I choose a nice restaurant for dinner, splurging on myself for a moment. I'm almost done with dessert—a rare treat—when my phone rings. Glancing down, I see Lydia's name – my last foster mom. I shake my head and send it to voice mail. I'll text her later. I'm forty years old. I don't need her checking in on me like I'm a teenager out past curfew.

She's always been overeager and nosey about my life. As if I owe her something for taking me in.

While waiting for my bill, I glance around the restaurant, zoning in on a couple in the corner. The guy's eyes are glued to his phone and the woman is obviously annoyed since she's been talking for the last minute without his acknowledgement. He yelps when she kicks him under the table, and an argument begins. I scoff, signing the bill. I don't need a relationship. Why jump into something when I will eventually go from happy to miserable? One-night stands are better.

The restlessness follows me out the restaurant. Not having the urge to go home, I head to my favorite bar. Danielle smiles at me as I approach the counter. "Fishing again, Adrian?"

"Eventually I'll find what I'm looking for. Isn't that how it works?"

"A friend with benefits?" Danielle scoffs, sliding me a beer. "That sounds more up your alley, but I think it requires you to at least be able to make friends."

"I have friends."

Danielle arches an eyebrow. I shrug. "Just because you don't know them, doesn't mean I don't have them."

"Get one here and the next round is on me," she offers.

Dipping for my phone, I text my friend from grad school, Jeremy. We haven't spoken in ages, but to my pleasant surprise, he replies. I offer him free beer if he meets me at the address I sent him. Again, he responds right away, telling me he'll be there in five minutes. I nurse another drink until he joins me.

Danielle scrutinizes him with a frown as he sits. "You actually know this dude, right?'

"What, Adrian? Hell yeah. We go way back to grad school."

She grumbles, but gets us both scotch on the rocks. We catch up for a while, then I catch the ring on his finger. "You're married?"

He looks at it and beams. "Yeah. You remember Rachel, the girl I had a crush on in grad school. I asked her to marry me a year ago and she said yes. I've never been happier."

My brows lift. "Really?" Back in college, Jeremy was the wild one, vowing never to settle down.

He nods. "Don't get me wrong, it's work sometimes. We're not perfect, but we're at our best when we're together. And let me tell you, it's amazing not being pressured to be my best self all the time. We actually have burping contests and on Fridays, we order pizza, play a game to decide desert, then lie around in our most comfortable clothes doing absolutely nothing."

"That doesn't sound ... awful."

"Nah. You just have to find the right one. That's the real challenge." He raises his glass to me. "Any woman catch your eye?"

Danielle chokes on her laughter and excuses herself to help other patrons. Jeremy looks at me, his brown hair shorter than I remember, the glasses on his nose new. God it's like I haven't known anything about his life even though we get together every few years.

His phone rings and he looks at it before asking me to hold on. "Rach?"

"Again? Okay. I'll be home soon." He sighs. "Our daughter got broken up with."

"Wait a minute. Daughter?"

"Well, she's Rachel's daughter, actually. In my eyes, she's mine too. We also have a six-month-old boy."

"How old is your daughter?"

"Thirteen." He shakes his head. "Basically, it means that a guy said no to holding her hand. She's a little romantic."

"Well, thanks for the beer and catch up," I say. "Go handle your business, man."

"And good luck finding the one." He pauses. "Congrats on that businessman-of-the-year award, by the way. Always knew you'd kick ass."

I raise my glass to him, then look around the bar for a woman who will do for the night. It must be the liquor fucking with me, but none of these girls look like the 'one' or the 'one for tonight'. None of them have strawberry blonde hair, for one. There's none with curves like a winding road, with long, shapely legs that seem made to wrap around my waist.

Which proves I've got it bad with Brooke.

When I get home, I make myself a bourbon on the rocks, have a second one when the first doesn't work and scroll through my contacts. I see many potential options for the night, but only one woman stands out.

The one I'm sure is either already asleep, or will tell me to fuck right off.

And maybe that's what I need.

Before commonsense chips in, I click her name and hold the phone to my ear.

"H-Hello?" I hear music in the background. It's after midnight. Why is she awake? "Adrian?"

"Are you still out?"

"I thought we agreed no business calls outside of work hours."

"This isn't a business call," I say, unbuttoning and unzipping my pants.

"Are you okay?"

I'm sloshy and lightheaded thanks to the alcohol. "You're killing me, Kitten."

The music fades, letting me know she'd left the main area for someplace quieter. A tingle runs up my spine when she lets out a breathy whimper. I edge my pants down and stroke my already hardening cock. "Ruining all my control and composure."

"Should I apologize for it?"

"No, you should come take care of it," I growl, tightening my hand around myself.

"Take care of ... oh." A softened groan. "Adrian, we already agreed we ... we wouldn't—"

"We don't need to *work*, Brooke. We'd both enjoy a night together. I'd make sure of it." I swallow my groan as I picture her on my bed, blushing, wearing absolutely nothing at all, her delicious, curvy body under my hands. "You can't tell me you're not curious."

"You're drunk." She moans, the sound hardening my cock. "Adrian, you're drunk."

"And right." I smile as she sighs. I can hear the agony. She's wound up tight as I am. "You liked kissing me, didn't you?"

"It was a slip up."

"That was me at peak innocence. Don't you want to see exactly how naughty we could get together? Especially tonight, while you have a babysitter."

"I don't screw around, and I really don't screw around with drunk men."

I don't hide my groan this time as I thrust into my fist. I pant and let my head fall back. "Then let's make a deal."

"Negotiations? Now?" But her voice is all breathy and sexy.

"If you hang up and don't listen to me come, I won't behave myself on Monday."

With that in the air, I stroke my cock, giving it all my attention while picturing Brooke on top of me, riding me hard, her tight pussy gripping my cock.

"Fuck," I groan.

"Oh, my God, Adrian," Brooke whispers in the phone. "I can't believe you're—God."

"You have a choice, Kitten," I hiss, quickening the pace of my strokes. "All you have to do is hang up."

But the line remains open as I disappear into the fantasy once more, her soft moans bathing my ears as she tells me how good I am, how good I feel inside her. I plunge deeper, burying my entire length inside her. Her fingernails curl into my skin as she falls apart in ecstasy. Just before I come, I look at my phone and see her end the call.

It doesn't matter. She listened long enough. I finish into my palm and my hips keep jerking as my climax lengthens. There's no denying I want Brooke. My post-come clarity makes that inescapably fucking clear. Which is a problem. In this perfect moment where everything lines up, I can't have her. It would destroy her, destroy our working relationship, destroy my focus.

Even though she's constant temptation, I have to behave. Even if it means fucking someone new every damn weekend. I'll have to do it. I have to ignore her. Have to get over this stupid schoolboy crush and show my body what it actually wants.

Brooke isn't it.
She can't be.
She won't be.

# Chapter 13

### Brooke

I can't focus on the rest of my night out with the girls. Not after that call. Adrian touching himself with me on the phone was a level of hot I've never experienced. I've never done the whole phone sex thing. I never saw the appeal.

But hearing him groan and grunt as he got closer and closer, the little panting breaths, picturing his face flushed and every inch of his body on display. I couldn't help imagining myself beneath him, his hard strokes bringing me to a long-awaited climax.

The girls try to get me back on the dance floor, but I'm so over tonight. I'm too tipsy, too horny. Very vulnerable. I don't want to do something I'll regret tomorrow, like, find Adrian's address and demand that he fuck the sexual frustration away. So, I bid the girls goodnight and head home.

Adrian is terrible for me. He's like a whole mountain of double chocolate ice cream. I got a taste and I want more, but I won't be able to stop if I get a second helping and that it will ruin me completely. Ruin my diet, ruin my stomach, and make me hate ice cream and chocolate forever.

That's what being with Adrian, even once, will do to me.

I'm sure that one night with Adrian would be fantastic. He has the confidence of a man who knows how to make a woman feel amazing in bed. And sure, Stacy talks about any guy more than seven years older as if he's a geezer, but Adrian definitely isn't. Plus, that soft side he has, the one I've seen with Ben is so damn spell-binding that it makes me gooey and ready to curse or sin or whatever else is required to have him for a little bit longer.

But if I let myself budge at all, if I give more than I already have, there won't be any coming back from it. I've never been able to do the one and done thing. Even after my husband left, I couldn't grab a guy at the bar and take him home. I tried. I got too nervous, flaked, and ran off.

Because what if Ben saw? What if the guy was terrible in bed? What if I was terrible because there was no connection? And why should I waste my time with men who aren't going to stick around when I can give myself pleasure instead?

So I do.

I strip out of my 'girls night' dress and lay naked in bed. I stroke over my body, trying not to think about anything other than my own hands. Not Adrian's steely gray eyes. Not that bit of stubble on his cheek from Friday. Not the way his hair falls in his face when he plays ski ball, or how his breath felt across my throat, the way he licked into my mouth when we made out.

My knees shake as I circle my nipples. I pinch them gently, rolling them between my fingers. One hand sinks low on my belly, over the little roll that I haven't been able to kick thanks to my love of ice cream, then lower still.

I stroke the growing wetness between my legs, pushing one finger in as I whimper. Adrian's groans were so hot.

The way he called me 'kitten', that hungry look in his eyes, all of it keeps me on the edge as I tease myself, thrusting my fingers in and hitting that pleasure point that drives me insane. I whimper and throw my head back as my own moans fill the air.

All at once, I'm done. Panting, I roll on my side as my body keeps moving and grinding, wanting more than my fingers can give. I pull myself through a shower and try again. "I don't want Adrian. He's damaged. He's terrified of commitment. He's only good right now because he's chasing me. The second he gets me, he's gone."

I sink on the floor with a sigh. "Because I'm easy to leave, anyway."

That one thought always does the trick to sober me up. It reminds me why I don't want one night stands, why I can't handle a casual relationship. Greg used me then left me, taking my whole world with him. He showed me that anyone, no matter how good they seem at first, can be a snake underneath.

At least Adrian is up front about who he is. But if I sleep with him, I'll still hope he stays because that's how I am. Ever the hopeless romantic, positive if I work hard enough I'll find my prince charming, the man who can be real and honest with me, a good man, a good father.

But Adrian will never be that man. Even if a part of me wants him to be.

LIKE EVERY OTHER SUNDAY, I throw myself into spending time with Ben. We run through the sprinklers, we play tag, then we go over to Stacy's to borrow her pool so he can wear himself out and have a great time. I'm relaxing by the poolside when Stacy joins me, wearing a white bikini that contrasts with her brown skin and sunglasses that are even darker.

She sits on the lounge chair beside me, gesturing to Ben with a tilt of her chin. "What's with the bruise?"

"Bullies at school." I shake my head. "It's a whole mess, but we're dealing with it. Slowly and surely."

"He has to be able to stand up for himself. How about I teach him to throw a real punch, or tell him where to kick?" Stacy offers. "One time and they'll leave him alone."

"Or they'll come after him twice as hard. Those little monsters keep trying to convince the staff that Ben is the bully."

Stacy's thick eyebrows lift. "Have they met Ben?"

I sigh. "I worry for him, Stace."

"Babe."

"I try so hard to stick to normal work hours and to really be there for him, but I keep wondering if there are things that only a father can teach, that only a father can help with." I rest my chin on my knees. "And the only guy who's taken any kind of interest in me isn't father material."

Stacy twists on the seat to face me, her face registering surprise. "Girl, you've been holding out on me! Who's the guy?"

"No one you know. But, Stace, he's totally hot." I drop my head against the back of the seat with a sigh. "He wants me, and the feeling is mutual."

"So get you some sex and move on," she suggests. "Just because you're a mom doesn't mean you don't deserve a good lay, right? You missed out on all the fun in college since you had Greg. Get it now."

"Stace...."

"I mean it. You'll feel so much better once someone else makes you come. Plus, women with that 'recently fucked' glow attract other men. Men who might be good fathers."

I consider that until Stacy nudges me. "But just to be clear, you don't need a man to be enough for your son."

"I feel like he's missing out, though."

"Look, you give him the love of more than two parents every single day." She motions to Ben, who's happily doing backstrokes in the pool. "He's well adjusted, he's kind, he's smart. He's not eager to beat up his bullies. You've raised a really good kid and that's all *you*. He doesn't *need* a father. He only needs you."

I hug her tightly, then we join Ben in the pool where we keep him busy until sundown. After a shower and a snack when we get home, I curl up with Ben on the couch.

"Are you okay, Mom?" Ben asks me when I've been pausing with the remote too long.

"Of course. I've had a lot on my mind lately." I give him a reassuring smile then turn on the TV.

Ben snuggles up to me. "I like Adrian," he says suddenly.

Surprised, I lean back to stare down at him. "You do?"

Ben nods. "He's a good friend to have, right? A good person."

"He can be when he wants to be." I nudge him. "But the jury's still out on him, my sweetheart." The last thing I want is for Ben to get attached. I can handle a broken heart, but my son, it will devastate him. It took him ages to get over his father leaving him. I don't know if he'll survive another heartbreak.

---

I RUB MY BURNING EYES, brushing a stray lock from my half-combed hair. A soft yawn escapes my lips as the beeping from the coffee percolator lets me know my morning pick-me-up is ready for me. I'm exhausted from tossing in bed all night with the raging battle between my body and head. I don't want this ache for Adrian. My instincts scream at me, begging me to not let him in. But the more I resist, the stronger the urge to lose myself in him.

Just one taste.

One taste, and I'll walk away.

I can handle a fling, can't I?

A sudden knock on the front door makes me pause pouring the coffee into my cup. Adrian strolls in a second later, and my stupid heart starts dancing for joy. I ignore its wild fluttering and return to adding cream and sugar to my cup.

He doesn't say a word. A gentle creaking tells me he's sitting down. I turn and see him in my seat, an audacious smile on his face.

"Good morning to you, too," I say. "You're sitting in the wrong seat."

He smirks, adjusting himself on the chair. "Am I?"

"Can you move, please? Don't think I won't sit on you."

His smirk widens. "I dare you."

Huffing, I set the cup down and march over to sit on his lap, powering on my laptop.

Two hands stroke up my sides, my shoulders, finally along my neck and into my hair. "For turning me down on Saturday, you're eager to be on top now," Adrian says in a gravelly voice.

Realizing my mistake, I start to rise, but he pulls me back down, my ass grinding on his erection. A soft moan leaves my mouth. Adrian yanks the scrunchie from my wrist and puts my hair into a ponytail. He pulls it back and kisses across my neck.

"This ... we're supposed to be working," I pant.

"You were late." The growl against my skin makes me shiver. "I should punish you for that."

"I'm not your employee," I argue.

"Luckily you're not." Still, his other hand rubs my hip. "And, lucky for you, your skin tastes almost as good as your mouth."

As if he has to prove it, he licks up my throat. This has to be a dream, right? It has to be. There's no way Adrian is throwing himself at me. He gets chased, he doesn't do all this to get women. He doesn't have to.

"Are you uncomfortable, Brooke?" he asks against my ear.

"No," I admit.

"Do you want me to stop?" His fingers brush my knee, slowly stroking along the skin of my inner thigh.

My logic is screaming, demanding that I get off him, leave the office, and be done with Adrian entirely, no matter what that means. But I'm so tired of fighting him. I'm exhausted all around and maybe Stacy's right. Maybe I need a good lay. I can do it without emotion, even if this last week with Adrian has proven he's capable of more than he thinks.

"Kitten," he purrs against my jaw. "I need an answer."

"Why?" I try to move again, and he groans. "Why me?"

"Because I tried to pick someone up at the bar and I couldn't. None of those women measured up to you." He nibbles my throat. "Because I can't get you out of my head." This time he jerks my hair back, so his mouth is nearly against mine. "Because I'm tired of behaving."

"But I hung up." It's the stupidest thing to say. "I didn't listen to ... to you ... finish."

Adrian groans and lets me go, showing some restraint, but all I manage to do is stand with my ass against my desk. He towers over me as he gets up, putting his hands on either side of mine, blocking me in.

Normally this would scare me. It should scare me, right? He's bigger than me, muscular as hell, and he knows it. But all I feel is hunger. I want him. And no amount of self-talk is going to change it.

"Do you want me, Brooke? Or am I seeing things that aren't there?"

"You're not. I ... I do," I whisper.

"Then all I need is one word." He loosens the tie at his throat, starts working on the buttons. Slowly, he pulls off his jacket and shirt, revealing the sexiest torso I've ever seen. His broad shoulders, thick arms, the taper of his waist. He's seriously sex on a stick. We should market modeling companies or gyms with his body. "Just one."

"Oh my," I breathe.

Adrian chuckles and guides my chin to his face. "That was two ... but thank you."

I blush beet red. "I ... we're in my office."

"That couch looks plenty big enough for us," he murmurs, finger brushing across my bottom lip.

His gaze sizzles across my skin and I itch for more than this light touch. He licks across his top lip. "I can't focus on work when we share an office. I'm too busy thinking about you, wanting you."

"You're a scoundrel," I whimper, watching as he reaches for his slacks. He pops the button, then goes for the zipper. As he shoves them down, revealing more skin, more muscle, and a huge, thick erection that puts everything I've seen until now to shame, I lose control of my mouth. "Delicious."

"You can find out," he pants. "I want you. Exactly as you are. Right fucking now."

I think I nod. I must do something that says yes, because the next thing I know, Adrian's yummy mouth is on mine. He kisses me like he can erase every trace of anyone else who's ever touched me, like I'm his and his alone. But his hands are so gentle. He guides me closer to him, strokes down my back, gently palms my bottom.

His hard body, demanding mouth, soft hands, it's a combination that I can't even pretend I don't want. I moan and against his mouth and stroke over his shoulders, savoring his silky skin stretched over the hard plane of muscle.

"Let me make you feel good, Kitten," he purrs against my open mouth.

"Please," I whisper, surprised I'm capable of speaking. "Please, Adrian."

He grins and jerks my dress over my head, tossing it to the side. Pressing his lips to mine again, I feel the rumble of his eagerness in his chest. "Good girl."

# Chapter 14

### Adrian

I peel away Brooke's bra and panties, lifting her into my arms. Her legs wrap around my waist as she keeps kissing me. I'm breaking all my rules with her. I'm that fucking desperate to get over this crush. Fucking her will do it. It does every time. Once we fuck, the questions will be gone, the curiosity sated.

But as I lay her down on the couch, I'm really fucking worried she's going to ruin that too. Because she's gorgeous, better than my fucking fantasies. Her breasts are full, her belly not flat, but still cute, and those damn hips, so curvy and pointing me right down to her pussy, shaved and perfectly nestled between her thick thighs.

"Adrian, you're making me self-conscious," she whispers, covering her pussy with one hand and her breasts with her arm.

I pull at both; angry she's ruining the view. "You're gorgeous and I want to enjoy looking at you."

"Enjoy it by touching me," she challenges.

I groan and climb on top of her, one knee nudging her legs open, so I have access to every bit of her I want. I stroke down her shoulder as she touches my side, gently at first, soon with more curiosity, stroking along the scar I got when my appendix was removed.

"Do you ..." she starts, then looks up at me. "Is this okay?"

"That's my line," I murmur, kissing her hungrily.

And every kiss I get only makes me want her more. When her body rolls to meet mine, I can't hold out. I kiss across Brooke's neck, then lick over her cleavage. She moans, throaty and wonderful. I suck her nipple between my lips and push her thighs apart so I can tease her with a finger.

She pants, the threat of her nails running along my back. God, she's perfect. Perfectly sweet, perfectly soft, perfectly loud. I swirl my tongue around her nipple as my finger makes the same path around her clit and she lets out another moan as her body arches against me, offering even more.

I bite softly, then kiss her again, licking deep into her mouth before pumping two fingers into her wetness. Brooke's legs try to close around me, but she can't make it happen with me in the way. Her legs open right back up for me. She wants this as much as I do. Her blush, her wild hair slipping out of the pony already, the way she keeps those dark eyes on me as I finger her.

"I was thinking about you when I called," I mumble. "About you riding me, how good and wet you'd feel around my cock."

Her lips part, but more moans pour out, no words. I push a third finger into her, and her pussy tightens around my fingers, clinging tightly, like her body's afraid I won't let her finish.

"You're better than I thought you'd be, Kitten," I purr, licking over her lower lip before she sits up and kisses me.

I blink in surprise, but accept her arm around my neck, her fingers threading through my hair, her hips grinding against my hand as she tries to find release. I curl my fingers and her mouth opens against mine before her head falls back.

"Adrian!" she moans my name.

I groan in response and fuck her faster with my fingers. I want her coming, I want her thinking of no one but me when I'm inside her. When she finally comes for me, her pussy squeezes my fingers so tightly and she arches her back so hard that I'm afraid I've broken her. She goes limp on the couch, panting hard, her pulse reverberating through her until I swear I can hear it when I lick over her neck.

"So good," she whispers.

I chuckle. "Those were just my fingers, Brooke. I think you'll like my cock a lot more."

"Yes." She nods eagerly. "Please."

"You want to ride me? Feel me deep inside you and come again?" I ask.

"Please, Adrian."

I sit down and pull her onto my lap. She rolls her hips, spreading her wetness over my cock again and again. I forgot all about a condom. I told myself I'd behave today, before this vixen sat on my lap and ruined all my self-control.

"I'm on the pill," she says, as if she read my mind. She rolls her hips again, dragging a groan from me. Just feeling her hot, wet pussy on my cock is nearly enough to drive me insane. "I want you inside me."

"So dirty," I growl, adjusting my cock so I'm tapping her entrance. "Keep talking to me like that, and you'll get a second round."

She laughs softly, sinking down on me, not inching down, not teasing, but taking. Fucking hell, if she were any more like me, I'd hate her. She rides me without hesitation or insecurity, bouncing while rolling her hips, circling them, moaning and hitting where she wants without letting me feel left out.

I thrust into her every time she comes down as she grips my shoulders hard. I take one breast and wrap my mouth around her nipple, sucking and licking as I guide her hips. She feels better than my hand and so much better than she was in my dreams.

Better than just about any lay I've had in the last year. Her firm ass hits my thighs every time she comes down and I can't resist grabbing a handful of her and jerking her closer to me. Her lips part as she looks down at me, my lips wrapped around her nipple, groaning as she gives herself over entirely.

"Fuck, you're gorgeous." I groan, tangling my hand in her hair and dragging her down to kiss me as her nails scratch down my arms.

My stomach tightens. I'm getting close. I can't fucking help it. I can usually go as long as I want, but Brooke makes control next to impossible. I can't think about anything but her gorgeous body, the sounds she's making, how she smells like an exotic rainforest, and feels like heaven itself.

I bite her throat, then soothe the mark with a kiss when she hisses.

"Fuck me," she pants.

I come to a dead stop and meet her eyes. "Did you just curse?"

"Fuck me hard, Adrian," she orders.

I pick her up and drop her back onto the couch, holding myself over her as I slam into her tight pussy, taking everything she offers and more. I cup her ass, jerking her leg over my shoulder so I'm even deeper inside her.

"Adrian," she moans. "Just like that."

"Such a dirty girl for me," I snarl, nibbling her bottom lip. My arms shake as I try to restrain myself. She's still too sweet for the kind of rough sex I like. "Keep talking."

"You feel good." She groans, tugging on the back of my neck. "So good."

I shudder. "I need you to come again."

"It's your turn," she argues.

I snort and push my hand between our bodies, taking a moment to look at exactly how well her pussy is taking me. How my cock disappears, then comes out shiny and wet. It's a fucking sinful view.

"Adrian!"

I rub her clit as I fuck her, determined to make her come again. If she's only ever come once from sex, she's about to learn exactly what a man should be doing for her. Her eyes start to roll back as her lips part, and she grips the couch in one hand and my hip in the other.

Writhing under me and making her hair a mess, she stops thinking and just feels, exactly what I was hoping for. Her back arches and she raises her hips to meet mine with every thrust until my vision is hazy and I'm panting and groaning right along with her.

Fucking hell, this woman is too much. She's far too much. And I can't hold out. I'm too close, too –

"God!" She yells and comes apart for me, pussy tightening until she drags me with her. I see sparks, my body shaking and shuddering as I thrust deep inside her and finish.

Her leg falls to the side and I can barely hold myself up over her. She strokes my face, shocking me and I instinctively grab her wrist. Brooke arches an eyebrow at me, then tugs me down to lay on her chest. And I can't resist. I can't tell her no. I can't do a damn thing but lay there as my heart keeps thundering through my body.

There's no denying. I can't run anymore. I am falling for this woman. That's why it's different. I respect the hell out of her, I like spending time with her and her kid, and damn if she doesn't make me feel like no other woman has in years. It's not an option not to call her. It's not an option to ghost her.

No matter what, I have to see her in the office, I have to work with her, and I can't just … think. Because she's right here. I can't call her a cab. The second I walk out of this office has to be perfectly timed or I'll be lucky not to take a stapler to the head … or watch her cry.

Fuck.

By fucking her I've fucked myself because I can't do this. Despite what I feel for her, I can't trust her. I can't give her more than sex. And her fingers, stroking through my hair, petting me as she comes down from her high is going to rip me to shreds. If I don't break things off with her, she's going to break me. One piece at a time.

She'll distract me, charm me, ruin my empire brick by brick until all that's left is some scared, useless little kid who never got attention or love or a second glance. I'll be a pathetic husk of a man and I refuse to be that.

I clear my throat and start to move, but she makes a frustrated sound and tightens her arms around me. "Cuddling is mandatory."

I smirk despite myself. "Even if it's workplace sex?"

"Sex with me means yes," she whispers.

Brooke's already thinking again. She's waiting for me to leave, I'm sure of it. She knows my reputation. She threw it in my face when I asked her to be my fake ex-wife.

She knows this won't be, can't be, more than sex. She doesn't need to know why. I start to move, but her fingers keep petting me, stroking down my neck until I shiver. She hums in her throat.

"Think you'll be able to focus on work in a bit?"

"Yeah." It's a lie and I know it. Because now I have to balance this lust that's already threatening to come up again. If I can't be everything for her, I might as well be nothing. And I'll work on being nothing but an asshole ... in five minutes.

She wraps a leg around me and sighs as she squeezes me gently. "That might have been better than breakfast."

Okay ... maybe ten minutes.

## Chapter 15

### Brooke

After ten minutes of cuddling, which still feels too short, Adrian gets up and starts getting dressed. I make myself do the same. I desperately want to clean up, really don't want to think about this. I just want to forget.

But sex has never been that good, ever. I've never let my lust get the best of me, never felt revived or refreshed by having sex. I've never let anyone seduce me at work, not even my ex-husband who tried more than once.

"Just loosen up a little, Brookey. You're the boss and it's sexy as hell. Come on, we'll be quick," Greg used to say.

I'd always tell him a professional environment has to stay professional. I'd remind him that some lines shouldn't be crossed. Then I'd kiss his cheek, tell him I love him, and get to work. So why wasn't it that easy with Adrian?

And worse, why do I want him to stay? Why do I want to think that he felt what I felt while we had sex? Because that was more than a quickie. It was more than a workplace romp in a coat closet to scratch an itch.

Hell, sex has never been like that for me. So all-consuming, soul-branding, earth shattering. The things I said, the way he held me, talked to me, all of it was more than I've ever experienced and more intimate than I expected.

Instead of focusing on the rising emotions that threaten to ruin me, I smooth out my dress and take my seat, focusing entirely on the laptop screen. I review an email he sent and clear my throat. "So. Sal's daughter sent over some footage?"

"Yes." Adrian's voice is cool. No. That's a lie. It's freezing. It's like the man who made love to my body no longer exists.

He moves closer. The scent from his perfume gives me a heady rush, leaving goosebumps on my skin. I keep my eyes locked to the screen; afraid he'll see the emotions I'm trying to hide. "That's great. We can review edit it together."

"I have a team assigned for that task, Brooke."

Great. Another thing I can't do. "Well I can crop bits of it and post them on social media. I have an account that has quite a bit of traction. And he's going to do the punch card, so we're set there. I already have a bunch of them printed. Over three hundred."

"You're quick on the draw," he replies.

I shift in my seat, still feeling the wetness between my legs. "Then it sounds like we have everything in order."

"I'd like you to take a look at another project. Sal referred a friend who asked to be 'put in the think tank' in his words," Adrian says. "I'll have Ms. Masters send over the file so you can review it."

Surprised, I look up at him. "You're hiring me for another partnership?"

He nods. "Are you surprised? You're great at what you do, Brooke. It's a pleasure working with you."

I can't help smiling. "I like working with you too, Adrian. Granted, I hated your guts at first, but you've redeemed yourself."

He chuckles. "I'm glad to hear it. We'll talk more on this new contract when the time allows."

"Okay." I nod.

He's silent for a while and my eyes flick to him. He rubs his jaw as he watches me. "Are you?"

From the tentativeness in his eyes, it's obvious he's not asking about work. "Yes," I reply softly.

"Okay." He nods. "You won't need to come to my office. If you have questions, I'll gladly answer them via email. It's approaching my busy season. Last week I had some wiggle room, but I have three new clients to address this week as well as—"

Ah. Here is it. He keeps talking, using those long sentences and more words than necessary. But I can cut through the bullshit. He's making it clear that what we did meant nothing to him. At all. He doesn't want more. He's satisfied now.

So I let him talk, watching him. I bet he's never had to actually have this conversation. I swallow my disappointment. I knew what I was getting into. I stop him by touching his arm. "I get it, Adrian. I'm glad you don't want to monitor me anymore."

He blinks a few times and his teeth click together. "As long as there's no confusion."

"None at all." I walk him to the door of my office and offer him my hand. "See you next week, if necessary."

"Brooke." He nods.

I nod back. "Mr. Thorpe."

He tenses at the formality, looks at me for a long time, then clutches his fist into a hand and walks out like I've insulted him. I shut the door and press my back to it, closing my eyes.

"Stupid, Brooke," I hiss at myself. "Did you really expect anything different? He was being nice to get his foot in the door and you gave him no reason to stay."

No. It's not on me. He never stays. That's his rule. I take a few deep breaths and shake the depressing thoughts from my head. Work. Work is more important. So I throw myself at it. I take care of Sal, sending him everything he'll need and posting some snippets of the videos his daughter sent.

Liz emails me the file and says she wishes she got to give it to me in person, that she can't wait for another girl's night. And that's how the week goes. Adrian hardly speaks to me, even over email. Liz handles everything. It's getting on my nerves.

He's a coward. Can't even face me after fucking me. Even my ex-husband was better than that and that's a really low bar. Adrian isn't an asshole, he's weak. He's scared, and he's unwilling to compromise.

And just as I resign myself to hate him, I receive an email asking me to come in on Friday.

Surprise, surprise. I glare at my computer. "Are you listening to me, Adrian? Don't want to let me off the hook even though you won't keep what you catch?"

I watch my phone and email, almost expecting a reply. Nothing. At least he didn't bug my office to make sure I don't talk about our little bit of fun. No. I'm not going to let him get under my skin.

I send a chipper reply saying I'll be there bright and early at nine thirty. He sends back, ordering me there an hour earlier and I say that I appreciate his eagerness, but unfortunately, since I'm not an employee, I'm a partner, he has to compromise.

Sure, it's sassier than I probably should be, but it's not because of the sex. I promise myself that. Because it's not. It's me reminding him that he's not my boss and can't order me around like he does the people on his payroll, no matter what's happened between us.

I don't get a reply and head home for the day. Stacy comes over and Ben plays video games with her. He's asked about Adrian once already and when I told him that he's a busy businessman, he accepted it with a shrug and hasn't asked again. He liked having Adrian around, but I'm glad he didn't get attached. At least, I'm the only one nursing the wound from Adrian's subtle rejection.

I smile as Stacy playfully shoves Ben and he shoves her back with a laugh. Glad that he's distracted, I get some housework done. Ben falls asleep on the couch by the time I'm done. After putting him to bed, Stacy and I huddle on the couch with a bottle of wine between us.

"How is everything going at work?" she asks.

"Really good. I'm actually in the 'good' area instead of 'fine.'" I stick out my tongue and she laughs. "I'm saving up to send the little man to the camp he keeps asking about and I don't have to worry about going on the ramen noodle diet to do it."

Stacy hi-fives with me. "That's a huge win! We need to celebrate." She swirls the wine in the glass.

A mischievous look in her eye stops me cold. "What is that face, Stacy? I don't trust it."

"What do you mean? I'm totally innocent. I think we should go out, or you should come over for a little party I'm throwing this Sunday."

"What kind of party?"

"Just a party, jeeze. Friends coming over. Adults to hang out with. A barbeque," she says. "Would it be so bad to be around people your own age?"

"I have a seven-year-old," I remind.

"And parents who'd love to spend time with him. It's not an over-night affair, Brooke. You can leave by eight and pick him up and get him bed," she insists. "Please? We can even invite Liz and her boyfriend. After meeting her, I *have* to meet him."

I try to keep my frown, but it's next to impossible. "Fine. But no funny business. I don't trust that smile and I *can't* trust you if you're planning things."

"I'm a good egg. Ask Ben," she says.

"He says that because he's heard you call yourself that so often. To get out of trouble. With me," I point out.

We finish our wine, I hug her, and promise I'll consider the 'innocent' party. Soon enough, it's morning I'm in the elevator on the way up to Adrian's office. No. Mr. Thorpe's office. Because that's who he is here. He's not the Adrian I like. He's not the Adrian who hung out with my son as if it were second nature. He's not the Adrian I made love to in my office.

He's a different man here. Cold, distant, and all work. Which is exactly how I should be. Because one round of good sex and a few good actions doesn't make Adrian a good man. He's not necessarily evil for dropping me that quickly, but he's definitely not the kind of man I have space for in my life.

So I won't torture myself over him. I won't.

I check my watch, see I'm a little late, but I don't care. I stop at Liz's desk and she looks up at me with concern on her face. "You're late."

"A few minutes won't kill him," I reply casually. "Stacy is having a party this Sunday and she wanted me to invite you and your boyfriend. I can text you the details if you want."

"If I'm not here, I'll be there." She glances towards Adrian's office and winces. "He's glaring at us."

I glance through the glass and sure enough, his dark stare lashes me. I cut my eyes away and smile at Liz. "What's he going to do? Throw me over his shoulder and drag me into his office?"

"He's been in a terrible mood since Monday. No humor."

"Does he ever have some to spare?" I hand her muffin and coffee. "You deserve a raise for dealing with him."

She accepts my gift I walk into Adrian's office and sit down, taking my sweet time. He pushes his palms together in front of his face. "Time is money, Ms. Dean."

"If all you do is work, sure," I reply. "I emailed you and Liz everything relevant for Sal's file."

"We need to discuss our contract. It only covered one client. I'm not happy with your repeated ..."

"Push for compromise?" I want him to say it, to actually say it.

"Businesses require negotiation; however, you push the line too far. Every time." He growls, steely eyes about as warm as the Arctic. "Showing up late and taking your time with Ms. Masters, flaunting exactly how little our meetings mean to you ..."

"You're implying."

"I'm inferring based on your behavior."

I watch him quietly. Something Liz taught me to do. He holds my gaze until my face heats. This is the first time we've been alone since .... Well. I look away. "You're wasting more time than I did by chastising me."

"I want to be able to trust you in business matters."

"But trust doesn't come easily, does it?" I counter, not looking at him. "Which is why you micromanage me, insist on being looped into everything despite being the CEO, and won't step foot in my office after—"

"Are you complaining that I'm not warm and fuzzy?" he demands.

I look at my watch.

"Do you have somewhere else to be?"

"I'm not some rebellious high school kid here to be lectured by the principal. Talk to me like an adult, or don't waste my time."

"Don't waste mine," he hisses.

I meet his eyes again. Forcing a grin, I stand. "Then I'll leave. Clearly you don't need me for the client. Like you said, we don't have a contract for this one and it's not like I'm part of the deal. Thank you for the partnership and holding up your end of the deal, Mr. Thorpe."

"Ms. Dean."

I ignore him, walking to the exit. My hand curls around the doorknob.

"Brooke."

His low voice, the *almost* plea gets me to stop. That and hearing my name on his tongue sends heat between my thighs. I swallow hard as his chair creaks. He's getting up. I still can't make myself turn around. I won't. There's no space for him in my life.

I learn from my mistakes. I don't make them multiple times over.

Adrian was a mistake. A pleasant one, but a mistake all the same.

"Please sit down," he says.

"Why?"

"Because I'd like to do this civilly."

I turn and find him closer than expected. I drink him in, gorgeous, perfect, every bit of him put together and closed off. It's not me who doesn't have space for him. No. It's him. He doesn't have space for anyone else in his life. Nothing short of perfect is good enough. Which means that anything, person, situation that doesn't fit in with his definition of golden will fall short.

"And what is *this* conversation going to be about?" It's a change, one chance for him to try with me.

His throat bobs. "Work. We only have a working relationship, Ms. Dean."

He's making damn sure of that, isn't he? "Sure, Mr. Thorpe. Whatever you say."

# Chapter 16

### Adrian

I'm supposed to like obedience, but when Brooke is so flippant with me, I want to bend her over my knee and remind her who's in charge. Or worse, activate the privacy screen on my office and remind her how hard she came for me.

Which isn't allowed. Because I won't do more than fuck her. I'm not capable of that. She's got a whole life without me and that's what's best. Especially since she has a kid. A kid changes everything. I don't date longer than a week to begin with but mix a kid in and it's irresponsible to be with a woman unless the end goal is marriage.

Brooke sits down and watches me as I try to measure her temper. It's there, seething below the surface. She doesn't want to look at me because she doesn't want to be here. She wants to be done with me too.

That's supposed to be the best case scenario. Just like fucking her was supposed to end this damn crush, but it's made me greedy. And that's pissed me off. She's not allowed to break the mold, but here she is doing just that and flaunting it like our sex meant nothing to her either. Like she regrets it and me.

"You said we were going to talk about work. Please, go ahead."

That goddamn please. My hand hovers over the privacy screen button and I force myself to let it go. "The client wants our collaboration specifically. That is the condition of the contract. You didn't miss that."

"I didn't, but I'm not a stranger to no."

"Aren't you?" I ask. "Someone as sunny as you seems to be eager to please."

"Not all the time." She brushes her knee even though nothing is on it. "I'd accept the same terms as we have for Sal's."

"Forty-percent on this client. I'll raise it to forty-five if they renew the contract after three months," I offer.

"Fine."

No negotiation? From the queen of negotiations? Interesting. No. Frustrating. Why the hell can't I get a read on her? Why isn't she like every other woman? Set in her ways, predictable at some point, at least angry with me.

"I'll have the paperwork in a moment." I send Liz the request in an email. "Anything else you'd like to discuss?"

"The views on the reel I posted have increased greatly. Others have gone and posted their own. They're all positive and fun. I wouldn't expect anything less from Sal. Families seem to love his restaurant more than anyone since the food is so kid friendly and they still have coloring mats and hang up the art that kids leave," she answers.

"Any other ideas for this new client?" I ask.

She crosses her legs and rubs her knee. "I did have an idea."

I motion for her to continue.

"So ... we've talked about a few different methods with social media. We're doing well with the reels, doing well with the YouTube commercials, and so on. For this new client, we can adopt a similar approach, but I think we should take it a step further."

"Meaning?"

"Social media isn't the same for everyone. It goes based on trends and tries to market accordingly. If we can get some Facebook pages for the business and get people to start checking in, it will pop more on their friends' feeds and spread even further. A lot of restaurants spend more trying to make and sell shirts than it would cost to bump the advertising for us so, I think it would be a really easy sell. Plus, if it starts doing well, like Sal's, we could do keychains or magnets.

Cheaper, easier to transport, more people collect them, and it would be a reminder."

How has none of this crossed my mind? How is her business failing at all when she's able to roll with the changes in advertising this easily?

"And, like I said, podcasts and Spotify. It's a lightly tapped market overall and we could easily get involved, especially with local podcast teams. I actually found four channels that have more than three thousand subscribers each that are interested."

"You already did this?" I ask.

"Yes. Why wouldn't I? It's my job." She hands me a piece of paper. "We can talk to the client about it together, but there are a few ways to make it sound like the best option and get them to agree if they're on the fence. Subtle things. Nodding while suggesting it. It sounds silly, but it works a lot. With your reputation to back it, they'll agree."

Brooke tucks her hair behind her ear and puts on that effortless smile. Not only is this woman sexy, sweet, and genuine, she has a brain that might put mine to shame. Which shouldn't happen. This is my business, I've built it up from next to nothing. They were near bankrupt when I took over and now …

And I've built it up, on my own, with a team that followed my advice. I cultivated the best to join and somehow I missed her. Missed her completely and a part of me is pissed that she's able to one up me so easily while the other part is just … impressed.

Her brow furrows and I realize I haven't answered. "It sounds like a good plan for this client. I trust you to walk some of my team through it."

"Oh!" She gently touches her face, like she didn't expect me to agree. But I'm not missing out on what could be an excellent return.

"Anything else?"

"What else could there be, Mr. Thorpe?"

I keep studying her face. I try to find any trace of discomfort, any level of upset, watching for anything that I missed with Celine. But there's nothing. Like what we did and me backing off hasn't affected her. Before I can open my mouth, Liz comes in with the printed paperwork. I write in the percentages, the time frame, handing it to Brooke.

"I assume Celine is leaving you alone," she says as she signs.

"She is," I reply simply.

"Then have a good weekend and try to take some time off. I hear it's good for your state of mind." She stands.

I don't want her to leave, which drives me crazy. It's not because she's so uninterested, it's because I miss going back and forth with her. I miss her authentic smile, not this retail one which looks *almost* real.

She's more than the women I'm used to fucking. I knew that from the start. She has a son, she's tenacious without losing a smile, and she's so fucking patient it's grating on my nerves in a way I don't entirely hate.

"We will have to collaborate heavily in the beginning of this contract. Monday we'll have a join meeting with the client – here obviously," I say.

The corner of her mouth pulls up. "What, you don't think my office has charm?"

"Charm, asbestos, dust, bad lighting," I list.

She snorts out a laugh and waves. "See you then. You better bring your compromise game and your listening ears because I'm going to be like I was with Sal."

"It works, so I can't knock it."

"Almost a compliment, look at that."

"I'm capable of giving you more than an 'almost'," I reply.

She freezes, meets my eyes and nibbles her bottom lip. It goes right to my cock, tightens my belly, and makes me want to get my hands on her again. I know how delicious her mouth is and biting her bottom lip has been a recurring theme in my fantasies.

"See you Monday unless you have another stalker by then."

Without waiting for my reply, she heads out, waving to Liz. I rub my forehead in frustration. It shouldn't be hard to get over this woman. She's everything I don't want in a woman. She's too confrontational, she has a kid, she's practically begging for commitment while struggling for stability. I don't have anything to gain by being with her outside of business.

But my cock hardens as I remember her command to fuck her. And my heart lurches as I remember her hands in my hair, the way she cuddled me without planning our future, without demanding more than a few minutes of giving me affection, even without me asking for it.

God damn, I'm too fucking soft and too starved for attention. But I haven't been able to throw myself into trying to get another woman on my arm or been able to convince myself to accept the offers I've received. My friends used to say to get over a woman, you get under another, but that works for flings and break ups, not self-imposed removal.

It's not like some prince charming will sweep Brooke up, right? Not with a kid and work eating up her life. Not that I'd care, anyway. Hell, it would be better if they did. Then it would be like Liz all over again, even if I didn't have the same intense infatuation with Liz.

Liz sticks her head in the door, interrupting my thoughts. "Do you have that contract for me?" she asks.

I hand it to her and she scans it with a scoff. "Another partnership. When are you going to hire her?"

"She'd never accept me as her boss," I reply. "And I don't need someone disrupting our current team. Any updates or clients requesting meetings?"

Liz cocks her head to the side. "Check your calendar. I update it hourly."

I nod. "Thank you, Liz."

She lingers at the door. "Don't mess things up with Brooke. She's sweet and hard working."

"Meaning?"

"Don't be unprofessional with her." She points at me. "I mean it, Adrian. As a friend. I've watched you do things I don't approve of, but it's your life. Do me a favor and don't ruin one of the first friendships I've had as an adult."

I watch as she walks away. What the fuck is Brooke doing to my office? What is she doing to my head?

I make myself believe that it doesn't matter, that she's a passing thing and get through the rest of the day. I work Saturday as well, doing tasks that could be left until Monday. Five o'clock rolls around and I'm still not exhausted enough to get thoughts of Brooke out of my head, so I throw myself into the gym. After a grueling hour that gives me no relief, I shower and head to the bar, determined to find a woman for the night. But like the last time, I find no one who holds a candle to Brooke. Frustrated, I leave for home. It's not that there aren't attractive women, but my dick seems to be entirely focused on the one that wants a damn leash around my neck and the promise of more than a week in bed.

"No," I tell my cock as it taps my belly. "It's porn or nothing at all."

Fuck. This is what Brooke's reduced me to. Lying in bed alone at night, talking to my cock. Which clearly means I need an intervention, because no man should be stuck on a woman like this. It's a sign of weakness. It's a vulnerability I can't afford.

DID I MENTION WHO MUCH I hate Mondays?

I hate it even more this morning, because it means the source of my weekend torture will be coming into my office today. Seeing her will only increase the agony. I'm hanging by a thread, resisting the urge to keep my hands to myself. I don't want to surrender. Sleeping with Brooke will only complicate our working relationship, and I can't afford to let that happen. She doesn't know it, but I need this partnership as much as she does.

As I step from the elevator, I see Brooke talking with Liz at Liz's desk. I glance at my watch. She's early. This is a pleasant surprise. I bid them both good morning as Liz hands me a file.

"Come on, it wasn't that bad," Liz says to Brooke as I walk away. "I had fun, Julio had fun. It was a great time."

"You can say that because you were there with a partner. I can't believe Stacy roped me into that. I knew she was planning something and I still let her take me on a ride."

"She wants what's best for you, that's all."

"Yeah, after telling me that I don't need a man. And I'm sure of that than ever, honestly," Brooke replies, her voice wistful.

I close my office door and press my ear against it, listening.

"Oh? She said you were the romantic type."

"I am. There's someone out there for me and Ben, but I don't think I'm going to find him at a surprise mixer thrown by my best friend. Especially when she's all about me having fun."

"Because you're a bright person who works too hard. You need some balance," Liz insists. "Otherwise, you'll become like ...."

"Bossy boots?" Brooke says.

There's a short silence, and I wait, wondering if she'll mention our little fuck session. I breathe a sigh of relief when Liz says, "You can't *not* date for another ten years, Brooke. You're young and hot and son or not, you deserve to be loved and doted on. If you put yourself out there, I'm sure a good man will snatch you up in a heartbeat."

I open the door, startling the two women. "The client will be here in five minutes," I bark. "I expect both of you in the conference room before he gets here."

"Yes, Mr. Thorpe," Liz says, her work voice in place.

Brooke watches me with a wicked smile playing on her lips. I have no doubt she knows I was listening. But I don't care. She should move on. She should absolutely move on. The more I heard the surer I was.

I'm not romantic. I'm not commitment ready and I don't want to be 'fun' even if it wasn't terrible spending the day with her and her son. It's not the future I'm made for. I'm not sad about it. But seeing how easily she works with the client; how smart she is and quick and flexible ... I'm convinced she's an asset.

I can't stop myself from wondering if she's waiting for me to ask for more. Maybe I'd be willing to go a week with her. Maybe two. I won't make the same mistake of spending time with her son, but I could definitely enjoy more of her sweetness, more of her moans, her quick wit and liveliness.

When I'm ready, though. Once we don't have these contracts holding us in place. And she's a single mom. It's not like she spends her free time dating around, jumping between men and so on. So I have to wait a few months, entice her for a few weeks, and see what happens.

By then she'll change her mind about wanting commitment from a man. Or maybe I'll get her out of my head. I won't think about her every night. Won't turn up the radio on my way to work and nod along to the beat. I'll be my old self again.

We get through the meeting, but it's not quite as seamless as it was last time. Brooke and I aren't on the same wavelength, but she still charms the client, promises perfection and I back it up with my reputation. He leaves with a smile and an agreement that makes me and Brooke quite satisfied. She's smiling too, at least until she pulls out her phone.

"More trouble at school?" I ask before I can stop myself. And I nearly kick myself for the comment.

"Nope. They caught Ben's bullies beating another student, so he was cleared. But I got him a cell phone just in case," she replies.

"Good to know," I say.

"Yup. But can we stick to talking about work, please?" Her voice sounds cool although she's wearing a smile.

I nod. "I look forward to seeing Sal's numbers increase. And I may have to ask you to add some extra hours in this week," I say.

"Any day but Friday. I have plans."

With Ben, of course. I dip my chin. "Add one hour of work today, tomorrow, and Thursday. I may send you an email or two Friday and Saturday."

"No weekends," she clarifies. "Especially not at forty percent."

I rub the spot between my eyebrows. "Brooke."

"Mr. Thorpe."

Her formality shouldn't be getting under my skin. This is the kind of thing I wanted after my experience with Celine. I craved this level of understanding, the professionalism, all of it. So why the fuck are my boxers in a twist because of Brooke Dean?

"Replying to emails doesn't take hours. If you aren't up for the challenge, you should have made that clear early on. I had assumed that your ambition was backed by commitment."

Her eyes narrow. "I'm not the one who lacks the ability to commit. Ability to enforce boundaries, maybe, but not any issues with commitment."

She flips her hair over her shoulder, bathing me in her mouthwatering perfume as she walks out. No trace of the sunny woman that dazzled me for a fucking week. Good. Keep her icy and this will be easy, I tell myself.

And tonight, I'll spend extra time at the gym to make sure I don't have any problems ignoring Brooke from here on out. If I'm dead tired every time I see her, my body will stop craving her. It worked with sweets; it'll work with her too.

# Chapter 17

### Brooke

I think he gets off on riling me. He has to. Nothing makes him happy because he's determined not to let himself *be* happy. But I don't have that problem. Not anymore. Not since Logan, a guy I met at Stacy's party has been texting me.

Sure, Stacy's 'party' was actually a singles mixer with a very unbalanced guest list. Her friend Marie, Stacy herself, and me were the only single ladies compared to the three invited couples and no less than ten single guys.

Even now, after putting Ben to bed, I can't believe that she thought it would work. Two guys came onto me in a way I thought was exclusive to Tinder, but Logan scared them off. He sat with me for most of the night, when I wasn't clinging to Liz and her boyfriend for help. But the more Logan talked to me, the better I felt being alone with him.

Polite, straight forward, not flirting or handsy at all. It had felt ... nice. There were no strings, no long stretches of silence, no demands or expectations. Just good conversation that left me smiling and laughing most of the night.

Until Stacy acted like the middle woman and gave him my number.

My cell phone beeps. I smile at seeing another text from Logan on the screen.

LOGAN: Hi Brooke. I hope work didn't kill you.

BROOKE: Alive and mostly well here. Just put my son to bed and relaxing with a stand-up series.

Just like that we're texting all night. Then he gets sheepish before getting direct.

LOGAN: I'd really like to take you on a date. If you're free at any point.

BROOKE: Well ... Stacy did tell me to keep Friday free, I'm betting you're why.

LOGAN: I promise, I didn't set this all up.

BROOKE: Only Stacy has the guts to pull strings like this.

We laugh, but I accept. And why shouldn't I? Logan is wonderful. He's got a steady job he enjoys without devoting every waking moment to it. He's not on the rebound, he's not looking for quick sex. He's only two years older than me and Stacy approved.

Those are all good signs.

He could be *the one*, though my romantic heart is a bit jaded after how good Adrian seemed for that one week. Logan might have an uphill battle for him when it comes to my heart. But we set up the date and I work hard to get through the week, doing more than getting by. Ben is happy as can be and doing well in school again. I'm keeping up with work, even with Adrian dropping by on Wednesday.

He follows up with me on our new client and lingers after our meeting. I catch his eyes flick to the couch twice, and I try to calm my nerves. Adrian has made it clear nothing else will happen between us.

"So, Friday, I've set up a call time with the client. You're welcome to join."

"As long as it's during business hours, I'd be delighted." I give him the warmest smile I can.

"It's at four."

"Then I'll be there until five," I assure.

"Or until the call is done, Miss Dean."

"I told you I have plans. I can't push them around because you didn't remember." I shuffle some papers. "I gave you notice."

I'm sure his jaw is all kinds of tight. And I can feel his gaze on me without having to look. Butterflies flutter in my stomach, threatening to make me cave. But I won't. I can't.

He sighs. "I'll move the meeting to three."

My eyes meet his and there's a hint of the softness I remember. A lock of hair falls over his right eye, and I notice the faint, dark circle around it. It looks like he hasn't been sleeping well lately. I suck my bottom lip as I debate asking, then give in.

"Are you okay, Adrian?"

He stands abruptly. "Have a good day, Brooke."

"Not telling me won't make you feel better," I say.

He stills, his back to me, his fingers curled into fists. I stand up and continue. "I don't understand you. You say you don't like fun, but you had a good time when we took Ben out. You like control, but you changed the time of the call for me. You keep working yourself down to nothing to have a good life later when you could have it right now. And you won't even give yourself the most basic of things, something that would make you feel good."

"The last time I felt good in this office was the most unprofessional moment of my life," Adrian murmurs. "And it definitely didn't 'make me feel better' as you put it."

I flinch away from him. "That makes one of us then. I felt pretty good until you got dressed."

His hands relax at his side. "You knew what you were getting into."

"So did you, when you took Ben and me to that arcade. It's okay to be confused, Adrian. But I hope you know I can't wait around for you to figure yourself out. I want to live life, not wait for the perfect moment to enjoy myself."

He lets out a slow breath. "See you Friday, Brooke."

"Of course, Mr. Thorpe. I'll even be thirty minutes early to your office. Remember that I'm not available after five."

"Not even if the building is on fire," he says softly. I'm sure I'm not supposed to hear it.

---

"I AM THRILLED, FOLKS," Rufus Hannigan, our new client says on the other end of the video call. "Your ideas are fresh and forward-thinking. Sal was right. You are definitely what I've been looking for."

"Glad to hear it, Mr. Hannigan. Brooke deserves all the credit. She's the think tank that Sal told you about."

I glance at Adrian, surprised by the compliment. Throughout the meeting, he has been controlled, totally and completely professional. Perfect. Cold as ice. Very distant. Now, there's a bit of warmth in those steely eyes. The corner of his mouth turns up slightly.

After the video conference ends, I gather my things and start to head out.

"What if I need you for an emergency today?" he suddenly asks.

"Don't," I say softly. "You should take this weekend off too. See what life has to offer instead of work." He opens his mouth and I hold up my hand. "I don't mean bars and gyms. I mean things you enjoy. Maybe some more skee ball."

He chuckles, actually chuckles. "We'll see."

With that I head home, change into a cute, emerald-green dress that Ben approves of and drop him off at my parents. The dress isn't too revealing. It shows a hint of cleavage, some thigh, and doesn't hide my curves, but it's not like I'm putting myself on display either.

I pull up to the driveway of the restaurant, put on some dark lipstick and collect my nerves. It's been so long since I've been on a real date. More than a year. I fan myself quickly, then walk in, not wanting to be late.

Logan rises from the table as I approach. His thick, blonde hair and beautiful green eyes are like I remember. He's handsome, has a bit of a dad bod which I love (all the better for cuddling), and a nice little stubble coming in.

He looks me over and whistles, shaking his head. "Oh, wow. I should have taken you somewhere nicer than this restaurant. You look amazing, Brooke."

"What, this old thing?" I ask with a grin. He grins back, pulling out my seat before taking his own.

"I was honestly worried you only saw me as a friend – not that there's anything wrong with that – but I figured if I didn't ask you on a date, I'd lose the opportunity."

"I'm glad you did," I assure, taking his hand. "I'm excited to learn more about you. What you want in the future."

"Well the future is so hard to predict," he says, before thanking the waiter for bringing us drinks and bread. He apologizes and asks for more time to decide what to eat. When the waiter leaves, he blushes a little and squeezes my hand. "I have my dream job, but I really want marriage and kids."

"Careful, that kind of talk will get you kicked out of the locker room," I tease.

He smiles, then laughs loudly. "Oh, I know. Why do you think I completely ignore the gym?"

His eyes twinkle at me and I find myself fully committing to the date. He makes me laugh, isn't afraid to be silly or serious, and he talks about how much he loves being a godfather to his best friend's kid.

"I've watched Atlas grow up. I was there when he was born."

"Really?"

"This may not win me any points, but for the sake of honesty, watching my best friend's wife go through labor made me want to punch him for putting her through that pain," he says.

"It's worth it. My son is the best thing in my life. He's amazing and all the pain is just a faint, almost dreamy memory. Holding him made every minute worth it," I admit.

"How old is he?"

"He's seven and going on thirty," I joke. "He's smarter than any kid I've met. He just ... gets life in a way that I don't. It's amazing."

"Well clearly he gets all his smarts from you."

I bite my lip and find myself already planning a second date in my head. Already wanting to introduce Logan to Ben. It's premature, I know that. But I can't stop the instinct that tells me Logan means what he says.

He shows me pictures of his godson, eagerly sharing his favorite moments, then tells me how he keeps meaning to go to the gym to be in better health and give himself a longer life, but he loves pizza too much.

I suggest making it for him one night and he beams. "Is that an offer for a second date, Brooke?"

I blush down to my toes and nod. "It might be, but that seems too forward. Our first date isn't even over."

"Should I drink faster so I can get the full invite?" he teases, holding his water up like he's going to chug it frat boy style.

Giggling, I put my hand on the glass. "Spare your stomach."

"I'd like to go on a second date. In fact, I'm already hoping for a third," he says.

I hesitate. It's an old cliché, but clichés exist for a reason. The third date normally means sex and even though I don't want to think about another man when Logan is right in front of me, so good for me, and everything I'm looking for, my mind goes to Adrian.

The sex we had on the couch in my office.

"Is that too pushy? I'm sorry, Brooke. I just ... I feel like we have really good chemistry and the third date is when we can do something fun. Maybe rock climbing or a hike. If you're comfortable enough to be alone with me, that is," Logan says, starting to let me go. "If I made you uncomfortable."

"No!" I assure, reclaiming his hand. "Let's wrap up date number one and we can talk about two ... and three."

He grins and despite me grabbing for the check, he wins the tug of war with a smile. "You can pay for date two if you want to. I don't mind being the gentleman."

Logan walks me to my car while telling me a story about work. I try to hide my laugh, but don't quite manage when we get to my car. I rest my butt against the door and play with my keys, twirling them in my hand.

"I really had a good time, Logan," I say.

"A good enough time that I can ask for a kiss without getting slapped?" He asks, rubbing the back of his neck with a nervous, but eager look. He's so damn hopeful and sweet. How am I supposed to say no. "Hopefully? The longer this silence goes, the more nervous I'm going to feel, Brooke."

"I'd like a kiss," I whisper. "I'd like more time with you even more."

He beams and tugs me close, dipping me back until I crack up. He pulls me back up and tries to kiss me, but we're both laughing. He brushes my hair from my face. "Stacy might deserve flowers for this."

"She definitely deserves flowers, but chocolates are going to depend entirely on your kissing skills," I tease.

He presses his lips to mine. We kiss once, but I don't feel half of what I was hoping to. He pauses a moment, then tries again, nibbling my bottom lip, licking into my mouth, but we can't get the right beat. I want to like it so much. I want to enjoy the kiss and enjoy what he's offering me.

Because Logan is perfect. So I wrap my arms around his neck and take over, kissing him the way I want to be kissed. He melts into it and we finally find the right rhythm. His hand gently stroking down my back, then across my forearm is so soft and light that I shiver.

Dropping back down I see him blush. He nods. "Yeah, she's getting chocolates."

I agree and we promise to text each other, kiss again, and I get in my car. I touch my lips and try to stop the smile from spreading my face. I can't. Logan is *good*. He's good for me, good for my life, entirely wonderful.

Checking my phone before I pull away, I see a message from my parents saying Ben went down easily and to enjoy my night. Then three missed calls from Adrian. A text that says he needs me now, another one that says he's on the way over, then a demand of where I am.

I narrow my eyes at my phone, putting the weight on my gas as I head home. I text Logan I arrived safely, slowly guide my car door shut while taking a deep breath as I see Adrian waiting for me under the porch light. His hot, angry gaze scorches from me, but he's not the only one angry.

"Where have you been?"

"I told you I had plans," I say simply, ignoring the hardness in his voice. "My date was wonderful, thank you for asking. Feel free to hold all work conversation until Monday unless you're paying me for my time."

I get my key in the door, but Adrian follows me in and backs me against the wall, the toe of his shoes against mine as he glowers down at me. "You were *where?*"

# Chapter 18

### Adrian

There's no way I've heard her correctly. There's no way Brooke just got back from a date. There's no way she ignored an *emergency* like this because of a date. And beyond that, did she really move on that quickly?

She moved on faster than I did? That's a record in some book somewhere.

Her eyes dilate and she swallows as I keep glaring at her. "What's the problem, Mr. Thorpe?"

"Don't you "Mr. Fucking Thorpe" me," I snarl. "Sal had a fire. Half of his storeroom got burned down."

"What?" She gasps, pulling out her phone. "He didn't text me!"

"Because he's dealing with the police. We have to pause all advertising and figure out how to get him some support. We have a release for him on Monday and it can't wait. So tell me again." I push her phone away. "How a date was more important."

She frowns. "I didn't say it was more important, Adrian. It's not like I knew about the fire. I don't look at my phone when I'm out on a date."

"So if your son needed you—"

"Don't you bring Ben into this." She pokes my chest. "Don't. That is different entirely. I like Sal, I'd never wish for anything bad to happen to him or his business, but that is work. You'd know there was a difference if you had a life."

Really pulling out her claws, isn't she?

I narrow my eyes. "Sorry that a fire happened the one night you had a date."

"Sorry that you had to butt into my life and come to *my house* when I didn't answer the phone instead of taking care of it like you do everything else," she replies hotly.

"You are impossible!" My unsteady grip on my temper is gone. "Do you realize that? Absolutely, constantly impossible. Whenever I have a work-related request, you ignore or disrespect me! I get that you have a life, fantastic."

She arches an eyebrow at me.

"But you're making mine next to impossible and you don't even realize it!"

"What are you talking about?" she demands.

Pacing, I drag my fingers through my hair. I'm so tired of wanting her. So tired of being frustrated because I won't let myself have her. Exhausted from trying to get her off my mind each fucking day.

It was one round of sex, why is she under my skin the way she is?

"Adrian." She takes a step towards me.

"You were out on a fucking date. You've got to be kidding me."

"Adrian." Her voice is softer. "What's really wrong?"

"You. You are an entire fucking problem and you're too damn sweet for anyone else to see it. And you're too damn sweet for me to …" I cut myself off and try to take a breath.

"What?"

"You went on *a date*." I say emphatically. "Two weeks after we had sex."

"And?"

I slam my hand against the wall, far enough away that I'm not going to hurt her. She still jumps. Her eyes widen as I pant, trying not to touch her, to show her how well we fit together. How, even though I can't commit to a title or weekly dates, I could please her. I know how. I've proved it.

"Adrian. You either tell me what's going on or leave my house. I'm tired of the drama. I'm tired in general," she says to my chest, not looking at me.

"I like you, Kitten," I confess softly.

Her expression settles, and she's staring at me like she understands the effort it took for me to say those four words. "So you take the first opportunity to try to crash my weekend?"

"I like you and I'm fucking ... jealous that someone else took you out." I can't get my mouth to stop. Can't lock my jaw hard enough to keep the words in. My world is crumbling, just like I knew it would around Brooke. "I'm tempted to find out who you went out with, tell him he's not good enough for you, and ..."

"And?" she prompts.

"And I'm pissed at myself. A lot." I walk away then, sitting in the recliner and rubbing my forehead. "Apparently I'm a fucking idiot."

"You were jealous?"

"Who wouldn't be? I'm not exactly used to women tossing me to the side. I do the tossing."

"Adrian, you ignored me after we had sex. It was right back to business. You made it clear. And you made it clear again this week," she replies, kicking off her heels and stalking past me.

My eyes follow her, taking in the way the green dress shows off her legs, her elegant neck, contrasting with her strawberry-blond hair. Her dark eyes are so beautiful, and a light blush softens her cheeks. Her lipstick is smudged though, and it ignites something white-hot and dangerous in me.

"I'm no one, Adrian," she's saying. "I'm a single mom at twenty-seven, not some model. My ex didn't even get jealous of men hitting on me."

"Cuz he's a fucking idiot," I growl. But I try to calm my anger. I take off my jacket and loosen my tie, undoing two buttons on my shirt. "And so am I. I can't get you off my mind, Brooke. I've tried flirting with other women. I've tired working out. I've tried working. I even went to an NBA game this week. But you're stuck in my head."

She takes another step forward.

"It kills me that you can date another guy without even thinking about it. I'm pissed that you went out and let someone else kiss you, touch you, romance you. I'm pissed that I can't control how jealous I feel. I'm pissed that you're right so often. And I'm really fucking pissed that I'm telling you any of this because it's going to fuck up your expectations and—"

She sits on my lap and lifts my chin. She studies my face slowly, rubbing over my jaw. I catch her wrists and pull her hands away from me. "Don't."

"What?"

"Don't tell me what happened on the date and don't say anything. Apparently, I needed to confess my feelings, but you weren't supposed to hear it. So pretend you didn't."

"And if I want to do something about it?" she asks softly.

I finally meet her eyes. She's flushed, demure, and fucking gorgeous. I tighten my hold on her. "Brooke, you know ..."

"Your timing and mine are terrible. This is stupid. I'm painfully aware of how badly this could go. I know we want different things in life." She leans forward until her breath brushes against my lips. "But this isn't about logic or being rational."

A tremor teases my spine. "Don't say things that make me want to kiss you."

"You wouldn't be here or angry if you didn't want to." She pulls herself closer. "So decide what you want tonight, Adrian. Tell me."

"You won't like it."

"Let me decide that. I'm an adult," she says.

"I want to kiss you until you forget all about your date, until every trace of his mouth on yours is gone," I hiss. "I want to drag you to bed and show you exactly how much better I am than a boring dinner date."

She makes a soft sound and her lips part.

"More than anything, I want to make you crave me, get twisted up in me, and half insane over me ... so you know exactly how you make me feel," I say.

Before she can say a word, my lips crash down on hers. Our kiss isn't gentle. It's borderline warfare. Want and hunger, lingering jealousy and anger from our fight, a testament to all the lines we shouldn't have crossed that have brought us here, and the expectation of exactly what's going to follow.

She welcomes my tongue, but keeps trying to take control as she teases me with soft licks and nips at my tongue when I try to claim her. I shove my tongue down her throat and she sucks it, making me hard until I bite her bottom lip. She bites back, exploring my mouth with eager and hungry strokes while ripping my tie off, going for my shirt.

"Ben," I mumble, forcing my brain to stay on for all of five more fucking seconds.

"With my parents," she whispers, kissing across my neck as her hips roll on mine. "It's just us tonight."

"Thank god." I pick her up. "Bedroom. Now."

"Impatient," she chastens, but wraps her arms around my neck and kisses me hungrily. "Ask me nicely."

"Now, Brooke. Or I'll fuck you against a wall. You're going to fall asleep thinking of me, remembering exactly how hard I make you come. I'm going to make sure you forget every other man."

She groans and mumbles the instructions against my skin. I carry her to her room and drop her on the bed. I don't even bother with the light. I don't need it. My eyes have adjusted and I'm too impatient to wait another minute to have her.

Once I have my shirt off, I reach for her. She kisses me hungrily, stroking over my skin like I'm a fine piece of artwork that she has to memorize. And I actually feel it right now. A moan reverberates through me and she stands a second to let me pull her dress off.

I can feel a bra and panties. She definitely wasn't fishing for sex tonight. I lick over her cleavage. "Who's the last person to taste your skin?"

"You," she pants, rubbing down my back.

"To touch your sweet pussy?"

Another moan. "You, Adrian. Only a kiss. That's all he got."

"That's too much for my liking," I growl, focusing on her mouth again even as I work on stripping her.

She's not going to forget how I taste. She's not going to forget how right this is, how easily we fit together, and exactly how good we are at this. She jerks on my slacks and makes quick work of my pants.

I draw back from her mouth and look her over. Every inch of her is spell binding. I shove her back on the bed. "I didn't get dinner because of your radio silence."

"Want me to cook ... after?" she asks.

I lift her thighs, spreading them wide and stroking over her wet pussy. Oh yes, nice and wet for me and me alone. Someone else may have taken her out for dinner, but I'm the one who's getting a feast tonight.

"Adrian?"

I lick across my bottom lip. "You're my dinner, Kitten. And I'm starving."

Her hips roll as I kiss up her thigh. She squirms, but I hold her hands down. I'm not going to tolerate her interrupting me because she's nervous about her deliciously thick thighs or anything like that.

Brooke is mine as long as I am here. We don't need labels. We don't need date nights or promises. She needs me to make her come, to make her feel good, needed, all of it. In exchange for that, I want all of her.

"Adrian..."

I skip the rest of her thighs and lick over her slit. She hisses between her hips and I moan. She's delicious, like I knew she would be. Better than the finest whiskey. "*You* are worth the wait."

Her back arches as I lick over her slit again. I lap at her clit, trying every trick I've learned. I circle her clit with the tip of my tongue, flatten it as I lick across, suck and tease her, savoring each of her moans and the way her thighs keep trying to wrap around my head.

We're going to have a very good night. I grin, stop with the teasing, and begin my feast.

# Chapter 19

### Brooke

Adrian proves what he says about me being worth the wait by devouring me like I'm the last meal he gets while on death row. And he's magic, absolute magic. How can he be so cold when his mouth is so hot? My back arches and I grind myself against him, knotting my fingers in his hair and pulling him where I want him.

He groans and gives me everything he's got, pushing me over the edge. Drawing back, he licks across his bottom lip, still glistening with my wetness. I shiver and hold his gaze. He finishes stepping out of his underwear, showing every gorgeous inch of skin.

So much muscle layered on his body, the way his waist tapers in before his sculpted thighs. His hard cock standing at attention. I swear, he's a demi-god. But I shouldn't be doing this. He was a … well … he was terrible after the first time around and just because he knows what to say and can make me come doesn't mean that I should let him back into my life.

Adrian climbs on top of me and threads his fingers through my hair, guiding my head up until there's only a millimeter between our lips. "I'm going to kiss you again, kitten."

I nod, helplessly. Logic doesn't work around Adrian. Not when he's like this, warm and eager. He twists me up in so many ways, making me stupid and needy at the same time.

"You're going to answer a question for me before I fuck you."

A shiver teases my spine and goosebumps raise across my skin. "Okay."

"No negotiating?" he teases.

"I get three questions," I whisper, leaning towards him. "For after."

His lips curl up. "There's my girl."

Adrian's lips claim me again. His tongue thrusts into my mouth, sure and commanding. I keep my hands on the bed to push myself up as he plunders me, owns me with every new angle and, every lick, every near punishing bite.

When I moan, he pulls back, holding my hair so tightly I can't follow him. I know he wants more though. He's panting as hard as I am and his eyes can't leave my lips. "Tell me who's better."

"What?"

"Your date or me," he demands.

The answer is obvious. It's him. Adrian's kisses are scorching. They make my heart flutter, set my skin on fire, make need like I've never felt pool between my legs. No one, not Greg, not my first 'love' in high school, no one compares to Adrian.

"You," I reply.

He kisses me again and again. It's pure temptation and I'm not strong enough to resist. I stroke across his arms and he catches my hands. I pull them free. "Let me touch you, Adrian."

His throat bobs and slowly he strokes down my arms, fingers gentle and continuous. When he gets to my shoulders, he kisses across my neck slowly. He reaches my pulse point and licks across it before biting softly.

I stroke over his arms, savoring the muscle tightening under his skin. "I like touching you."

"Fucking hell, kitten," he growls and licks across my nipple, circles it with the tip of his tongue, biting softly, nearly massaging me with his teeth. My eyes flutter shut and a moan leaves my throat as his cock nudges against my pussy. "You drive me insane."

"I need you inside me," I beg.

He groans and pushes two fingers into my pussy. It's not close to what I meant, but I love it all the same. He nibbles my neck, then steals my mouth back. Pleasure teases my nerves and heat races along my veins. Adrian is like an addiction.

I thrust against his fingers and he kisses me again, more demanding, faster, lust on overdrive. I take everything he gives and then some. His tongue, his fingers, they work together to drive me closer to the edge of bliss. His thumb rubs across my clit and I can't hold back. I can't.

My head falls back, and I surrender. I kick every thought to the side as I dissolve into the most pleased puddle that's ever existed. A loud moan tears from my throat as I come apart. Adrian bites my bottom lip and licks across it as I come down.

"I'm not done making you come." He nibbles my ear.

Then he thrusts into me. No pre-amble, no warning. My back arches and I drag my nails down his back. He braces himself on his elbows over me as he devours my mouth. I whimper and rub my hips against his. He doesn't move, just rolls his hips, hitting deep inside me again and again.

"Please," I whimper.

"I'm deciding what to do with you," he says. "Exactly how I want to fuck you."

"Every way you can think of." My back arches. "Now. Please."

He lifts my thigh up, holding my ankle over his shoulder and thrusts into me. My lips part as a whimper escapes. Adrian thrusts into me again, sure and determined, the tendrils of heat spreading from my pussy. I moan and whimper, not afraid to be loud.

Adrian folds me in on myself and keeps kissing me as he fucks me, touching everywhere he can, maintaining total and complete control. I hold onto him as I get closer and see his eyes dilate, a little bit of pink in his cheeks as he pants above me, the hint of sweat on his hairline.

Oh, he's so good, so beautiful. I bite my lip and he grabs my chin. "Be loud, Brooke. I need you loud."

"Fuck," I hiss.

"Good girl. Tell me how good I feel. Tell me how much more you want."

"Harder! Please, Adrian, I need everything," I demand.

He moans and spreads my legs wide, pressing down until the muscles tense, but he's so deep inside me that nothing else matters. I can see the way his body rolls, how every muscle tightens and relaxes and I swear I'm hypnotized.

But he slams into me and I nearly scream as pleasure tears through me. Adrian smiles, a wicked victorious smile as I writhe under him. The orgasm tears through me and I let him hear every near scream that it drags out of me.

He jerks out and finishes on my stomach, letting out a groan that's so delicious and gravelly that I can't resist jerking him forward to taste it. He kisses me slowly, lazily. I grab for my dress and wipe my belly down before tossing it to the side.

Adrian flops onto his back and I roll towards him, expecting him to tell me he doesn't cuddle. Instead, he accepts me close and plays with my hair while watching the ceiling. "You have questions, Brooke."

"Is this another ..." My throat is sticky. "When you leave will it be the same as last time?"

"No," he says, but his hand falls off my hair. I hide my face against his shoulder. "But that doesn't mean I'm ready to be in a relationship."

"I understand that. I just..." Jeeze, words are so much easier to handle when I'm not naked and vulnerable and questioning every decision I've ever made. "I don't want to be your toy or a convenient fuck, Adrian."

"You're not convenient, Brooke." He chuckles, rubbing the back of my neck. His eyes finally meet mine. "You are impossible, entirely. You're not a toy, you're not a place for me to stick my dick when I'm bored."

I nod. "Then – not because you owe me – but because I'm curious, why no relationships or relationship adjacent things?"

"This isn't the kind of post-sex conversation you want, kitten." But his hand doesn't leave my hair.

I draw a sun on his chest and then kiss the spot. "You know my stuff. I don't hide it. I have a seven-year-old son. I was with one man for nearly eight years and married for five. You know my business is barely holding on."

"Brooke." He sighs, catching my hand. "I'd really rather not talk about this."

"We made a deal. Three questions. This is only number two."

"I know how people are and that's enough reason. Giving trust is like giving someone a loaded gun. People are only in it for themselves and the second someone or something better comes around, they'll leave. It's easier to leave first."

I keep watching him and he groans. "Fucking hell, woman. I have commitment issues, okay?"

I kiss his chest. "I'm sorry."

"For what?"

"No one is born with commitment issues," I say, pressing another kiss to his shoulder. "Which means you went through plenty. You have some years on me and I'm not going to pry, mostly because you would, and I like that you don't. It's one of the charming things about you ... but I'm sorry that you had to experience some of the worst in people."

He lets out a shaky breath. "I need you to stop being so sweet."

"Question three: are you okay spending time with me and Ben?"

"Shockingly, yes," he answers. "Not bad as far as kids go."

"Enlightening," I say with a laugh.

"Kids were horrible while I was growing up and I'm sure they still are now. Picking on whoever was smaller, being general pains in the ass. Ben is a good one," he says.

"Do you have siblings?"

His expression shutters, and he breathes another sigh.

"I know, it's more than three questions." I try to cling to him. "Adrian—"

"I went through a lot of foster homes, Brooke." He sits up, his back to me, and I notice a few scars across his back. I move forward slowly, stroking across a bad one and kiss above it. "It sucked ass. The stories suck and I'm not putting that burden on your shoulders."

"I have big shoulders."

He leans back against me, his head resting on my breasts like they're pillows. "I think mine are a little bigger."

I stroke through his hair and hesitantly trace his features, along the bump in his nose, his high cheek bones, and along his sharply cut jaw. His eyes close and he exhales slowly. I keep stroking his face until he turns into my palm.

I expect him to tell me to let him go, that he has to leave, or turn this back into work, but he doesn't. He lets me touch him. "Are you staying the night?"

"Never," he whispers.

"Just like you *never* mix business and pleasure? Or like how you *never* commit?"

"Second one." He holds up his finger. "But for you, I'm willing to compromise at cuddling and time spent together without a sex guarantee."

"Thank you." I kiss his forehead.

He smiles slightly, rubbing over my hands. "And I let you touch me. Another big win for you."

We tease each other a bit more, going back and forth until he gets dressed. He pauses when I walk him to the front door still wearing only a towel. His eyes darken with need as he jerks me against him. A soft breath leaves his lips as he holds the knot in my towel.

"What?" I ask.

"I'm offering you an out, Kitten. If casual isn't you, that's okay. You can tell me to fuck off right now."

I stay quiet, thinking about saying exactly that. It would make more sense, wouldn't it? We've had sex all of twice. We had a good week before that first time, then it was gone. We're good in business together. We should be able to do this, but I've never been casual when it comes to relationships. Especially when I don't know where I'm going to stand with him tomorrow ... but ... but I can't make myself take the logical option.

Adrian holds his breath and finally, I shake my head. Because I want this. I want him. If that means casual, I'll take it. I can handle it. I know I can. "I want you."

He kisses me softly. "Promise to answer your phone for me on weekends?"

"Promise," I breathe.

"Then I'll talk to you soon." He kisses my cheek.

# Chapter 20

### Adrian

All day Saturday, I question my decision making. Why the hell did I say anything? Why the hell did I show up at Brooke's place and let things get out of control again? Why did I offer her casual anything?

I enjoy fucking her, that's true. I can't get her out of my head and I'm not sorry for finally tasting her sweet pussy. But not putting a time stamp on anything? That's not like me. I don't set unrealistic expectations and I certainly don't engage with someone I work with. The only explanation is that Brooke makes me crazy.

Standing in the shower with the water beating down on the back of my neck and my head, all I can see is her unbothered face when she told me she was on a date. Sure, she's behaving differently than every woman I've ever been with, but I had this idea of her waiting for me. Of us working together, of us spending more time together while I really felt things out.

The one girlfriend I had just out of grad school, the one who lasted years, she's more like Brooke than anyone I've known. At first, the issues from my past made it hard for me to trust her. Over time, she worked to earn my trust. I let my guard down. We settled into a relationship, and for two years we made it work.

Until I stopped looking for problems, until I let myself be happy. Removing that guard, taking away that pressure from her shoulders was like removing a leash from a dog in a sausage festival. You think you have it trained, you think it loves you enough to stay, that it trusts you to know what it can and can't have, what will and won't hurt it, but it runs straight for the butcher who's distracted by a meat grinder.

And you lose it.

Just like I lost her. Found out from a friend that she'd tried snaring him. Found out from one of her friends that I should look at her phone under the name "Jamie". I did. Jamie turned out to be a 'he' who was getting more time with my girlfriend than I was. And was definitely getting a whole lot more attention.

Because I'd trusted her completely, she'd run. The game was over, she won, and she was tired of me afterwards.

And Brooke ... she has that same feel. The same magic that will get me to trust her so she can pull the rug out from under me.

"No," I tell myself, trying, for the life of me to hold onto sanity. "I'm smarter now. I'm going to enjoy what I can get and move on."

Come Monday, I show up to her office for a surprise visit. She's humming to herself as she goes through a file, jotting things down. Her hair is pinned away from her face so I can see that fresh glow there.

"Brooke?"

She jumps slightly and looks at me, eyes widening. "Oh, shoot. Did we have a meeting today? Did I forget?"

"No," I assure. "I thought we could do lunch."

"You mean actually eating right, not eating ..." Her blush says enough.

"I'm not going to complain if you're on the menu," I tease.

She gives me a frustrated look, but I see the smile trying to come out. Walking around her desk, I push her laptop to the side and sit down.

"I was working on that."

"Oh?"

"For Sal. I was able to get some work done for him this weekend, in terms of getting donations for repairs and putting a hold on the advertisements," she says. "And I was checking the funding page I set up. A few YouTube gaming influencers jumped on it when Ben decided to do a charity stream."

"Ben started this?" I ask.

"Sort of. I told him about Sal's and he showed me another gamer who did charity streams so we started it together over the weekend. Apparently listening to me scream whenever a zombie scared me was entertaining enough. We earned some money. Not enough to cover damages, but enough to help," she says.

I lift her chin, then kiss her. I don't know what else to do when she says shit like that. Her actions weren't to promote Sal's, though I'm sure she talked about it. She wanted to help him as a person, to achieve his dreams.

And that's so fucking sincere and genuine that I can't *not* taste her mouth to try to figure out what she's made of. I lick deeper, teasing her with different strokes of my tongue until she melts against me, stroking my sides, guiding me closer.

But I force myself to pull back before I get hard and start picturing everywhere else I can use my tongue. Brooke pants as she watches me. She licks over her bottom lip. "Lunch?"

"We either go get some, or you're going to become it," I warn.

She jumps up, fumbling for her purse. If she wasn't so damn innocent and infuriatingly upbeat maybe I'd walk away from her. As we drive to get some sushi at a restaurant I recommend, she sings in the car, off key, and too loud. She lets the wind tangle her hair without worrying about the strands that get loose and stuck on her.

"How do you do that?" I ask.

"Do what?"

"Just ... forget about work," I clarify. "You leave everything in the office?"

"I tried to tell you before, Adrian. There's more to life than work. I'm not going to waste time outside the office or the workday thinking about the job."

"Even though you care about the people."

"Of course. You know I care about them," she says, leaning back and putting her feet on my dashboard. Bare feet with each toe-nail a different color. She hums as she reclines in the seat. "But I care about me too. My son. My friends, my family."

I reach over to her, ready to push her legs down, but she catches my hand and slides it on the inside of her thigh, humming with the radio.

After grabbing food, we eat in her office – not exactly my first choice of scenery – but after lunch, I feed her kiss after kiss until she draws back and waves at her mouth.

"Is that a compliment?" I ask.

She grabs a bottle of water and downs the entire contents down her throat. Giving me a guilty smile, she sticks out her tongue. "I can't handle wasabi."

A smile starts to turn my lips up and I try to force it back down. "I thought you could handle a little heat."

"I can handle your brand of spicy just fine." She smirks at me. "Hot food is something else entirely."

"Well, I'd be a scoundrel to deny you my brand of spicy." I stand, pull her from her chair and drag her over to the couch.

Because I have no filter, no ability to resist her, nothing resembling control, I lick and kiss down her body as I undress her. Just as I kiss up her thigh, she covers her pussy. Shaking her head once, she pulls me back up.

"Not with that extra wasabi heat," she says softly.

But instead of pushing me away completely, she strips me slowly, worshiping me with every kiss she plants across my body, until she gets to my pants. Dropping to her knees, she drags them down and wraps her mouth around my cock.

"Brooke." I groan, sweeping her hair out of her face so I can watch her. She takes me slowly, tongue flicking over the base of my cock as she explores my length. I've got plenty of inches for her to take.

She gags as her lips meet the base of my cock and a low growl drags up from my chest. She slides her hot mouth toward the tip and her dark eyes rise to my face. She flattens her tongue over the head, and I clutch my fist at my side.

"Fucking hell, woman. You've been holding out on me," I breathe.

She smiles and takes me again, the same intensely slow, but delicious pace until it's like I'm going to lose my mind before I come. Every brush of her tongue feels amazing, but it's not enough. I need her faster, harder, sucking my cock like she needs me to live.

When she pops off again, I pick her up, walk her to her desk, putting her hands on top. "Stand right here."

"But—"

I swat her ass and watch her tremble. I kiss along her neck as one of my hands works her breast and the other rubs her pussy, teasing her slowly, like she did to me. Too slow, too light, nowhere near enough to make her come.

"Adrian," she pants.

"Did your date ask you out again?"

"I turned him down," she says shakily. "I want you."

I pat her clit lightly with two fingers. "Just me?"

"Just you, Adrian."

I groan and nibble her shoulder while dipping a finger inside her. She whimpers and rocks her body against me. I work two fingers deeper and stroke her clit with my thumb. "Wouldn't you rather have my mouth right here?"

"Yes." Her soft whisper leaves goosebumps on my skin.

"Maybe I should leave you all eager and wet for me," I tease in her ear before licking the lobe. "Let you think about the way you tease me."

"It wasn't teasing. It was build-up," she argues. "Making it more intense later."

"I can do that too," I murmur, pulling my fingers free of her pussy to tease her clit. Her thighs tremble and nearly tighten around my hand. But I keep my feet planted between hers so she can't move. I lick over her throat and kiss her pulse point while lightly teasing her clit. "What do you think? You like it?"

"Please Adrian!" she yells. "Please, I need you inside me."

I push my fingers into her again and she moans. "Like this?"

"No!"

"That's what you said, Kitten. Maybe you should clarify."

I love watching her shake, hearing her whimpers, witnessing her struggle with her logical mind. Fully dressed Brooke, ready to work Brooke, she would never beg. She would never use dirty words, curse, anything. And I love pushing her past that point.

"I need your cock inside me," she says in a low, husky voice that makes my cock twitch.

"Good girl," I praise, pulling my fingers free and thrusting into her.

Brooke moans loudly for me, rolling her hips back against mine as I bury myself deep inside her. I feed her my fingers. "See how good you taste? Why I can't get enough?"

She moans and licks my fingers, sucking them like she should. Once she has them clean and she's rubbing herself on me impatiently, I thrust into her completely and jerk her chin to face me so I can devour her mouth.

There's next to nothing better than tasting her mouth and pussy at the same time. Especially when I'm inside her while she's tight, wet for me. I groan and fuck her harder while thrusting my tongue deep into her mouth.

Brooke moans and sucks my tongue, flicking the tip of hers against mine as I fuck her hard. Her hands slip on the desk, pushing her ass against my hips and I groan.

Jerking her hips tighter against me, I slam into her again and again. I want to brand her with my cock, with my kisses, with everything I can. But fuck, she's too good. Her soft skin under my hands, her pussy squeezing my cock over and over, the breathy moans and barely muffled cries of pleasure snake through my veins and ruin my reason.

I pinch her nipples and her pussy floods with wetness. She yells my name as she comes, her body tightening, trying to arch back for me. But she drags me into her climax. I don't even have time to pull out. The thundering of her heart pounds throughout my body, the ecstasy from making her come mixing with my own pleasure.

Panting, I press my forehead against her back. I let myself slip out of her, then pick her up, bundling her in my arms like a child. I sit in her chair and stroke her back as she rubs my sides. Brooke nuzzles my throat and laughs once.

"What?" I demand.

"Before I knew you, I never understood how woman could be satisfied going into a one week relationship with you," she says. "I think I get it."

"Oh yeah? Ready to give me up on Friday?"

"No, but you're ... Being with you is like having all my reason ripped away the second you touch me."

"So I make you stupid?"

"Absolutely." She draws back and taps my nose. "I'm a complete idiot. Because otherwise, I'd never fuck a colleague in my office."

I can't quite contain my smile. "Another not-compliment."

"Not an insult either." She rubs across my shoulders. "Going to sleep with me every time you visit my office?"

"Every other time," I barter.

I cuddle her for a solid ten minutes and it's not torturous. It's a little forced, but not as much as it should be. I like the way she touches me, draws designs on my arms and sides. I like her breath warming my throat.

I pat Brooke's thigh when I'm ready to be done. She gets up and stretches. She looks ready for sleep. She yawns as she gets dressed.

"Sleeping during work time is a bad habit."

"So is extending lunch to have sex." She sticks her tongue out. "But you don't seem to mind that habit."

"I'm filled with bad habits, sweetheart." And she's becoming the newest irresistible habit.

# Chapter 21

### Brooke

Being with Adrian is now a full-fledged habit I can't kick. Not that I want to, anyway. I learn fast that he needs sex more than anyone I've ever met. In one week we've had sex five separate times. But when Saturday comes and he tries to get my attention, I remind him I have a son and I'm not on call. As much as I enjoy being with him, as much as it's like I'm on ecstasy or something when he touches me, I'm not about to give up time with Ben.

Since it's warm, I set up a sprinkler in the back yard, turn his little Home Depot playground into a mini water park like my dad did for me when I was little, then pull on a bikini with a pair of shorts. When Ben finishes his breakfast and comes out to see what I've been doing, his eyes widen with delight.

"No way!"

"Yes, way! We can't go to the water park, so it's coming to you, little man."

He hugs me, then runs in to go get changed. I put my hair up in a ponytail and spray myself down with sunscreen. I put a kiddy pool filled with water at the end of each of his slides and call it good. It's not much, not really, but it's taken me more than an hour to get set up for him. We'll have a good day. I'm sure.

I go inside to call Stacy and invite her over for some fun, but I see a text from Adrian. Before I can answer, he calls, impatient as ever. I let it ring three times before I answer. "You don't have anything better to do on a Saturday but send me texts?"

"Are you upset that they're not dirty? Do you miss my cock already?" He asks in that damn sultry voice he knows gets under my skin.

I walk outside, shutting the door and Ben whoops with happiness as he goes down the slide. "Come on, Mom! You'll fit too!"

"I made a water park. If you actually have swim trunks and aren't afraid of working a grill, I'd be willing to let you come over."

"Do I need water wings too?" he teases.

"You know what, for that sass, yes you do," I say with an easy smile. "We're around back."

"Got it. See you soon."

I don't actually expect to see him coming with burgers and water wings and swim trunks though. If anything, he'll stand in the shade and watch. Right? Sure, he showed Ben how to play skee ball and was happy to play the team games with him, but Adrian's not the fatherly type. He doesn't want to be.

And when we have been together, other than for work related meetings, it's been all sex and short conversations that acquaintances have at parties when there's no one else to talk to. I put on sunglasses and pull Ben for sunscreen before joining him. I get nervous going down the slide, but he cheers me on.

"Come on, Mom! It's not that high!" he says.

"I'm too big!" I say as I sit, and my thighs smoosh out to touch the edges.

"No you're not!"

I manage to get down the slide thanks to the thin layer of water and land in the pool. When I start to get up, Ben tackles me. He tries some of his fighting moves on me, always being gentle, then splashes me before he hugs me tightly.

"This is awesome, Mom."

"Well enjoy it!" I encourage.

"Can I invite Dustin over from down the street?"

"Sure!"

"Dry your feet before going inside!" I call as he dashes off.

I make sure all the hoses are working properly, then drag the huge bag of charcoal from the garage to the back of the house. I huff as I set it down and adjust my sunglasses. Cutting it open, I set up the grill, put on the smallest amount of accelerant I can and get it going. I jump as the flames lap at my fingers.

"A woman who can start her own grill. Nothing sexier."

I look up at Adrian's voice and my jaw nearly drops when I see him. Sure, he knew what was going on, but seeing him in a tank top and blue swim trunks, sunglasses balanced on his nose, water wings around his wrists, because that's probably the only place they'd fit and a bag from the store is so shocking, I'm not sure what to do with myself.

I burst into a laugh. "Adrian."

"You said water wings were required," he says, snaring my waist, glancing towards the sliding glass door before giving me a toe-curling kiss that steals whatever air is left in my lungs.

I might never recover from him.

He lets me go and shows me some burger patties and hot dogs along with everything else needed. Chips, soda, ketchup, buns. Everything. As he unpacks it, I stare, not sure what to do with myself.

I rub over my arms, then grab him before he can put anything on the grill. "Your water wings are definitely flammable."

He scoffs at them, then tosses them to the side. Before he can say anything, Ben comes out. He spots Adrian and gives a 10,000 watt smile before hugging Adrian tightly and to the man's credit, he ruffles Ben's hair.

"Hey, kiddo."

"Mom didn't say you were coming."

"It was a surprise," he says simply.

Ben accepts it, then turns to me. "Dustin is coming. His dad said yes."

"Great!" I say.

Ben goes to do another run through of the playground, runs through the sprinkler, has an all-around great time. Adrian grabs my butt when Ben can't see. I want to swat him, but I also don't want to draw attention. Adrian won't be around long. Whatever fascination he has for me will wear off and he'll leave. I don't need Ben confused. When I don't respond, Adrian tugs my back pocket, pulling my attention.

"Don't get handsy," I hiss.

Adrian lowers his glasses. "He's not paying any attention to us and he won't know if you don't react."

"Behave," I insist.

"Stop being so damn tempting and I will." He flips two burgers.

Dustin soon comes over, and I coat myself with sunscreen and do the same for the boys, before releasing them to enjoy the water slide. Adrian shoos me when I try to return to the grill, instructing me to have a drink and relax. I smile as I obey him, taking a spot in front of the grill where I can watch him work. He works the grill effortlessly, a contented smile—a huge anomaly—on his face.

I could get used to this.

But I won't.

Nothing good will come from wishing for a life I'll never have.

Adrian soon calls the boys over for food and they eat ravenously, talking about things I don't quite get in terms of video games.

"Have you played Overwatch?" Ben suddenly asks Adrian.

"Can't say I have." he admits. "Is it a first person shooter?"

"Third!" Dustin volunteers.

From then on, Adrian gets engaged in the conversation. He doesn't talk down to the kids, or doesn't make himself more approachable, he's just his normal self. As the day winds down, Ben offers to walk Dustin home. Adrian hesitates, then says he'll go too, that he needs to walk off the meat sweats, which makes both boys laugh.

He tells them to wait for him out front, pulling me close. "Leave this stuff up. I want to play with you in the water once he goes down for a nap."

I gape at him, but can't say anything since he's already half way around the house. So ridiculous. As if Ben takes naps. He goes hard almost all day.

My phone rings and I pick it up. My mom starts asking me how our weekend is, tells me how much she misses Ben, but I hear the car engine in the background.

"Where are you guys off to?" I ask, curious.

Mom tsks. "Oh, crap. We wanted it to be a surprise. We're coming to see you, honey."

I palm my forehead, glancing at Adrian who's still deep in conversation with the boys. "Why? Ben was there a few weekends ago."

"Well, we miss you both. We've seen a ton of Ben, but almost none of you!" my mom says.

"We want to be involved in your life. You're still my little girl, Brooke," Dad chips in.

I sigh. "I know. I have a work friend over is all."

"Well the more the merrier."

"Hopefully, you brought swimsuits," I say.

They laugh and I remind them not to get distracted by the phone. I hang up as Adrian returns with Ben on his shoulders. Not his back, his shoulders. Nervousness eats at me, but Ben keeps his hands on Adrian's head and Adrian has his arms around Ben's legs.

"Thought he'd like to know what it's like to be tall," Adrian explains, reading my face.

"Grandma and Grandpa are on their way!" I say through gritted teeth, looking at Adrian, who seems undisturbed.

He sets Ben down and Ben bounces around, filling up his water guns again. "We have to spray them right away, Mom."

"Not when they have phones, little man," I remind.

He huffs, but Adrian takes care of that, chasing Ben around, firing sparingly, acting like he's dead when Ben shoots him. Ben goes to check on him, then drags me over. "Mom!"

I look at Adrian then to Ben. "Go ahead, you know CPR."

"You gotta do it," he insists. "He's too big for me."

I put my hands on Adrian and he grabs me, jerking me down to the ground next to him to spray me with the gun. Ben does the same and they high five. I gape. "You two planned this!"

I'm not sure what's more surprising, that my son managed to get through the ruse without cracking up or that Adrian took the time to plan it with him. Adrian flashes a wide smile and Ben has them fill up the guns again. I shake my head at Adrian.

He shrugs and bumps my hip. "Where's the fun expert's sass now?"

"Apparently, I'm being shown up." I barely contain my joy.

My parents soon arrive, Mom immediately zoning in on Adrian. She shoots me a questioning look, one that doesn't disappear even after I introduce Adrian to them. I don't know what she's thinking, but I'm sure she'll make it known when we're alone. Adrian keeps his hands to himself, but my mom keeps looking between us like she's trying to figure things out.

Adrian tugs on his shirt a few times. It's hotter than normal for this time of year. And he's been running around, working the grill, all of it. Maybe he knows if he takes off that flimsy tank-top clinging to his mouthwatering body, I'll be a hopeless drooling mess. Forgetting where I am, I lick my lips, and then catch Mom's eyes. She raises her brows at me, and my cheeks burn like the time she caught me kissing a boy at sixteen.

The sun soon sets, signaling the end of my parents' visit. On the way out, I hug my mom and she whispers in my ear. "Is he a friend or an *adult* friend?"

"Mom!" I hiss, looking at Adrian and Dad talking to Ben.

"I'm asking. He seems like a good guy, just a little old for you. I'm putting him at late thirties."

"It's not like that. It's not a relationship or anything," I say.

"You're an adult, but I know how you work. You get attached to people. If someone doesn't want you entirely, if they don't want a future with you, you should move on. Get someone who's serious about settling down, someone a little closer to your age."

She's sweet as peaches to him when they say goodbye, leaving me frustrated, but with nothing to say. She's not wrong. I mean, Adrian hasn't settled down ... well ever as far as I know. He was never married. Never engaged. It would have been all over the internet. He hasn't even given a girl the title of 'girlfriend'.

But what we have isn't logical. It's physical and ... something else. It's thrilling and fun. I deserve that right? I won't do casual forever, but I can handle casual for a time. For right now. And Ben likes him.

Even if it's not forever, he's good for now. And that's enough. I'll make sure it's enough.

"Can I have another burger?" Ben asks, his face and shoulders getting redder by the second.

I gingerly touch his skin, making a mental note to apply aloe vera gel after his bath. "We forgot your last round of sunscreen, didn't we?"

Ben shrugs. Adrian motions for him to head back around and works on the grill while I empty the pools, hanging them up to dry. I turn off the sprinkler, take care of the hose and notice Ben half asleep on the lounge chair, his half-eaten his burger on his lap.

"Here, I got him," Adrian says as I reach for Ben. He gently nudges me aside with his hip and lifts my son, taking him—and my heart inside. I follow and take over after he places Ben on the couch. I towel him off, get him changed, put aloe on him and get him into bed. He's out before I can choose a book. I return to the living room to find Adrian looking around, probably taking in the mess's insanity. He pull me close as I walk by.

"Thanks for coming today," I say.

"Besides the unexpected arrival of your parents, I had fun," he admits, kissing my nose. "You're a little red too."

"Am not."

He pulls me to a mirror and pulls my bikini top down, showing exactly how red I am. But since his hands are on me, I can't think about anything else. "Adrian."

"Before you get sore, I'd like to have a little fun. I know how to keep you quiet," he purrs.

We have intense sex, with my hands pinned to my back while Adrian takes me from behind, giving me everything, making me lose myself so often my body is like jelly when we're done. Sated, we curl up on the carpet, his head on my chest while I play with his hair.

"Does it bug you that you're closer to my parent's age than mine?" I suddenly ask.

His jaw tightens against my chest, but he does give me an answer which is more than I expected. "Not until you said it like that."

"I don't think it's a bad thing. I just wanted to know."

"Always curious, aren't you?"

"Is *that* a bad thing?"

"Not when it's pushing someone's boundaries," he replies, his voice a little stiff.

I shift my weight so I can see his face. "Am I pushing your boundaries?"

He sighs. "I know that look, Brooke. I'm not about to argue over a trivial matter." He presses himself to me, making me aware of how hard he is again. "I can think of a better way to spend our time."

I open up to him, wondering if Mom was right about me getting too attached. Maybe I shouldn't have given Logan up so quickly.

# Chapter 22

### Adrian

Although it took every ounce of my willpower, I leave Brooke alone for two days and focus on work. I text her occasionally, but I manage to keep my dick in my pants where it belongs. I still can't believe I met her parents – by accident – but still.

Her dad was kind enough, didn't read into anything. Her mom on the other hand, must have said something for that damn question to come up. Not that her age bothered me, at least, not until she brought it up. Now I wonder exactly how stupid this whole set up is. What am I doing fooling around with a woman so young?

I brush away the doubt with the memory of fucking her twice that same night. The first time was needy, demanding, my hand over her mouth to keep her quiet since we couldn't wake up Ben. The second time was slow and ... gentle. Especially for me.

I'd worked aloe over her body, bit by bit, spreading it over even the unbothered skin until I was hard and couldn't resist. I'd been slow and soft with her, something I haven't done in twenty years.

And I'd nearly fallen asleep with her beside me. Nearly. I caught myself in time, taking her to bed and slipping out a little after midnight. The temptation to stay slowly faded as I put distance between myself and Brooke's house. Getting home to my empty bed didn't feel right, though. Still, I ignore the void in my chest and settle into sleep like I always do.

Two days without Brooke is like a lifetime. I can't survive a third day without seeing her face. Reaching for my phone, I text her, asking if she's interested in having dinner with me. Five minutes pass before my cell phone beeps again. A smile plays on my lips as I read her message.

Brooke: Ben and I are having lasagna. Care to join us?

Without hesitating, I reply, *I'll be there in half an hour.*

There's of plenty of work left on my desk, but I don't care. Anticipation lifts my spirits as I drive the short distance to Brooke's house. Ben opens the door excitedly, even though Brooke yells at him, reminding him to ask who's there first, that not everyone is nice.

Brooke smiles at me as I enter. There's no sign she's upset with me for not coming by these last two days. "Dinner will be ready in twenty minutes," she says to me, throwing a kitchen towel over her shoulder. "Can you set the table, please?"

She hands me a stack of plates and I set the table while Ben tells me about his day. I actually like the kid. He shows me some karate techniques he's learned, like kicks and chops and poses. I try to do the same and let him correct me when I get it wrong. It makes him laugh.

Then we have dinner. Only about halfway through do I realize that this is how normal families eat. No yelling, just talking about our day, laughing, enjoying the time. Not that I do much laughing, but I give encouraging smiles when Ben tells a joke.

And there's not one plate thrown. No bits of passive aggressive conversation, no sending Ben to bed early because he spills something or gets a stain on his shirt. When he's done, he goes to get a book and convinces Brooke he can read it alone.

Brooke and I talk, watch a movie, then I leave. We do the same thing on Friday. On Saturday, she surrenders her son to her parents, and we have a full day of overdue sex before we go see a movie together and I take her out for dinner at a four-star restaurant nearby. She scans the room filled with semi-casual-dressed diners then looks down at the simple jean dress she's wearing. "I don't think I'm fancy enough."

"You're perfect," I assure, squeezing her hand.

She snorts. "You have a way with words, Adrian, but not even you can make me believe I am."

It's on the tip of my tongue to cancel this dinner, take her home and show her how perfect she is. Instead, I guide her to the seat and pull out her chair. She doesn't need sex as reassurance. In fact, it would probably worsen her insecurity. Still, I make a mental note to change her mind, because she's perfect, inside and out.

I study her as we dine. She picks at the escargot, wrinkling her nose and that gets us into a conversation about food. Brooke tells me Sal's is more her cup of tea, that she's not used to fancy dining. She's never had a meal like this in her life and maybe that's why.

I don't like that she minimizes her own opinion. So when she starts to put another escargot on her fork and looks at it with barely contained dread, I guide her hand to my mouth. I wrap my lips around it, sucking it off the fork.

Her eyes widen and her cheeks flush.

"Thank you," I say politely.

"Adrian—"

"If you don't like it, don't eat it, Kitten. I'm not offended. I might be if you order off the kid's menu though."

She bursts into giggles and shakes her head. She tells me about how she did just that when her ex-husband took her to a French restaurant. "He was mad for a while, in that silent, brooding, punishing way. I'd rather someone yell instead of going silent. Silence is worse," she says.

"Really?" I doubt she's ever really had someone yell at her before.

"Well, yelling isn't great, but I at least know why they're mad. It's not me projecting past experiences. A conversation is better, but silence ... my mind goes crazy and I expect the worst."

I nod. "Good to know."

At the end of the meal, I suggest we walk along the river. We find a swinging chair and Brooke runs to it, kicking off her heels and beaming as she pushes the swing much higher than its meant to go. I join her, calming the motion.

She looks over the water, the lights of the city just beyond. "Adrian ... I think it's time for a check in."

"Is it?"

"We've been doing this for two weeks now," she points. "Your flings usually last one week."

"I'm not ready for a relationship," I blurt, some pre-recording that falls out of my mouth whenever the time is right.

"I know." She scoffs, nudging me. "I'm not about to ask you to be my boyfriend. I wanted to say I appreciate what we're doing. I like spending time with you, but I like the space too. It's kind of nice."

"You're not saying that to spare my feelings, are you?"

"You have feelings?" She gasps. "Something other than anger and lust?"

I roll my eyes.

She kisses my cheek. "No. I'm saying it because I mean it. I didn't think casual anything would work for me, but I like it. I want to make sure you do too. Especially after having dinner with Ben and me."

"I do like it," I say.

"Good, because I'm gossiping about you tomorrow."

I give her a side glare. "Brooke."

"Not by name," she promises, slipping her feet back into her shoes. "But I can't lie to my best friend. Stacy's been a little mad since I refused that second date with Logan. She doesn't like when her matchmaking skills are put to waste."

"Just tell her you weren't interested in him," I advise.

Brooke sighs in response. I slide my hand around her waist, pulling her close and kissing her temple. It feels natural, even if I can't remember the last time I've done any kind of public display of affection.

"Were you interested in him?"

She glances up at me and away. I turn her chin toward me. "Just tell me, Brooke. I'd rather know, just like you would."

"I was," she mumbles. "He wants to settle down, have a family. He has a godson he's crazy about and we had things in common. It was the best date – called a date – I've been on in ... Jeeze eight years."

"Your ex-husband didn't take you on dates?"

"A few, but they started feeling like the same routine over and over again. Or we'd get in one of those silent fights. The last two years he was really distant. Always tired from work," she says. "Sorry, it's like I shouldn't talk about him around you."

"I'm not offended," I say. "You can talk about him whenever you like."

Brooke stares at me for a moment, pushing to her feet. "I'm ready to go. Can you take me home, please?"

We quietly walk to the car, and the silence continues on the way home. I turn the radio on to a pop station she likes, but she doesn't sing along. Halfway on our journey, she turns to me.

"Are we exclusive, Adrian?" I gape at her and she continues. "Obviously, you'd be pissed if I was dating anyone else, right?"

"I can't handle more than one woman at a time. I work sixty-five hours a week and spend another ten at the gym," I reply.

"Okay..."

She's clearly not satisfied with my response, but I'm glad she doesn't push it. I can't handle a conversation that will inevitably get deep. I don't want to face my feelings right now. What I want is Brooke pinned under me, begging me to fill her. She doesn't need sex as reassurance, but I do. It's the only way I can control these voices in my head, the ones telling me to trust Brooke with my heart.

BROOKE BITES HER LOWER lip, fingering the hem of her shirt. "I don't know, Adrian. I think—"

"Don't think, Brooke. Just do it. I'm offering you a break. You've been frazzled at work, and Ben has been having a hard week at school. Let me give you a day off Mom duties."

She's still tentative. It's right there in her eyes. I don't know why I'm volunteering to spend time with Ben—the last thing I'd consider doing a week ago—but I want to ease the burden from Brooke's shoulders, if only for a short time.

"Ben likes me. We'll call it babysitting. You can pay me if you want," I push.

She glances out of my office to Liz. "Well...I could use a girl's night."

"So schedule one and put me to work. I can handle it," I assure.

Saturday rolls around, and within two minutes of being alone with Ben, I start questioning my confidence. I stare at Ben, waiting for him to tell me what to do. He stares back.

I clear my throat. "So ... what's a normal thing to for a babysitter to do?"

Ben shrugs. "I don't know... order pizza? Watch movies?"

I nod and order a pizza. I try to think about the things I wanted to do as a kid. Other than eat a full meal and not get yelled at, anyway. I always wanted to stay up late. Other kids in school talked about blanket forts. Some said their babysitters were hot, or they got to have all the foods their parents didn't allow.

"Want to build a fort?"

"We can defend it like knights!" Ben says. "Mom never plays swords with me. Says it's too rough."

"Let's do it."

We get to work on the fort and Ben keeps insisting we get higher so I can fit in it. By the time we're done, it takes up half the living room. We eat pizza, down way too much ice cream, raid the candy stash, fight each other with swords. Ben stabs me, right between the arm and my side. I fall over dramatically, like I've seen in movies.

When I peek open one eye, I see him taking a picture. I try to swat the phone, but he holds it out of reach. "It's for Mom!"

"No way, little man." I flip him upside down and he laughs, presses a few buttons and tosses his phone. I turn him in a circle and he demands it again, saying it's like a rollercoaster ride.

At least my muscles are good for something I suppose. When we settle into the fort, we play a multi-player game and I only realize he's asleep when I beat him. The high of victory is blown there.

I pull a blanket over him and sets his head on a pillow, watching him for a few minutes. I've never wanted kids. My experience as a kid was fucking hell, so I ruled it out, but now ... Ben isn't the kind of kid I used to have to deal with.

He's pretty cool. I've genuinely had a good night tonight. I didn't miss beer. I'm not half as overwhelmed from a shit work-week. I actually ... actually liked playing games with him and not feeling the pressure to be put together and perfect. And I'm exhausted.

But I try to clean up some, get laundry started, pick up the mess we made of popcorn, put some of his toys back, clean up everything but the fort, which is how Brooke finds me when she comes home.

"How was it?" she asks me, her eyes scanning the spotless room with awe.

"It went well, I think. Ben had a good time."

"Is he in bed?"

I point to the fort. "Nope. Passed out playing video games."

"Good." She kisses me softly, then again, and again.

I groan and fist her hair in my hand. "Are you drunk, Kitten?"

"No. Just all loosened up," she says, taking my still damp hand from dishes and leading me around the fort.

"And where are you taking me?"

"I'm not sure if you're sleep-over ready, but I'm going to show you how much I appreciate you."

"Sounds dirty."

"Good." She opens her bedroom door, jerks me in and locks it behind us. "Because it is."

We go two rounds of sex which reminds me that I need to introduce this woman to ball gags while Ben is at home. I welcome her to cuddle me after we share a shower. She rubs my shoulders and my back, peppering me with kisses while massaging me.

"Since you took care of me so well, do you want to talk about how hard your week was?" she asks.

I shake my head. "Not particularly."

"Might make you feel better."

"Your hands are taking care of that perfectly."

But somehow, I still end up venting. By the time I'm done, Brooke hugs me, resting her cheek against my back. No one-upping my story, no telling me to get over it because this is the job I chose. Nothing like that.

A soft, nearly miniscule voice in my head says if this is what settling down feels like, I might like it. But happiness is a trap. I know that. I have to wait for the other shoe to drop, because there's no way this can last.

After getting Ben into bed, we curl up on the couch with a movie until she falls asleep. I tuck her in, staring at her for a moment. What the hell am I doing living a happy family life? I know what happiness is. This can't last. The fact that we've made it this long is a miracle.

Whenever I leave, whenever she takes a while to answer her phone ... I'm waiting for her to point out our issues. To point out how much time I give work. Waiting for her to say she wants someone else and toss me to the side without a care.

There's a huge part of me that wants to commit to her, but that will destroy the comfortable dynamic we have going. The second I give Brooke a title, she will take advantage of me, my trust and ... and I can't handle that. So maybe it's time to start pumping the brakes. To take control back.

But I look at her asleep, hair a mess, still naked, completely unworried and my heart thuds painfully.

No.

I'm not doing this.

I won't fall deeper than I already have.

I get dressed, start to leave, doubling back to check on Ben, as if he's mine or something. Another no. I shouldn't care. But I turn on his nightlight and leave while promising myself I'm going to figure this out. I don't have a choice.

# Chapter 23

### Brooke

Somehow, I've managed to keep Adrian interested in me for an entire month. Technically, a month and two days. I realize it on Monday when he texts me that he's thinking about me instead of work. When I ask why that's bad, I get a picture of his hard on.

Which leads me to flash my parted legs.

He warns me that he doesn't have lunch plans, but he sends me a schedule request. He wants *me* for lunch. I approve it and smile to myself. I smile even more when he follows through, eating me out and letting me return the favor before we actually get food. His cell phone rings, interrupting our contented moment.

It's work, of course. After ending the call, he rises, giving me a quick peck on my cheek. "I'll miss you more when I leave," he whispers, before kissing me full on the mouth.

It's corny and makes me laugh, but he's been different since he babysat for me. He let me fall asleep, then tucked me in before leaving. But his texts have been dwindling down. He hasn't invited himself over at all (which means I keep extending the invitation), and even though they're small changes, easy to overlook when I don't think too hard, it worries me if I have nothing else to do.

Luckily, Ben doesn't give me much time to miss Adrian, who definitely likes to keep me busy physically. I've been having plenty of good sleep when my head hits the pillow at nights.

But for some reason, I'm not quite contented anymore.

Tuesday, Stacy comes over. After we have dinner with Ben, he dances off to his room. "Adrian said I was better with the sword this time, but I want to beat him the right way."

"Keep working on it and you will!" I promise before wincing.

"When's he coming back over?" Ben asks.

"Um, I don't know. We can invite him," I offer.

"Good. I like Adrian."

With that he's gone, leaving me with a best friend to deal with. She glares at me. I open my mouth and she holds her hand up. "Please tell me that I didn't hear what I thought I did."

"That my son is going to be an excellent swordsman?" I ask, hoping to distract her.

She drums her nails on the table. "Please tell me that he messed up the name or that there is another Adrian in your life. Because if I think for a second that you are dating that asshole, I'm going to have to send you in for a brain scan."

"Stacy—"

"Are you fucking kidding me, Brooke?" she demands in a whisper. "I set you up with the perfect man. The kind of man who wants to settle down, the kind of man that wants everything you want! And you trade that for a dick who won't commit?"

"How do you know he won't commit?"

She raises her brows at me. "Because I read the tabloids, Brooke. I've seen the 'woman of the week' on his arm in each issue. He's a player, through and through."

"He's good to me. He's good to Ben. He said he didn't want anything serious and I don't think I should jump into anything serious either. I've been divorced for a while, but I have dated no one since then. Not for longer than *one* bad date," I say.

She starts to talk, but I cover her mouth. "He treats me *well*. We've gone on dates. He takes me *and* Ben out. He's babysat Ben twice. We have amazing sex, we have dinner here. There's a lot that could go wrong, but it's going right."

"For now. But men are good at 'for now' type of things. The stuff that doesn't require much. And he knows how to do it because he's older and has been with at least a hundred women." She huffs, grabbing wine and pouring it for both of us. "I mean, you realize he's thirteen years older than you, right? Your mom is only eight years older than he is."

"Yeah, I'm aware."

"And he never settles down. Whatever is possessing him to act like this is going to leave his body – since it's obviously a demon. Are you really okay with that? You're okay with him going off and fucking other women when he's done playing family? Will Ben be?"

"Like I said, there's a lot of potential problems, but he's trying, and I enjoy our time together."

She keeps staring at me as I drink. Sure, there have been more than a few times after our fun times where I can see his walls come up from innocent questions. I really only know the basics about him. Beyond that, he's a closed book. He doesn't talk about when he was young. He doesn't talk to me about his feelings. Not to mention, he can switch to work mode in a snap which means any flirting gets me a glare. It's almost as bad as whiplash.

I finish my entire glass as Stacy keeps staring like I have a terminal illness. I rub the back of my neck with a sigh. "I don't like thinking about when he'll leave."

"And it should be an *if*, Brooke. You're worth more than this."

I swallow hard and set my glass down. "Until he gives me a reason to worry, I'm not going to."

"He already has. By not making you his girlfriend, he's leading you on. He's letting you get your feelings involved when his aren't. You'll start seeing it now. Mark my words. You'll see that he's all talk unless sex is involved. He's not going to be bringing flowers for you or toys for Ben. You'll see."

And I do.

Much sooner than I expect.

ADRIAN HAS BEEN IN his head throughout dinner. He's quieter than usual. When Ben asks him to play swords after we've cleared the table, he says he's tired and had a long day. Ben's smile melts and instead of rubbing the top of his head, or saying next time, Adrian apologizes and says when Ben's an adult he'll understand.

I get Ben taken care of for bed and suggest a movie. Adrian angles to the bedroom, but since I should be starting my period any time, I offer a blow job instead. He thinks about it, shaking his head, saying he should go since he has an early morning meeting, anyway.

He pecks my lips and heads out.

No texts for three days. No come-ons. No flirting.

Thursday, I log on the internet, searching the tabloids to see if he's been with anyone else. He hasn't been spotted with another woman so far, but the thought is stuck in my head.

I'm about to leave work early to get Ben from school when a knock comes on my office door. Before I reply, it opens and Adrian steps in, very casual, as if he hadn't ghosted me for three days. Whatever. I'm not going to let him see how his behavior bothers me.

"Hey."

"Hey." I say, pulling my purse over my shoulder.

"You're heading out?"

"I got in a little early and worked through lunch, so yeah," I reply. "I wanted to surprise Ben and get him right after school."

"Is he having trouble with those bullies again?"

"No," I reply, catching a look on his face. "Are you okay?"

He threads his fingers through his hair and worry bubbles up my throat. "Sal ... Mr. Hanson. Oh no. Is Mrs. Hanson okay."

Adrian hugs me. "She's fine. Mr. Hanson took her to the E.R. with severe dehydration yesterday, but she recovered enough for him to take her home today."

I take an uneasy breath and Adrian calms me. "I wanted to let you know, I'm going to be busy this week. I won't have time for dinners or babysitting."

"Okay." I draw out the word and pull back. "Are we still ... are we still doing this?"

"Yeah." His brow furrows. "Why? Do you want to give that other guy a try again?"

I narrow my eyes. This question resurfaces whenever I try to get some reassurance from him. Is there another guy I want instead? Is there someone else trying to sleep with me? The jealousy was hot the first time. Now it's starting to feel like possession that he doesn't get to have. I have feelings for him, and I've made that clear. I include him in my life constantly. I tell him I like him, that I like us. He's the one holding out.

"I haven't talked to Logan since the night he took me out. And contrary to what you believe, guys don't exactly pick up single moms on girl's nights or in the car line at school."

"No, but they'd snap *you* up in an instant," he argues.

I put my hand on my hip, glaring at him.

"You're hot as fuck, Brooke. Sexy and smart with a smile that I'm pretty sure could bring about world peace." He huffs. "I've seen people in my office stare at your ass."

My throat closes for a moment. It's still strange to have anyone be jealous over me when Greg wasn't. His friends would openly hit on me, stand too close, call me pet names, and he told me I was imagining it.

"Well, they can look all they want." I stare at him directly. "They don't get to touch."

His shoulders drop and he kisses me softly. "I'm sorry for upsetting you, Kitten. I'm stressed."

"Did you go to the gym? That usually helps," I offer.

"Getting you loud and wet while watching you come does even more for me," he teases, his silky voice giving me tingles.

Well... I still haven't started my period. "Quickie?" I offer.

He gives me a smile and lifts my chin. "I don't do quick. Text me once Ben's in bed. If you're up for it, I'm all yours."

His words trigger a flutter in my stomach, and I take a deep breath, dropping my gaze to his chest. He shouldn't say those words, not when he doesn't know how I take it. To me, it means he's going to stay. That I'm the only woman he's seeing, that I'm the only woman he wants.

Adrian kisses me hungrily, showing me exactly how much he does want me, then walks me out of the building on trembling legs. His fingers brush mine, almost like he wants to hold my hand. I brush my fingers over his and rub his hand with my thumb.

He adjusts himself carefully, working his tie back into shape. "I really am going to be busy, Brooke. Work and sleep are demanding my attention."

"You said that before, Adrian, and I understand. I told you that."

He nods, and there a flash of guilt on his face before he opens my car door. I ignore the drop in my stomach, giving him a forced smile before driving away.

---

I CLOSE THE OFFICE door behind me, my bag falling from my hand as I spot Adrian sitting on the couch, his thumb stroking his bottom lip. It's hard to read his expression, but his stiff shoulders relax as I move farther into the room.

It's been four days since I last saw him. Four days since he made me come so hard, I passed right out afterwards. Four days after he snuck out of my bed and left without saying a word. Four days since I cried myself back to sleep while reminding myself it's just a fling, that

I shouldn't get emotionally vested. My heart is still struggling to get the message.

I drop my purse on my desk, feeling the heat of his scorching gaze on me.

"Hey."

"What's up?" I reply, summoning a calm expression before facing him again.

"You tell me. There's something on your mind, isn't there?"

I abandon the laptop I'm about to turn on and close the space between us. "Are you ending things between us?"

His brows shoot up. "No. Why would you ask me that?"

"Because you left without saying goodbye. Plus, I haven't seen you in four days."

Without warning, he reaches for me, pulling me onto his lap. "I've been busy. That's why I told you in advance."

White-hot flames of desire threaten to consume the questions in my head. I resist the urge to surrender long enough to ask, "You'd tell me if you wanted out, right? You wouldn't string me along, would you?"

"Of course, I wouldn't, Brooke. You know how straightforward I am."

He smothers my next question with his mouth, and I surrender. I'm helpless. And I've been horny as hell lately, when I'm not verging on pissed off. Nearly six weeks of this not-relationship and I still don't have a grasp on the man I'm seeing. It's driving me crazy.

After two rounds of sex that leave me dizzy and in some kind of pleased, half-asleep pile, Adrian drags on his pants and pulls my head onto his lap. We lay in silence until he clears his throat. "I want to be honest about something."

I turn my head to look at him. "Oh?"

"I like spending time with you, Brooke. You and Ben, but it makes me uncomfortable too," he says.

I try to sit up, but he holds me there. "Let me talk before you do."

Based on his tone, this feels a hell of a lot like a breakup. I swallow the lump in my throat.

"I don't want to keep coming over to your house. I'm afraid to let Ben rely on me or trust me. Trust is ... not good." He takes a moment, organizing his thoughts. "I've been in the foster system since I was a baby. The foster homes weren't great. The second I trusted someone; it was like opening myself to getting hurt. Because I'd take them at their word."

I nod, understanding at once. "And you don't want to hurt Ben, right?"

"Right." His jaw tightens for a moment. "I don't want him getting used to having me around, so you should come to my place Thursday or Friday instead. If your parents don't mind."

"They won't." Because I won't tell them I'm going to see Adrian. They don't like him. Not after Stacy told them his company had been poaching my clients. My dad is a little more willing to give him a chance because he's Ben's hero, but they're both suspicious. Especially now they're aware of his age. "Let's shoot for Friday."

"If something comes up—"

"I'll tell you," I finish. "In a month or so, Ben is headed to camp. Thanks to our business agreement, I can afford it. He's excited. He's never been to summer camp before."

"I will see him before then."

I trust Adrian to keep his word, even when he helps me get dressed and leaves without a kiss. He doesn't call or text until Thursday asking if we're still on. I tell him yes, but I'm not sure what I'm going to be walking into.

Just like I have no clue what next week is going to hold, not with him acting like he has been this last week. He's unpredictable, and I hate it.

But it's not enough to discourage me. I want this. I want him, even if it's for a few hours tonight.

So I slip into lingerie I've never worn, pulling the tag off before I grab a dress, then ask Adrian for his address once I drop Ben off at my parents'. For all I know, this could be goodbye. He hasn't texted me today either, so maybe he's forgotten, or is asleep ... or has started seeing someone else. Adrian never promised to *remain* exclusive. He only said he was too busy.

God, I'm so queasy. The uneasiness has been with me all day. I take several deep breaths, but it doesn't help. I'm nervous about tonight, that's all.

I chew my bottom lip as I step into the lobby of his apartment building half an hour early, already intimidated by the elegance of the space. Adrian is far out of my league; why would I imagine he'd want more than a fling with a girl like me?

The elevator doors open ahead of me, and I stop short when I see Celine walk out. She's wearing a just-got-fucked look, with her tousled hair, rumpled blouse and smudged lipstick. She smirks at me while passing, running fingers through her hair, her hips carrying an extra swing. I watch her go, my heart faltering.

No.

Adrian wouldn't dare.

But, what are the odds she'd been with someone else in this apartment building? Adrian and I aren't exclusive, but he wouldn't dare invite me to his apartment after he's been with someone else, would he?

The queasiness in my stomach gets worse than before. My eyes flick to the elevator and I almost turn around when I get a text from Adrian, saying he has dinner all set up and he can't wait to see me.

Ok, I'll give him the benefit of the doubt until he gives me a reason to leave, I think to myself before taking a breath and getting on the elevator.

"The second he does, I'm gone. No regret. No looking back. No tears." I say out loud, even though I have a sneaking feeling that being done with Adrian, no matter how we end, won't be that easy.

# Chapter 24

### Adrian

I pace in front of the door, restless, hating that I'm so eager to have Brooke here with me. This wasn't a part of the plan when Brooke and I first hooked up. I shouldn't be making dinner and changing my outfit twice. My sweaty palms are an anomaly. The racing of my heart was only ever triggered by a session in the gym or the adrenaline from blowing the company's profits through the roof. It's like I'm losing control and I don't like it.

Goddamn Brooke. Bubbly, sweet, sexy Brooke.

I'm already trying to figure out what to do with her. I should let her go. Now is the time ... but I don't want to. I don't want to walk away from her. I want to be with her and Ben. I miss being there for dinner. I miss hanging out with the kid.

And that's fucking terrifying. It's a trap. I'm not cut out for family life. Once this honeymoon phase is over, the rose-colored glasses will come off. We'll break up, and my business will have a gaping hole in it because she'll want nothing to do with me. I'll ruin us both.

But at some level, I have to look out for myself. My company is *my* baby and it needs nurturing care to outlive me. And it will outlive me. I can do a relationship once I've made sure of that. I can sit down and relax. Or I can find the right woman. One that takes me at my word, stays home and is the perfect housewife. A woman who makes logical sense. Someone who either isn't going to break me or doesn't have the power to.

The knocking on the door pulls me from my thoughts. I open up and see Brooke standing there, chewing her bottom lip. She doesn't even look at me as she slips out of her shoes and walks in, the hem of her dress swinging which each step. My eyes travel upwards, taking in the outfit that clings to her body without being slutty. Her glossy hair hangs in loose waves over her shoulder, brushing her lower back. She's wearing makeup, enough to emphasize her natural features. Her skin has a glow I didn't notice before. She's classy and sexy, and tonight she's mine.

"You're so damn beautiful," I breathe out, unable to help myself.

She looks up at me, studying my face. She's been doing that more often recently. "I ran into Celine in the lobby."

I frown, her unexpected response throwing me off. "And?"

"You don't seem surprised," she replies, her expression falling.

"Why should I be?"

She huffs. "Why did you invite me here, Adrian? Better yet, why would u use me to scare her off if you'd planned to be with her, anyway?"

I stare at her. Now I'm confused. "What are you talking about, Brooke?"

"I'm talking about you sleeping with your stalker," she makes air quotes, "right before you invited me to your apartment."

"I did no such thing, Brooke."

"Really? Because her hair was a mess, her lipstick smudged. She looks like I did after you—"

I interrupt her. "Don't accuse me of something I didn't do. If you saw Celine, she must've been with someone else. I wouldn't touch that woman if someone paid me to."

She stares at me, chewing her lower lip.

"Believe me, Brooke."

"I *shouldn't* believe you based on your reputation and the fact that you keep pulling away ... but I do." She says it quietly. "I'll believe you until you give me a reason not to."

I take her hand and draw her close to me. She takes a staggered breath. "Please, Adrian."

"Please what, Kitten?" I ask.

"Please be honest when I ask you this question. No bullshit, no shortening, no cop out about it not being fit for a date or whatever this is."

Really, not a date? Do I actually have to say the fucking word for it to be important to her? Or is it that word that matters so much. I clench my jaw and wait for her to speak. I can't let my temper get the best of me. I can't.

"Have you been in a relationship before? A real one, not a one week something? But a real one, with a girlfriend?"

"Of course," I reply, wondering where she's going with this.

"Not a high school fling either. Those don't matter."

"We're going to agree to disagree there, but yes. I was in a two year relationship once." I walk her to my dining table that overlooks the city. I pull out her chair, pushing it in once she sits. "Is that so surprising?"

"Relieving actually." She lets out a breath I didn't realize she was holding onto. "Why did you break up?"

"Are we really doing an interrogation instead of a date?" I ask, a little sharper than I mean to.

"If it's the only way for me to get to know you, then yes," she says simply.

"And why are you so desperate for more? I told you we'd be casual, Brooke. That doesn't mean you get to pick into every bit of my life and constantly demand more of me."

She stand and puts her hands on the table, glaring at me. "I am trying *so* hard to trust you, Adrian. I trust you to be around my son, which is new for me. But I don't even know who you are! My Mom thinks the worst of you. My best friend keeps saying your bad for me and I can't defend you other than saying I like being with you, that you make me feel good and valued. Seen and heard. That you appreciate me for who I am, whether that means as a mom, as a colleague you respect, or when I'm being silly."

I stare at her. She takes a few panting breaths and sits back down, wiping at her eyes. "I don't call you my boyfriend, but I can't call you a friend either. I need *something*."

"Or?"

"There is no or." She plays with the ends of her hair. "I don't make ultimatums."

I don't know what to say to her. That I keep waiting for some shit to hit the fan? That I'm too happy for this to be real? That I suck at commitment? That I don't want to half-ass anything in my life including relationships? I'm not sure I can give my whole self to a relationship.

"Please, Adrian," she whispers.

"You asked if the relationship went badly," I reply. "It did. She cheated on me. Had been for a while. I don't know if it started after a bad fight or something else. Once I stopped looking for problems, they found me. Once I stopped ... looking into everything, stopped worrying and went out with my friends, was myself, she didn't want me anymore."

"Is that why you don't do commitment?"

"Every time I've trusted someone with myself, shown them who I am completely, not held back, I get tossed. I got passed over by foster homes because they wanted the younger, polished kids. I was too rough around the edges. Soon, I became what they expected. I figured, why bother trying if they were going to replace me, anyway. Happened with my ex. Happened with friends once I started getting successful and wouldn't give out money or take care of the bar tab every night or wouldn't hire them. I'm only as good as what I can provide. I understand that."

"A few assholes don't speak for the whole population," Brooke argues.

"So if I didn't give you the contract, would you have helped me from the goodness of your heart? If I didn't make you come, you'd still sleep with me?"

She rolls her eyes. "You're fishing for a fight."

"I'm asking questions. I'm *allowed* to do that, right?"

Her lips tighten. "If you didn't offer me the contract, but had *explained* things to me in full, yes. I would have helped. No matter what an asshole you are, you don't deserve a stalker. If you didn't make me come, I would have shown you how so we could have a good time. I like having you over and cooking for you before we watch a movie. That's a date to me."

Fuck. I scrub my hands over my face. Brooke gets up and comes over to me. She straddles me and rubs the sides of my neck and up through my hair. "Me trying to understand you isn't me trying to get ammunition for later, Adrian. It's because I like you ... dummy."

I snort, but when she kisses me and holds my gaze, my heart beats in a new pattern. I want to believe her more than anything in the world. I want to trust her. I rub her hips. "How do you ... trust me? Even when you shouldn't?"

"I will trust you." She kisses the corner of my jaw. "Until you give me a reason not to." She kisses my cheek. "Because I don't believe anyone is all bad."

I wish I had that luxury.

I help Brooke to her seat, then serve dinner by candlelight. Brooke seems impressed by my effort, although it's miniscule. She's even more fascinated with the asparagus-stuffed chicken breast I made, and I tell her of my two-year stint at culinary school before I found my calling with advertising. Halfway through the meal she gets a little pale, and when I enquire, she assures me she's okay.

"I've been a little queasy all day, but I'm sure it's nothing," she says.

Before I reply, she asks where the bathroom is and hurries that way. I can hear her throwing up and glance at what's left on her plate. She barely ate half of what I served her. The food is good; I'm sure of it. It wouldn't result in a reaction that quickly.

I gently knock, a bottle of Pepto-Bismol in my hand. She groans in response, so I open the door. Brooke moves to the sink to rinse her mouth out, spits, flushing the toilet before taking the bottle from me.

"I'm so sorry. I don't even know what happened."

"You don't have to apologize." I gently pull her into my arms. "Is it stress? Are you getting sick?"

"Ben was a little under the weather earlier this week. Maybe it took some time getting to me." She sighs.

She's a little warm. I turn on the shower, keeping the water cool and slowly undress her. She groans. "I can't have sex right now."

"I'm not asking for that."

I strip myself too and we get in the shower together. I take my time washing her down, including her hair, holding her under the cool water. Brooke looks up at me and smiles slightly. "See, I can trust you."

"Don't sass me when I'm worried about you," I grumble. She nuzzles into my neck and I rub her side. "Am I doing this right?"

"What, no one took care of you when you got sick?"

I shake my head. "My last foster mom wanted to be involved in everything, but I was sixteen when I got to her. I didn't want her babying me. I knew how life worked by then."

"Everyone needs some extra care when they're sick," she murmurs. "Thank you for giving me some."

We sit there until the water is icy and not once do I consider letting her go. I help her get dressed in one of my shirts so I can send her dress out to get cleaned and we watch a movie together. She pulls me down and takes my lips for a deep kiss.

"You're a good man, Adrian," she murmurs against my mouth.

I hate her giving me such positive feedback. It's addictive. Easily addictive. But my mouth works without my brain. "I like you."

She smiles and steals the remote when the movie is over. "I want to show you my favorite movie. Don't laugh."

"I can't promise it."

She puts on The Princess Bride and I smirk. "Some of the best dialogue in any movie I've ever seen."

She kisses me again. We spend the first half of the movie making out. We take a break once the sword fighting starts, but we're back at making out by the time we're done quoting the movie together.

I can't *not* have her. Not when tonight was so random and emotional and so fucking sweet. When I toss my own shirt to the side and lay Brooke back, I pause. "Is this okay, Kitten?"

"Yes." She nods. "I feel good enough for this."

"Then I'll work on making you even better."

She moans as I slowly unbutton my shirt. It's never looked better than on her. I kiss each bit of revealed skin until she's naked under me. I stroke through her hair. "I like when you touch me."

"I like touching you." She strokes over my chest. "I like being with you."

I groan and let her take off my slacks. Once we're both naked, I'm still not ready to dive into her. I feed her slow, lazy kisses. Brooke whimpers and strokes down my back, holding me like something precious.

God damn, how the hell am I going to have a life without her when something as innocent as this makes my heart threaten to explode? I kiss across her neck, pausing as I realize what this pleasant warmth in my chest really is.

Fuck. I might just love her.

# Chapter 25

## Brooke

Adrian hovers above me, a tremor sliding over his biceps. He takes a ragged breath as I stroke his face. "You're beautiful, Adrian. You know that?"

"Fucking hell." He groans and kisses me hard, hungry, fingers digging through my hair before he pulls me up and on top of him.

I make a soft squeak which lets his tongue deeper in my mouth. My eyes roll back and I cling to him. So intense, so warm, so perfect. Adrian is perfect. Casual is a word, but what I feel for him is so much more than that.

He's good with Ben, he's so good with me. I've seen so much good in him, so much to love and hold and enjoy. I cling to him, feasting on his mouth so he knows what I feel even if I won't say it.

His cock robs against my pussy and I groan, trying to adjust us so he's inside me.

"You're too good for the couch," he hisses.

Carrying me to his room, he keeps feeding me kisses, licking down my neck. He drops me onto the bed and hops up with me, continuing mapping my body with kisses and soft licks. Nothing rough or rushed.

Like he's memorizing me. Sitting back on his heels, so I can see every gorgeous inch of the man in front of me, his intense gaze, flushed face, chiseled jaw with a light sprinkling of hair, his muscular body and hard cock. He's a god, not a man.

And this god is kissing along the inside of my calf like he won't be satisfied until I'm trembling and begging for more.

"Adrian," I pant.

"You have no idea what you do to me, Brooke. How you make me feel. What you make me want." He groans, nipping the inside of my knee.

"What do you want right now?" I whisper

"To make you come until you can't move." He's so dirty. "I'm going to start with my mouth." He licks up my thigh. "Once you come a few times, I'll move to my fingers."

"A few times?" I gasp.

"I'd eat you out for every meal. Your pussy is better than alcohol or food." He drags me further towards him, curling me so my lower back rests against his chest as my legs dangle towards my face. "But I can't resist fucking you."

"God…"

"So once you've come for my mouth and my fingers, when your voice is all hoarse and sexy and you're ready to curse for me, I'll fuck you." He licks across my slit. "I'm going to cuddle you, finger you once you start coming to, and watch you writhe until I'm hard again so we can do it all over."

"Adrian, please," I whimper.

He wraps his arm around my hips and pushes one of my legs down as he devours my pussy. Licking and sucking and driving me insane. I can't even move to get more of his mouth on me. All I can do is watch.

Adrian groans and his eyes shut as his mouth works. Seeing his face like this so different, so new, so … fuck. I grab at the sheets as I try to get my feet on his shoulders and take more of his tongue. He's licking into my entrance, teasing me with slow, teasing lashes that sets my skin on fire.

"Don't stop!" I demand. "Just like that. Oh fuck, Adrian!"

He groans and licks faster, his nose brushing my clit as he fucks me with his tongue. I come, shocked he was able to get me to the edge that quickly. But, as promised, he doesn't stop. He focuses on my clit now, lapping and sucking as his hands tighten on me.

"Adrian, I—"

But I don't have the words. Pleasure keeps waving through me, pulsing like my pussy is. I whimper as his tongue keeps up the torture, changing when I get used to a pattern. Faster, slower, everything I need and more.

Holy fuck. I doubt there's a man alive who's better at oral sex. Adrian has to be a god, a mind reading god, to be this good. The second orgasm is even better than the first, he lets my hips move as I ride it out, but I'm not even sure I'm going to come back down.

Adrian flips me over, putting me on my knees in front of him. "You taste so fucking good, kitten."

"Mmm," I hum, all I can manage.

"I'm not quite done with you. Come here." He drags me back and spreads my ass, licking across my pussy again. I fist the sheets and he groans. "So wet and ready for my cock, aren't you?"

"Yes." I gasp as he buries his face between my legs again. "Yes, please. Please, Adrian. I need you inside me."

He groans and keeps feasting on me. Trying to move means he locks me into place, licking even deeper, teasing new spots that leave my legs shaking and my heart thundering in my chest.

I want more than his mouth, but holy shit does he know how to use it. My eyes roll back and I bite my lip, trying to stay quiet. Adrian's hand comes down on my ass and I let out a sound I'm not proud of. It's wild and needy.

But I come, obedient without him needing to say a word. I moan his name and slump against his bed. Adrian kisses up my back slowly. So much gentler than he was with me. He gently guides two fingers to me and my lips part.

"Ohh, yes," I groan.

"I know how to please you, Kitten. I know what you like." His fingers curl inside me deeply. Then he taps that spot that drives me wild. "And I'm a very determined man."

"Ambitious," I agree.

"Unwilling to stop until I hit my goal." It sounds like a threat laced with something sweet and soft as he whispers it in my ear. He keeps fingering me from behind while rubbing his cock against my ass. "So many positions, so many ways to make you come."

"Try them all," I encourage.

"You're not mad at me anymore?" He nibbles my ear lobe. "Still trust me?"

"Not mad," I promise.

"And?"

"Yes!" I roll my hips to take his fingers deeper. "Yes. I trust you."

"Good." He licks up my throat. "Glad that's mutual."

I blink, wanting to push on that admission, but his damn fingers are so good. I can't hold out or focus on anything but how he's making me feel. I come again, soaking his fingers as my legs clench around his hand.

Adrian moans. "Good girl."

I roll over to face him and kiss him hungrily. Adrian groans and lets me lead as I wrap my hand around his cock. He groans and lets me touch him, lets me kiss him, until suddenly, he sits up.

Licking over my puffy bottom lip, I watch as he squeezes his cock. "I'm not ready to come."

"But, I've already done it four times." Why the hell am I complaining? Adrian is the only one I've ever come more than once with. I should enjoy it.

"And you're going to come again." He promises.

This time it's his mouth and his fingers. I'm hopeless. I come again and Adrian licks into my mouth so I taste myself on him while he tries a third finger inside me, fucking me with them as my body writhes for him.

"Please!" I beg when he draws back. "Fucking please, Adrian. Fuck me."

He groans. "Not yet."

"I want you inside me." I say, "I need your cock deep in my pussy."

That ruins him. He growls, pulls his fingers out and thrusts into me. He holds still for a moment, looking at me. "A feisty kitten."

I drag my nails down his back. "I have claws."

He groans and fucks me like he needs me. Something wild and unrestrained. But he doesn't hurt me, doesn't hold me down, only tugs at my hair, touches me, strokes me, loves me. That's the difference. I experience real emotion, affection between us. And I'm not imagining it.

It takes me even higher. I give in entirely, submit. Adrian kisses me hungrily, drawing each one out as he pounds deep and hard. I shiver. "I'm close."

"Come for me, Brooke," he pants. "Please."

That 'please' pushes me right over the edge. I come, clinging to him, burying my face in his shoulder, going hoarse as I float away on cloud nine. Above me, Adrian comes too, groaning low and long as his hips jerk against mine. He pants and collapses next to me.

We're both sweaty and sticky even so, when I stay in one place, offering him some space since he's not crazy about cuddling, he jerks me to him, wrapping my arm around his middle as he cuddles me.

"Where did you think you were going?" he demands, low and gravelly.

"Nowhere."

"Good. You're mine until I say so."

My body shivers with pleasure as I kiss his chest. I want to be his for longer than a night or a date or a week. I want forever. God, I want a lifetime with this man. Adrian's heart softens against my ear, then he threads his fingers through my hair and guides me up.

"What's going on in your head?" he asks.

"Nothing."

He shakes his head, still sexy and rumpled despite our very long fun. "There something on your mind. Tell me."

Sighing, I rub his side. "You've been pulling away from me."

"Brooke." He sighs too and lays back down. "I've been busy."

"I'm not arguing, but what I said is still true."

He compromises with a "Maybe," but doesn't offer me anything else. I lay my head back down. Why do I want to know when it will hurt me, anyway? He'll hurt me. I knew that going in. I close my eyes and take a slow breath.

"I'm going to get a shower," I announce.

"Want help?" He sits up, ready to follow.

I force a smile and shake my head. "No. I'm a big girl."

But in the shower, I actively fight the tears. Why am I so emotional? Maybe it's a side effect of whatever sickness has been bothering me. I reach for Adrian's shower gel, taking a sniff before pouring a little on his loofah. My head suddenly spins, and I gag, bending over with the urge to throw up. There's nothing but air. Still my stomach keeps hurling.

I glance at the bottle shower gel, confused. Why is such a pleasant scent making me ill? I've never had a reaction like this in a while. It reminds me of when—

Oh, God.

It reminds me of when I got pregnant with Ben.

Shit.

My veins turn to ice. No. Please be wrong. Throwing up, emotional, and I was so angry earlier, so jealous, so turned on and ready to go. Mood swings.

I'm late too. By two weeks. My always consistent cycle .... This is seeming a whole lot like I need to take a test. I manage to get through the shower, then collect myself before leaving the stall. Do I tell Adrian now, or wait until I'm sure?

He's already using the ensuite shower, so I sit on the edge of his bed and wait for him to return. A dozen questions run through my head, the most important one being; how will Adrian take the news?

"Everything okay?"

Startled, I jump to my feet as he comes back into the room, wearing only a towel and droplets of water. I swallow hard, debating whether to do the test now, or to enjoy what I have for a little longer.

"You're not feeling sick are you?" he asks, leaning against the doorway.

I shake my head. "No. I'm okay."

He walks to me and tips my chin up, kissing me softly. So hot and cold. He rubs his thumb over my cheek. "Come lay down."

Decision time. Screw it. Once I do the test, we have to get real and don't I want just one more good night with Adrian? No regrets. I take off the towel, dropping it on the floor and his eyes drink me in.

"Bed. Now."

And he follows through, making me come over and over, everyway he can think of until we're exhausted. He doesn't rush me to leave, just holds me as I start to fall asleep. I give myself a bit of sleep and wake up to see him laying with his arm on me, like he's afraid I'll leave.

My heart actually *hurts*. Of course it happens now. In the worst possible time.

Because I know, in my heart, that tonight could lead to so much more with him, we could take our time and get into this relationship. We could take our time and get there. But time isn't something I think we have.

Because Adrian is easy to predict in at least one way. If I'm pregnant, he'll leave. Maybe he'll toss some money my way to take care of the baby, but he'll be gone. I'm sure of it. He doesn't want to be a dad. He doesn't want the happy family, not until it fits into his schedule.

My eyes water as I look at him, sleeping on his back, completely at ease. He's never been more attractive. Rumpled, completely at ease, naked. He's beautiful. And not mine. But I smile, gently move his arm and try to move as quietly as possible through the house. I find my dress on the floor and pull it on.

My stomach growls, reminding me of my half-eaten dinner. I check his pantry, wondering if he has any bread, and as I find the bag, his hand strokes down my side, startling me.

"Hungry?" he murmurs against my ear.

"Yeah. I woke up starving," I say, turning to kiss him.

Adrian grunts, answering my kiss with one of his own. It's more demanding, leaving me weak in the knees and ready to forget my hunger for a while. But Adrian insists on making me a sandwich and we eat together, laughing easily, talking, avoiding the big question in my head. Adrian rests his cheek on the back of his hand, watching me.

"What?" I ask.

"I enjoy our time together, Brooke. You're unlike any other woman I've ever met."

"Is that a compliment?"

He nods. "Most women I meet want my money or title. I worked hard to earn it, but they want to grab it for themselves no matter what it takes. They play different games, but I know a woman on a mission when I see one."

"My mission doesn't involve getting anything from you," I assure him.

"I know." He takes my hand. "You have goals for yourself, for your son, for the people you love and that's amazing to me. You're beautiful, driven, your approach to our business is amazing."

I'm not sure what to do with all these compliments. So I just grin and kiss him. We wash the dishes together, then I contemplate what's next. Does he want to me to spend the day with him? Do I ask?

Adrian stretches, yawning loudly. "Are you heading out?" he asks.

"I don't know.... Do you want me to stay?"

He shrugs. "If you want, I guess."

He's trying to be subtle, but I read right through his response. Shaking my head, I dry my hands on the kitchen towel. "Think I'm going to head out," I say.

"Are you sure?" he asks me.

"Yup." I get dressed, accept the kiss he gives me and promise to text him when I get home. Of course, I stop by the pharmacy and get a pregnancy test. Once in the house, I make my "I have to pee" dance to the bathroom and impatiently wait for the five minutes. My phone dings and I look at it, expecting that to be the timer, but it's Adrian.

I text him that I'm home, send it, then see the positive response on the test.

Yup, I'm home, and I doubt I'll be back at his apartment ever again. Based on his response earlier, he won't take the news well. I sit on the toilet and rub my belly. It doesn't matter if he wants this baby or not. A smile tugs at my lips.

Ben is going to have a little brother or sister.

# Chapter 26

### Adrian

I should have told Brooke why I'm pulling away. She would understand. She's proven that time and time again. She wouldn't go running, maybe she could even fix things. But I'm torn. Half of me wants to run. Especially after that thought where I might love her.

How natural it felt falling asleep with her. How easy it was to be myself around her. Everything with Brooke – the things that matter – they're easy. Even when it's hard, we work at it. Like the conversation earlier.

I glance at my empty bed. After the text last night, I haven't heard from Brooke. Surprising. And I hate that she's not here. My home has never felt so warm. Maybe, if we can keep up this pace, we can really be something.

We'll get to where I'm comfortable with trusting her with the hardest parts of my life, not only with the basics. Enough to never grab her phone when she leaves or think she'll run to another guy.

I'm trying.

There's a soft knock on my door. It's the middle of the afternoon. I'm not expecting anyone, but I hurry to answer, anyway. Opening the door, I'm surprised to see Brooke standing there. She seems nervous, her throat bobbing as she swallows. Stepping aside, I let her inside. What are you doing here?"

"Kiss me, please?" she says.

I pull her against me and take her lips for a deep, hungry kiss. I'm not going to complain when she offers herself to me. But I can tell something's bothering her. She's anxious, she's not fully in the kiss. I draw back and look her over.

"Are you still sick?"

"Not sick. I wasn't sick." She motions to the couch. "We should talk."

"Are you ending things with me?"

She laughs once, a humorless dry sound that rubs me wrong. This is not any kind of Brooke I'm used to. Her pushing my hand away when Ben is around, her work mode, her around her son, her with me. This is different from all of them.

"No. I'm not." She bites her lip and doesn't fumble when she finds something in her purse. She swallows.

"What is it?" I hate how upset she is. "Talk to me, Kitten."

She sniffs, looks at me and smiles softly. "I'm pregnant, Adrian."

She hands me a stick and I stare at the word "pregnant", imprinting it on my mind. She's ... fuck. "You were on the pill."

"Today's the first day I haven't taken it in six years."

"So how ..." I can't wrap my head around it. I just can't. It's not in the plan. Brooke wasn't a part of the plan. This, a baby. Holy Fucking Hell. "How?"

"It's only 99% effective, Adrian," she whispers, the smile melting.

Brooke puts a protective hand on her belly, like she's afraid I'm going to take it from her. She still hasn't met my eyes. Fuck. I'm not ready for this. I'm not close to ready for this. It doesn't match the plan, it doesn't match anything at all! What am I going to do?

Frustrated, I drag my fingers through my hair. "I need to ... I need to think about this."

"Adrian—"

"I don't know what to else to say, Brooke!" I yell, tossing the stick. "I need to think."

She swallows and sniffs. "Okay. How much time do you need?"

"This is huge, Brooke, so I don't know," I snap. "I'll call you."

She hurries out of my apartment as I slump to the floor. I turn off my phone and dig the heel of my hands into my eyes. I'm not sure what to do about this. I don't know how to plan for this. And I have no one to talk to.

Fuck.

Turning on my phone, I almost call Liz, but at the last second, I reach out to my old friend Jeremy, inviting him over. He comes over in half an hour, whistling as he looks around my apartment. "Damn. This is nice, Adrian."

I nod, closing the door behind me. "Thanks."

He catches my dry tone, turning to me with a frown. "Are you okay, man?"

"My girlfriend is pregnant." I say, unable to hold it in. I don't even choke on the world girlfriend. Brooke has me that twisted. "I ..."

"Congrats, man!" He pats my shoulder. When he sees my expression, he falters. "Um, congratulations, right?"

"I don't know. I mean ..."

"Talk."

I spill, as much as I can. Saying how unplanned it is, how it doesn't fit into my life, how I'm not even ready for a serious relationship, let alone a baby. Who can possibly be ready for all of that all at once?

I turn my phone off as it rings again.

"I can't do this, Jer." I whisper.

"Why not?" he asks innocently.

"Because I—" I sigh, palming the back of my head. "I don't know."

Jeremy nods, as if he understands anyway. "Look, man, I was struggling with finding a new job when Rachel told me she was pregnant. It was hard. I wasn't ready for another kid. I don't know if it's possible to really be ready."

"So what should I do; go old-school and marry the girl, become a dad and balance that with my long work hours?" I snort. "That's not me, Jeremy."

"It could be. If you choose to do that. It's a decision, Adrian. You make them at work all the time or you wouldn't be the CEO of a billion-dollar company. But this one isn't about numbers. It's morals, it's happiness, it's where you're willing to compromise."

I nod.

"But you can't leave her hanging. You have to give her an answer. You've *got* to talk to her sooner, rather than later."

"Even if I lose my control?"

"Yup." Jeremy says. "But tonight, let's have a drink—or two. You'll figure out what you want afterwards."

But even after Jeremy walks me home because I'm beyond wasted and drops me in my bed, I don't know what I'm going to do. I like Brooke, more than like her honestly, but a baby?

Fuck. What am I supposed to do about that?

---

I GIVE MYSELF SUNDAY to sober up, then I distract myself with work the entire Monday. I'm in the office until eleven, arriving home to find several missed calls from Brooke. Sighing, I dial her number, pressing the phone to my ear. There's no running anymore. I have to do this.

"Hey." Her cool tone puts me on the alert. She's upset, and rightly so.

"Hey. I'm sorry for the delay. I needed to think."

"It's been two days, Adrian." Her voice tremors, like she's holding back tears. "The anxiety has been killing me. This wasn't planned, but we're having a baby."

"Brooke—"

"I don't want to raise another kid on my own, okay? I don't just want you to be a dad. I want to be with you."

God, the pressure weighs so heavy on my shoulders. I rub my forehead. "Brooke-"

"Just please, please consider it. I can't not have the baby. I want it. And I want you. Please don't ask me to choose. I can't." I can already hear her crying and the threat of anger on her sobs. "Adrian, say something!"

I swallow hard. Thinking of a life entirely without her is so fucking cold and unbearable. But I'm going into this with full honesty. Which means starting with the hard part. "You have to hear me out all the way."

"So you're leaving."

"Just listen, Brooke," I insist. When she proves she can stay silent, I continue. "I'm not ready for a family. You know that. I haven't even been ready to call you my girlfriend. I really like being with you and Ben, but this is difficult for me."

"So you're leaving. I didn't get myself pregnant, Adrian!"

I grit my teeth. "If you'd let me finish—"

"I don't want your fucking money. I don't want anything if you can't own that this is your responsibility too. But you won't. Because everything in your life has to be perfect. Your image, your business, everything. And I'm not! The baby won't be."

"Brooke!"

"Well we don't need you. Just fuck off. I'll raise this baby all by myself and try managing my son's emotions since you're not only leaving me. Don't call me. Don't talk to me. Liz can handle everything between us at work. We're done."

I stare at the phone when she hangs up, then dial her number again. It rings out to voicemail. I give up after several tries, plopping down on the couch with a hefty sigh. I'm not ready for what Brooke wants. The white picket fence, two kids and a few dogs, school drop-offs, dinner at six life isn't for me, but I wanted to try. I wanted to be there for her and Ben. It would have been hard at first. That's what I tried to explain. She didn't give me a chance to say it.

I take a shuddering breath and run both hands through my hair. She gave me an out, though. I should take it, right?

---

I DIG THE HEELS OF my palms into my weary eyes as Liz enters my office. She takes one look at me and turns on the privacy screen, then sits in front of me.

"What's going on with you?" she asks.

"What do you mean?"

"You look like hell. And that's saying something for you." She motions to me. "Didn't shave. Your shirt is rumpled. Tie is knotted, not tied. Your hair isn't done. You even have bags under your eyes... should I continue?"

I wave her off. "I get it."

"So, are you are going to tell me what's wrong?"

"You'll hate me, Liz. And I can't have you quitting."

A knowing look crosses her face. "Ah. Brooke. You ended it," she says with a sigh. I can see the anger there.

I shake my head slowly. "I didn't mean to. I didn't want to. I didn't say the right thing. How does anyone do this shit?"

She watches me with surprise as I stand and pace. I rub my hand over my mouth. "She didn't even let me talk! A conversation means both people talking. I should have done it in person. I should have been there so I could have wrapped my hand over her mouth and made her listen."

"Creepy."

"I had so much more to say." I deflate into my chair.

"So why don't you try again? If there was more for you to say? If she's worth it..."

Brooke is worth every effort I could possibly put into her. But she doesn't want me involved. She made that clear. "I tried calling several times. She doesn't want to hear from me."

"I shouldn't tell you to go after the girl who doesn't want to be chased because that's ... bad. But she was upset, Adrian. You can push on that."

"That's the first time you've called me Adrian." I distract her purposely.

She snorts. "Focus."

"I'm not going to step back into her life if I'm unsure. I'm many things, but I'm not cruel and I'm not a sadist. I won't hurt her like that again."

"You want to be there." Liz stands up. "The only thing stopping you is you. I know you, Mr. Thorpe. Better than anyone."

"Don't tell your boyfriend."

"I was here when you brought this company from the brink. You put *everything* into this company. You didn't stop. It didn't matter what obstacle came up. It didn't matter when you had to invest your own money. You kept pushing."

I nod.

"You are unstoppable when you want something, but you *have to* want it. So you're right. If you're unsure, leave her alone. Because she deserves someone better, who will support her through everything and chase her right now."

Liz takes a slow breath, and the silence between us drags out. All of a sudden, she drops the files on my desk. "Saturday, I'm going to talk to her. She's my friend. I'm going to hear all about it. It's your choice to tell me."

"Tell me what?"

"Whatever straw broke your back and made you panic enough to scare her into yelling at you. Brooke doesn't yell. As your assistant, I need to make sure whatever you're trying to hide stays hidden."

I hesitate, but Liz has a point. If there's anyone but Bridget that I trust in this world, it's Liz. She's never let me down, she's never confused me, she's made everything in this company – and by extension my life – work.

"Brooke's pregnant." Her eyes widen. I nod once. "An accident, but all the same."

She sits back down, staring at me deadpan. "Fuck."

"Unprofessional," I comment before I can stop myself. "But yeah. Fuck. We had a dinner date at my house, and she was a little ill. I wanted her to spend the night, but she was all ready to go, dressed and antsy. Then, the next day she knocks and hands me a stick and teaches me birth control isn't as effective as I hoped."

"Seriously?" She waits for me to confirm and shakes her head. "Fuck. She must be so overwhelmed."

"Yeah." I rub the back of my neck.

"No wonder she was emotional on the phone. You did what you do when you're stressed and draw things out."

"I wanted to start with the worst and get to the best part."

Liz meets my eyes. "What?"

"I was going to stay, Liz. I wasn't going to leave her. I'm cold, I'm calculated, I can be an asshole, but ... damn I have a heart."

"Were you staying for her or the baby?"

I shrug. "Both. When I was drunk, after she told me, I almost ordered balloons to send to her. My friend stopped me, but I did buy a book of baby names and a 'how to' kit for building a crib. Don't know why, but ... it wasn't the worst thing to think of. And I really like Brooke."

"Then go get her, you giant, flaming idiot!" She yells at me. "God! For an intelligent CEO, you're such a dumbass."

"It's not that easy. Not when she doesn't want me. Not if I'm not sure I can commit now. That I can handle this."

"Get your act together." She clicks the privacy screen. "Because if you don't, you're going to lose her permanently. There's no coming back from you leaving after this news."

I fold my arms on my chest with a sigh. "I know."

# Chapter 27

### Brooke

I can't believe Adrian. I didn't even need the words. His tone, the lead up. I knew it. He doesn't want this baby. He doesn't want to be with me.

With tears running down my face, I rub my belly. "It's okay, baby. I'm a really awesome mom. I'll take great care of you."

It's the first time I've said it and believed it. Once I sob myself out, I get out of the car where I'd gone for privacy when Adrian called. Ben is still asleep, thankfully ignorant to everything going on. I wish I was that young again. That I could sleep that easily.

I get ready for bed and lay down, lying in the dark thinking about how I prepped for this. I cried when he ushered me out. I cried the first time I called him. I cried the next day, at the office.

Ugh. I'm so tired of crying and none of it prepared me for losing Adrian ... again. The first time was easy. One week of connecting with him and one round of sex. But we'd been going on eight weeks.

I know him now; how silly he can be, how good he is with Ben. I've seen his dedication for what it is, his drive, his focus. He cares without even realizing how much.

Like that one night where he covered the sharp corner of the dinner table when I bent to get Ben's toy off the floor as if it was nothing at all. He didn't even notice he did it. Just like he didn't notice how much his face softened for Ben.

There was so much he didn't see about himself.

It's a miracle I get through the day, but Wednesday, after work – an early day for me – I drive over to Stacy's. I cannot bear this burden alone anymore.

She takes one look at my face and pulls me into her arms. "Hey, babe, what's wrong?"

I burst into tears again. She leads me to the couch, and I tell her everything. She rubs my back and to my surprise, she cries with me. "I'm so sorry, Brooke. You loved him."

"I never said that."

"It was obvious." She wipes my eyes. "Ben loved him too. It was only eight weeks and one week before, but I saw you fall for him. When your mom told me about how good he was with Ben, how she saw him playing with him and spending time with you guys, I wanted to be wrong."

"You shouldn't talk to my mom about me or my partners," I grumble.

"Whatever. Look." She grabs my shoulders, staring into my face. "I'll be a kick-ass dad, okay? So, that little bean in your belly doesn't need to worry. It's going to have so much love. Unconditional, all-consuming love."

I pat my belly and sigh. "Is it stupid that I still wish he'd come and sweep me off my feet? I told him not to talk to me again, but if he wanted to ..."

"I can't believe he's done with you," she says. "I mean, he said it right?"

"He said he's not even ready to make me his girlfriend. That he's not ready for a family." I snort.

"That's a bummer. I was kinda hoping he was."

I glare at her. "What gives? You told me he's no good for me."

"I know." She rubs the back of her neck. "And he's old as balls, but he made you so happy and I wanted to be wrong once I saw it. I saw how you changed, even if I never got to see the two of you together. I just ... I hoped for the best."

"Me too."

"And he was coming over for dinners, babysitting Ben, actually taking you on dates. I mean, that doesn't seem like a guy who doesn't want to be in your life."

"A baby changes things." I sniff. "And now I get to tell my parents I'm pregnant and alone."

Stacy squeezes my hand. "You're not doing this alone, babe. I'm here and believe me, I can handle a lot."

I hug her again, deciding to tell my parents tomorrow. I make myself wait, because a part of me, that damn hopeless romantic, swears that Adrian will come back. But my phone remains silent. He hasn't emailed me. Liz is handling our business, just like I asked. If I went to his office, would he even want to see me?

Chewing my bottom lip, I decide it's not worth trying. It's not. Because I can't handle another rejection. It will destroy me, and I have to be strong right now. I pat my belly. "Don't you worry, baby. You're going to have the best big brother and very happy grandma and grandpa. Aunt Stacy is going to spoil your rotten."

"Damn right about that," Stacy suddenly says behind me, making me jump. I didn't hear her come in.

She grins at me, dressed to the nines although we're only having dinner at my parents' house. She's holding a cake box with three envelopes on top. "You ready to go?"

I nod, rousing Ben from the couch where he's been stuck watching TV while we wait for Stacy. There's a mysterious smile on her face as we drive over, and she turns to me as she pulls into my parents' driveway.

"Okay, don't be mad, but I have a surprise for you."

I cock my brow at her. "What did you do?"

"It's only a little prop for the announcement," she whispers, her eyes shifting to Ben in backseat. "I want your folks to know this is a celebration, not an incident."

"But it was an incident."

"Was, but no more." She hugs me. "I'm here for you, Brooke."

I hug her back. "Let's get out of here before I start tearing up again."

My parents are as excited as Ben when they see Stacy, especially when they see the cake box. My mother tries to take it, but Stacy wards her off gently, explaining it's a surprise. Anxiety takes over during dinner. I'm an adult, but my parents' opinion is still important to me. I'd hate for them to be disappointed with this news, considering how happy they are right now.

Once dinner is over, I clear my throat, giving Stacy a tilt of my chin to show I'm ready.

"So, our lovely Brooke has news," she says. "Open the envelopes."

My heartbeat races as I watch them. Mom opens hers first. I bite my thumb as she scans the card.

"Oh my." My mom's eyes shoot up to me, her expression unreadable. "Really?"

"Wow." My dad rubs his chin.

Ben jumps up. "I'm gonna be a big brother?"

I nod. They hug me and Ben bounces around, so excited, saying he has to start getting stronger faster. Stacy distracts him with cake as my parents pull me aside.

"I hate to ask this, honey, but is Adrian the father?" Mom asks.

"Yes," I reply, bracing for the worst.

"Why isn't he here with you to celebrate?" Mom asks. "Is he working late again? That's not going to work when the baby is here. He's got to be diligent and if he's not I'll drag him from his office."

I try to laugh, but my eyes water. My dad sighs and pulls me to his chest, making me burst into tears. He strokes over my head, reminding me of when I was little. "Did he leave you, Brooke?"

I nod.

"Fucker." It's the second time I've heard my dad curse. The first time was when I told him my date stood me up at prom. I didn't hear his reaction after I told him that Greg left me. "Why did he leave?"

"I don't think he's ready for a kid, dad. Adrian's work comes first."

My dad lifts my chin. "He's not good enough for you, princess. You deserve more than a workaholic."

"I really liked him," I whisper.

"Oh, honey." My mom hugs me this time. "I'm so sorry. Why don't you and Ben stay here tonight? Take tomorrow off work."

I sniff, wiping my face. "Okay."

We eat cake, but I can barely keep it down. Ben enjoys the sugar high as he and my parents play board games. Stacy plops down beside me on the couch as I watch them, kissing the top of my head. "I can still key his car, you know."

"No." I shake my head. "No interaction."

"Alright, wifey." She kisses my cheek and says bye to my parents before heading out.

Once Ben hits the wall, my mom tucks him in, but he won't chill until I come in. He touches my face. "You're sad."

"I'm very happy," I assure.

He swallows hard. "Adrian isn't going to come over any more is he?"

My eyes water and I get in bed with him. "No. He's not."

"Is he a bad one in disguise? Just a mean bully?"

"Is that how he was with you?" I ask.

Ben's lip trembles. "No." He hugs me. "I really liked him. He was fun and made me feel good."

"I know, Ben." I hug him tightly.

He tells me his favorite memories of Adrian, counting them down. I'm surprised three of them are from their night together when I wasn't there. But he gets to number one. "I liked when he came over for our water park day. You smiled so much, Mommy."

He put me on his shoulders and made me feel tall, he let me plan everything for you to come save him. I wanted you guys to kiss."

"Ben," I whisper.

"He's good for you, Mom. Can't you get him to come back? I like him being at the house, even when he tries to clean faster than me," Ben continues. "Please, Mom?"

My heart breaks for him. I get him calmed down, reminding him he's going to be a big brother and we have a lot of preparing to do for the baby. As he falls asleep, his snotty face against my shirt, I hear him.

"I love you enough for Adrian and me."

I close my eyes tightly, trying to stay strong for another five minutes. I kiss the top of his head. "I love you to Pluto and back."

I slide out of bed once he's asleep, then sit on the couch. My dad sits next to me and wraps his arm around my shoulders, curling me against him almost like it's an accident. Unable to hold back the tears, I cry into his shoulder.

My dad nods. "I know, honey."

"Why couldn't he stay? I loved him." I sniff. "Why am I never good enough for them?"

"Tell me the whole story, Brooke. All of it. Every detail." But he doesn't look away from the TV.

I go over everything about us ending. Adrian's behavior when I first told him about the baby, how I called and texted and he didn't answer. How I tried to prepare myself because I knew it would be too much for him. Then to the final conversation.

When I finish, my dad turns off the T.V. and looks at me.

"He didn't leave you, Brooke."

"Yes he did!" My voice raises a little before I lower it. "It was obvious, Dad—"

"You knew he wasn't ready, and you kept putting words in his mouth. He asked you not to interrupt. Do you think there might have been more?"

I swallow and shake my head. No. I'm killing the romantic inside me right now. She's never right. She always gets me to this point, over and over again. Because that's my life. That's how it goes.

"Yeah, him using his long sentences like he does when he's being careful. Him artfully saying he didn't want me or the baby. That we wouldn't compare to his plan and that's all it would have been. It would have taken more time, that's all."

"I don't like he hasn't corrected things. But you jumped the gun. I've always been direct with you, Brooke. I always will be. It's how I love and guide you. He didn't say he was leaving, you did."

I sniff and wipe my eyes.

"You told him to leave you alone, that you were done, that you didn't want him contacting you. A good man will obey your wishes, even if there's a miscommunication. Until you open the door or something reminds him that you're worth getting, he's not going to fight."

"Why not?" It's whiny and ridiculous, but I don't care.

"Rom coms aren't real, princess." Dad cups my cheek. "He's not going to come storming through the front door, sweep you off your feet, and give you a ring. Issues require fixing, not talk."

"I guess."

"If he walked in right now and begged for you to come back, would you?"

"No," I reply at once. I'm stubborn. It doesn't matter that I want him.

"Exactly. He has to prove himself. And you didn't even give him the chance to talk when he asked for it, so how are you going to expect him to put in the work, to fight, to prove himself now?"

I groan and shake my head. "He wouldn't have stayed, Dad. I wish you were right. I wish I could believe you, but Adrian is a creature of habit. If he had called me his girlfriend, told me he loved me, anything like that, I would be banging on his door right now."

My dad looks up when Mom comes in. As she walks by, he reaches around and pinches her butt. She giggles and swats at him. "You're a terrible man."

Somehow, I see it now.

They don't have to say the words for them to be obvious. Those damn three words can be laced into so many other things. Like saying he trusts me. Like being willing to open up. Like babysitting my son, telling me he respects me, even in business.

Holy crap.

What if Adrian's in love with me, but doesn't know it yet?

# Chapter 28

### Adrian

My foster mother has called no less than five times, so when she calls the sixth time on Friday, I answer. "Hello, Lydia."

"Hi, honey!" she says brightly. "I've missed you so much. I haven't seen you in a whole year! I'd really like to have dinner with you to catch up."

I tap my desk. "Tonight?"

"Oh, I'd love that, Adrian! I can't wait. You can choose the place."

"Okay." I don't even know why I said yes. "At seven?"

"Perfect. I'm so excited to see you, honey. I'm sure you have so much to say after a whole year. I love you."

She hangs up and I shake my head. Always wanting to know everything and be overly involved. I'm surprised she hasn't walked into the office. I glance at the door, then at Liz. Liz who has been getting progressively angrier and less professional as time has dragged on. She wants me to go talk to Brooke, but ...

I shake my head and finish getting through the day after making a ten thousand dollar donation to Sal's restoration fun – personally, of course. When I text Lydia to meet me at her favorite bistro in town, she sends me a whole slew of emojis.

I get to the restaurant ten minutes early, and while I wait, I battle with the urge to text Brooke. I'm sure she has a doctor's appointment coming soon. I shouldn't go, but I should make sure the baby's healthy, right? It is mine ... kind of ... to a degree.

I scrub over my face, my finger hovering over the call button on my screen.

"Adrian!" Lydia comes in, as bright as ever. I tuck the phone away, standing when she reaches out to me. She hugs me tightly, confining me against her chest, reaching up to pat my head, as if I'm not taller than her. Like she used to do before I hit my growth spurt.

She's nearly seventy, but I don't think anyone's told her. And I don't know how she misses her white hair in the mirror, the laugh lines and crows feet on her face, the thinning of her lips, and has she shrunk?

"Lydia."

She scoffs at me, then holds my face in her hands. "Still handsome as ever, my son."

Her calling me son has never felt right. I was hers for two years. Granted, she didn't want to let go even when I was in college ... or grad school .... Or working on businesses. She sits down and leans towards me, bracing her elbows on the table and ignoring the menu.

"What do you want, Lydia?" I ask, gesturing to the menu.

"As always, for you to be happy and tell me everything," she replies, misinterpreting my question. "Go on."

I shake my head. "There's nothing going on with me. What about your life?"

She waves her hand casually. "Retirement is a joy, but your father is bored as can be. He's taken to building bird houses."

She pulls out her phone and shows them to me. I'm impressed by how beautifully they're painted. Lydia flicks through them and nods with a proud smile. "He builds them, we paint them together, then we sell them for cases of beer or flowers, or a few dollars."

"You could sell them for so much more."

"Why would we? We have nothing else to do. He gets the wood no one will use from a welding and fabrication shop and we get to do it together. That's the best part of retirement. Just George and I being together. We went on a cruise this year which was lovely, got to feel like drunk teenagers again. I even got him to go swimming in one of those Mexican sink holes with me."

A smile teases at my mouth. George – steady, calm, rational George – swimming in a cenote and drinking like a frat boy is something I can't picture. She keeps talking about the cruise, stopping only to order a BLT with a fried egg and a coke. Her same order every time.

"Now you, dear. What have you been up to?"

I go over my businesses, but she watches while slowly shaking her head. "I always knew you'd be successful. You're so driven and focused. You've always been smarter than me too. I'm so proud of you."

"You shouldn't be." It slips out before I can stop it.

Lydia reaches across the table and rubs my hand. "Why not, son?"

I clear my throat. "Why do you call me that? Why do you ... always push for more with me? You had me two years. I don't get it."

"We decided to foster you and wanted to adopt you so badly. I didn't give birth to you, but you have been my son since the moment you stepped into my house. I love you, and you weren't always interested in that. I tried to make you welcome, to make sure you felt like we were your home, that you could trust us, but you just pushed away."

"You were clingy," I grumble. "Over excited. Overprotective."

She laughs lightly. "Like most mothers are. I wish we'd found you even five years earlier. Before life hit you so hard." She looks at my big hand and sighs. "But you never wanted our love. You always said you didn't need us. I tried so hard to be a part of your life, to get you to let me in and you just ... didn't want it. You kept pushing me away."

"And you kept trying," I point out.

"Of course I did." Her face softens, reminding me of when she first showed up at the group home.

She'd ignored the cute ten-year-olds and came right at me. The matron had tried to push the younger kids at her, but she was determined to choose me. I didn't want to go. This was the only home I knew, and I had two years left to wait it out.

Lydia keeps rubbing the back of my hand, bringing me back from the past. "I love you, Adrian. I tried to change how I approached you, but I wanted you to *know* I loved you. What's bringing all this up now?"

I swallow. "You'll be disappointed with me."

"And you're too old to care about me being disappointed," she teases.

A smile tugs at my lips again, but when I realize how fucked up I've been to Brooke, it sobers me. "I was ..." Might as well call it what it was. "There's a woman I've been dating for a few weeks..."

I tell her everything. I don't hold out on my first stupidity, leaving her right after sex, meeting her son, having dinner with her, playing with them both at her house, treating her son, how much I enjoyed it, how much it scared me. When I get to the part about her pregnancy, I hesitate.

"She sounds wonderful, Adrian. A good companion for you. A really good woman overall. And you, being a good role model for her son. Showing how far ambition and drive can take you, but when to put it down and have fun."

She's making this so much harder and doesn't realize it. I swallow hard. "She's pregnant."

Lydia gasps. "That's wonderful!" She catches the look on my face. "Isn't it?"

"I never wanted kids. Not after mine abandoned me. I don't know how to be a parent. I didn't want to mess it up, but I was willing to try, but I tried to spell out how unready I was, so Brooke knew exactly where I stood. But she cut me off and put words in my mouth and I let her."

Lydia palms her cheeks. "Oh, honey."

"But I'm not ready. I never even considered settling down with a woman until I was ready to retire. And now I'm looking at a whole family. How can I be ready for that? How do I know I'm going to stay? She already has one ex-husband."

"Do you want to give her up?"

"No," I whisper, the first time I've admitted it. "I miss her so much, Lydia. Her son too, though that seems weird to say."

"So go get her."

"She told me not to talk to her!" I exclaim. "What kind of man would I be if I ignored that?"

"Sweetheart, you're one of the smartest people I know, but you can be so dense when it comes to people. If she realized you had one foot out the door, then yes, she reacted that way to protect herself, especially if you start out with the worst."

"Work from the worst to the best, isn't that the best way?"

"Not with people. And I'm sure it wasn't in person."

"It wasn't."

"If you want her, you're going to have to fight for her, Adrian. And if you didn't want her, this wouldn't be weighing on your shoulders. You're pushing her away, like you pushed me away, because you're not used to be being loved. And now you're pushing your baby away too."

"She'd raise it well."

"And alone. With two. I'm sure she's strong enough to handle it, but you won't get a second chance at this." She swallows. "And you want this, even if it's terrifying. George and I weren't sure we were going to help you. We wanted you to feel loved, safe, to have a good life."

"I fucked up, Lydia." It's nearly a sob that leaves my throat. "I don't know how to fix this."

She rounds the table and hugs me from behind. My hands spread over her arms, then I stand up and hug her back. She sniffs and hugs me tighter. "It's okay, son. You'll figure it out. Trying is half the battle. Just try. Show her you want to be involved. It's not going to be easy."

A tear rolls over my cheek. "I want her. She's so ... amazing. She brings out so much in me. It's terrifying sometimes, but I like who I am with her."

"That's reason enough. Go after her, Adrian. I want to meet her, and I'm dying to meet your baby when it gets here."

"Finally ready to be a grandma?"

She stifles her own laugh and hugs me again. Once our dinner is over, I try to call Brooke. It goes to voicemail. I leave a message, saying I want to see her and talk about what's happening between us. I'm not doing this over the phone again. If I'm going to fix it, it will be the right way.

Which means doing some research.

Arriving home, I ruin my Netflix and Hulu selections with plenty of rom-coms and actual romance movies. I take notes, not knowing what else to do. Flowers, saying what I feel and think without worrying about my pride.

And that's just for Brooke. How am I going to fix things with Ben? As it is, I've probably already made him feel unwanted. So I'm going to have to fix that too. Not to mention, I'm sure she's told her friends.

Saturday is a mess of overthinking and watching movies I can barely stand until I can't take it anymore. I just can't. Because I don't know if any of this shit applies to real life, let alone if it will work to get Brooke back.

Groaning, I rub my hands over my face and dial Liz's number. She picks up after the first ring. "Mr. Thorpe?"

"Adrian right now. Can you meet me at the bar on fifth street? I'd like to figure things out," I say, getting ready to head there. Danielle will be surprised to see me with a girl when I walk in.

"Depends on what we're going to be figuring out."

"How to get Brooke back."

"Oh god. I'm going to have to teach you how to beg." I can picture her rubbing her forehead. "Okay. Let me get Julio too. He got me back after a fight. He has experience."

"What, mi amor?" I hear a man in the background.

"Change of plans." She muffles something, then laughs. "Yes, later. I promise. Ten minutes."

"Thank you."

I'm going to get Brooke back. Whatever it takes. As long as it's not too late. And I refuse to accept that it is. I want to prove I had no intention to abandon her, Ben, or our unborn child. I'll tell her exactly what I feel, including that damn L word. That I trust her, that I want her more than anything else in this world even when we're bickering.

It shouldn't have taken me nearly losing her to figure that out, but considering I hate my own bed since she's not in it, how much colder and empty my life is without her, how unfulfilling working seventy hours a week is when I don't have our family dinners or anything else as a reward for it ... I definitely can't accept that we're over.

Worse, I can't even look for a happy future that doesn't involve her.

Somewhere between the dates, the sex, the weekly dinners with her and Ben, the times we went out together, cuddled, read to Ben ... somehow I fell in love with her and I have a feeling this isn't the kind of thing I can bounce back from.

And I don't *want* to bounce back from it. I want her. I'll give up my apartment for a suburban home with plenty of room for a family.

I'll give up working so much overtime. I'll give up the gym, all of it. She's worth it.

"She's worth everything," I correct myself as I get in my car and head to the bar. "Everything I can possibly give. Please don't let it be too late."

# Chapter 29

### Brooke

I leave the doctor's office, still hearing the quick little heartbeat in my head. It's early, only two full months pregnant, but there's life inside me again. Ben bounced when he heard it and kept trying to point out the baby to me.

He's excited as can be.

But now that we're in the car, he doesn't even stare out the window. He kicks his feet against the back of the seat as I drive. It's been a hard time without Adrian. Ben misses him and wants him back. He doesn't want to play swords with me. He doesn't want to build a fort, nothing. Hell, he's even put down video games.

When we get home, I sit with him on the couch. "It's Friday, Ben. What do you want to do?"

He shrugs.

I sigh and cup his face in my hands. "I'm so sorry things didn't work out with Adrian, little man. I wanted them to. You did too. But that's how it goes sometimes. You can love someone, you can want them in your life forever, but sometimes it's not enough."

"That's dumb," he whispers.

I wrap my arms around him, not sure how to respond. I'm exhausted all the time. I don't know if it's because of the baby or because I miss Adrian constantly. I shouldn't. Not after our fight, our breakup. But not being able to text him is so hard. Not hugging him. Making love to him. Just simply being around him.

Why do I have to miss the asshole so much?

Hell, I haven't cooked since we ended things. Because I'll miss him at the table. Sleep doesn't come easily. I lie staring at the ceiling, wishing I'd heard him out. Wishing I'd been more patient. But I'm still frustrated with him because he left.

Why would we have that conversation on the phone? Why hasn't he come to get me if I cut him off? No. My dad's wrong. Adrian doesn't want to be with me.

Saturday, I try to keep Ben busy. I tell him all about camp, how he gets to be there in one week and he perks up a little. We set up an obstacle course and he helps me in the garden we've decided to grow. Plenty of different plants since we chose them together. Tomatoes, jalapenos that neither of us will eat, flowers, cactuses.

But when we go back inside, shower, and curl on the couch to watch TV, I see the cloud come back over his face. "Ben ..." I squeeze his hand.

"Did Adrian leave because of me? Like the bullies at school said? Am I a bad kid?"

"No!" I hug him. "Don't you ever think that. Adrian liked you so much. It was me, honey."

"But you're so cool and nice and pretty," he whispers. "He must be a bad person to not want to be with us."

I don't know how to argue with him right now. I don't even know if I should. There's not really a 'how to guide' with this kind of thing and Ben is past the age where he believes blindly.

"Let's watch a movie, okay?"

I put on the live action George of the Jungle, one of his favorites, and I see him start to smile a little. We settle in, and I start to relax when my cell phone rings. It's Liz. I sigh, answering the phone. "Is this a work call because I made myself clear about overtime and—"

"Girl. I'm at a bar with Adrian," she says. I hear the commotion in the background and can't doubt her.

"What?"

"Well, Julio's with me, but so is Adrian!" She clears her throat. "Brooke, he wants you back."

My heart dances, but I will it to stop. "That's cruel to say and you know it."

Especially because that hopeless romantic thinking is going to rear back up and it was hard enough to kill yesterday.

"I'm serious," Liz insists. "He's here asking for advice on how to get you back, how to apologize, how to fix things."

That's impossible. "How drunk are you, Liz?"

"I'm not! I'm telling you so you can prepare. Make him beg, Brooke."

I pat my still flat belly and look at my despondent son, only smiling for Brendan Frasier swinging into a tree. "He'll have to do more than that. It's not just me he hurt."

"I know. Hence the heads up."

I hang up and sit with Ben. My leg bounces and I force it to stop. Another thing that reminds me of Adrian. I had to have picked it up from him. My temper, well that's obviously the hormones ... and maybe a little bit him because he brings it out in me. Always turning me in circles and making me crazy.

"What do you want to do tomorrow, Ben? Now that schools over and out?"

He shrugs. "Can we play putt-putt?"

"Absolutely." I ruffle his hair. "We'll even go to the one with the animals."

He nods. We read together and I fall asleep in bed with him. I wake up with a stiff back, a cramp in my neck, but Ben is curled against me, holding me tight. We haven't done this since Greg left.

If I tried to get him to lie down, he'd find his way to my bed and I'd wake up, sure that some kind of predator had gotten in the house to see my son. I run my fingers through his hair and shake my head.

We don't need Adrian. Just like we didn't need Greg. Not really. We're a family all on our own. We have a great day doing putt-putt, then I put on Lilo and Stitch while Ben colors and draws.

I take care of dishes, laundry, and picking up around the house, keeping my hair back as I clean. Just as I'm working on the sliding glass door, I hear a car door slam. Oh no. I tell Ben I have to take care of something outside and shut the front door.

There's Adrian, as Liz predicted. He has one hand tucked behind his back, a video game in the other, and a frown on his face. Why would I expect any different? I put my hand on my hip, trying to glare despite the little thrill that jumpstarts my heart.

No.

No way. He doesn't get to walk back in. Not after hurting me twice. Not after leaving me. No. Because that would mean my dad is right and I can't take another hit like that.

Adrian approaches slowly, his cautious eyes on me. "Brooke."

"Why are you here?"

"You didn't answer your phone."

"Because we're not together and it's not work related." Why does it take so much effort for me to keep my tone?

The hand behind his back produces a bouquet of my favorite flowers. Stifling a gasp, I stare at them a long time before taking them. "What is this for?"

"The start of a very long apology." He hands me a video game too. Something called Man eater. He nods to it. "For Ben."

"This doesn't fix anything, Adrian."

"I know."

"So why are you here?" I push.

He scratches the back of his head and pushes his sunglasses to the top of his head. His eyes are rimmed with red, with bags under them, and the short stubble tells me he hasn't shaved in days. For the first time, Adrian Thorpe is a mess. His clothes are rumbled, his hair longer than normal. He actually looks his age.

"Because I refuse to do anything over the phone with you again." He clears his throat. "It took me too long to do this. I should have driven over here right after our phone call."

"Oh, to keep telling me all the ways you aren't ready?"

"Will you stop interrupting and let me talk?" There's the anger.

I flinch and take a step back, sucking my bottom lip.

"I wanted to be honest and that meant starting out with where I was. Because I'm not ready for this, Brooke. It was never in the plan and I'm terrified," he says softly. "But you ... you're a once in a lifetime kind of person. A deal I'd be stupid to pass up."

I watch him, trying so hard to control my face.

"You and Ben. It shouldn't have taken me so long to figure out and I know that, but I wanted to be sure. After everything with Greg, I couldn't do this until I was sure how I felt."

"How do you feel?" I ask.

"Like I'm going insane without you. Life is so bland and empty. Work doesn't do a thing for me. I just ... it's like I'm missing something huge. Like ..." He groans. "Fuck, talking about this shit is so hard."

I nearly give him the flowers and game back.

"I'm trying," he says quickly. "I am. I want to be with you and Ben. I want to be where we were before you left my apartment. I've never wanted someone to spend the night so badly, but you were all dressed to go, and I thought that maybe you were ..."

"I was leaving you?"

"Yes."

"I've always been up front, Adrian. I told you I liked you. I told you how much our time together meant to me. I told you how much I liked having you at dinner, that I trusted you, that I cared about you. I said it all."

"And you're good at it!" Still, he doesn't move towards me. "But I'm not. Nothing in my past is an excuse for how I've held back. I know that. I was just jaded and scared and overwhelmed. It wasn't excusable for it to take this long for me to come and correct things."

"Correct things?" I parrot back.

"You really think that I wanted to leave you?"

With a huff, I drop the flowers this time. "Let's rewind this, Adrian. You said that you weren't ready. That this wasn't the plan. That you weren't even ready to date! Why would I stay on the phone to listen to you crafting sentences that make it seem okay that you're leaving me?"

"Because if you wouldn't have interrupted, like I asked, you would have found out that I wasn't leaving," he hisses. "You would have heard, that even though I'm not ready, I wanted to be with you and Ben. I wanted to see this through. That we could work towards everything."

"Easy to say now." I shake my head. "You're plenty good with your words. You've proved that or nothing would have happened between us. Because I knew – I knew you were going to destroy me from the start."

"Brooke."

"You need to leave, Adrian. Take the flowers and the game. I can't let you in until you decide it's too much and leave. Even if *I* still trusted you, if I thought you'd stay, I can't do that to Ben."

His face twists with pain and he looks at the front door. "I should have talked to him."

"And now you won't. I'm not going to drag him through this again. I won't. He deserves more than a father who barely speaks to him and you, who made him feel special, had him questioning if he was the reason people kept leaving."

"Brooke, please." He takes a step forward. "Please, there has to be a way for me to ... to say what I'm feeling and make it make sense."

"You already said your piece. I just ... I can't trust you anymore, Adrian. Your reaction to me being pregnant. The fact that you made me wait three days. That you ...." Where are all my words? The harsh ones that I had ready for him.

Adrian takes another step forward. "Tell me you don't want me."

"I just did!"

"No, you're giving me the logic. You're telling me Ben doesn't want me. That you don't want me to hurt him. I want to know about *you*. Just you."

"There is no 'just me'!" I insist. "That's what you don't get! I'm about to be a mother to two kids. They come first, not me."

He just keeps watching me. "You know exactly what you want, Brooke Dean. *I* know that I want you. No woman has ever twisted me up like you have. No other woman has ever made me feel a fraction of what you have. I would give—"

"Stop." I shake my head and push the game back into his hands. "Just stop, Adrian. The hypothetical doesn't interest me. The sweet talk doesn't interest me. More unfulfilled promises. Me always wondering which kiss will be the last one ... I can't do it. There aren't enough pretty words in the universe for me to consider this *again*."

He lashes me with pleading eyes. "At least let me be involved in the baby's life, Brooke."

"File for custody then," I growl, refusing to let his eyes soften me.

Adrian looks at my belly and shakes his head. "I would never take a child away from you, Brooke. If you don't want to see me or talk to me, I'll go back to honoring that request, like I was."

I swallow, trying so hard not to cry right now.

"I was led astray. I talked to Liz and my foster mother about this. They said I should throw myself on my knees and beg your forgiveness, but I should have known better." His smile turns up slightly. "I've always said if you were any more like me I'd hate you. And I'd hate this."

"Words are easy, Adrian," I whisper, taking another step back towards the door so I don't do something stupid like throw myself at him. "Actions are harder."

"And it's impossible proving I'm trustworthy to someone who has every reason to stay away. I understand Brooke. But you're going to have to say it. Tell me to leave you alone entirely, or I'm going to keep trying for this."

I scoff. "Just go get laid, Adrian. You used to be good at that right? Picking up a new girl every week."

"Not interested. I want you. Only you."

"Adrian." I fumble for the doorknob. "I ...." He waits, patiently, so unlike him. He doesn't demand an answer, doesn't force me to talk, just stands there. "You should go."

"I will. And I'll see you again soon."

My heart flutters a little, but I'm going to rope my heart into place. Because this won't end well. He's proven that twice, hasn't he? So why, why in the world, would I even allow a chance at a maybe?

"I'm going to fight for a third chance with you, Brooke," Adrian says simply.

Without replying, I shut the door on him and sit with Ben to enjoy the movie.

"Are you okay, Mom?"

"I will be," I assure him, hugging him tightly once more. "We will be."

Even if it murders my heart now, I refuse to let another man devastate me like Greg did when he left me. I won't walk into a situation like that willingly. I can't trust that Adrian is going to stick around. His commitment issues are too much. I'm not going to set myself up for failure and I certainly won't break my son's heart again.

I won't.

No matter how much I want to run out the door and jump into Adrian's arms right now. I won't. I'm stronger than whatever infatuation is between us. Because I refuse to believe it's love. Love isn't this painful.

# Chapter 30

### Adrian

On Monday, I drop by Brooke's office before she arrives. I leave flowers and a card at the door and hope she'll get them. I ask her to stop by the office whenever she can, that I'll push meetings to the side as long as it means another conversation.

I have to show her I'm consistent. That I'm not going anywhere. I don't want to annoy her. I won't stalk her or lose my brain like that, but I'm not going to disappear into the wind. I can't do it. There's no chance of it. Not when she makes me so emotional.

I sigh heavily as I turn, the tip of my shoe bumping the door.

"Come in!" she yells.

I glance at the time. Eight thirty. She's way earlier than I expect. I consider it for half a second before picking up the flowers – a different set than I brought yesterday – the card, and walk in. Brooke looks up at me, hair down, simple day dress on, eyes wide.

"Adrian, what are you … why are you …"

"You said there weren't enough words. So I'm taking the actions I can … without being overbearing." I set the flowers in a vase I see, sure it's dusty, but not caring. I hand her the card. "You don't have to read it if you don't want to."

"Did you put a check or something in it?"

"No."

She narrows her eyes and opens the letter. She clears her throat my cheeks burn. "Brooke, I miss you. I miss you every night when I get into bed alone and I miss …."

Her eyes scan the letter and she swallows hard. "I miss playing with Ben. I miss seeing you both smile and knowing that no matter what happens, you're not going to yell at me, kick me out because of a small mistake, and that my day will be brighter because of both of you. You really are sunshine and Ben is going to become an amazing man because of your love and dedication. He's lucky. I want to be lucky with you both."

"I mean it," I whisper. "It's easier for me to write my feelings than say them."

She nibbles her bottom lip and plays with the envelope. "Why can't you move on? You could have anyone you want."

"Apparently, that's a lie, Brooke." I sit in the comfortable chair on the other side of her desk.

She glances at the clock. "You're going to be late to your office."

"Yes." I consider that. "Liz will take care of things."

"You're not even worried?"

"You're talking to me. That's better than going through paperwork that Liz can absolutely handle. I've been stifling her talent for too long. She could probably handle more than half of my job responsibilities."

Brooke swallows. "I get that you're sorry. That's fine."

"That's progress."

"But you still have commitment issues, Adrian. We can go back and forth all the time, but that is still there. I thought my ex-husband was going to stay. I thought we had everything, but he still left."

"I'm not him," I say simply.

Brooke opens and closes her mouth before curling her hair around her finger.

"I'm not him, Brooke. You can compare us, but I kind of want to strangle him at the moment." My hands curl around the edge of the desk. "He had you. He had Ben. He had everything I'm willing to fight for and walked away from it."

"So did you."

"No! I didn't!" I stand up. "And I'm not walking away now. You want me to give up my position to prove it? You want me to camp out in your front yard? Want me to be a babysitter every single day over summer? I will do it all."

"Why?" she asks. "It wasn't even three months, Adrian."

"Because I fucking love you, Kitten." I say, deflating. I sit down in the chair and face the wall, rubbing my jaw. "It took meeting with my foster mother to realize how much I suck at seeing things clearly when emotions are involved."

"The one you told me about? The one who was overbearing and always breathing down your neck?"

"That's how I saw it. She reminded me of what it was really like. She wanted to be involved, to really be a mom and I didn't recognize it."

I can see her taking me shopping for prom, the one I didn't want to go to. She'd showed me how to tie my tie, as if I didn't know, insisted on taking photos, gushed over me. I'd seen it as her faking it, trying to have the perfect family, but even when I'd been rude and picky, she'd never changed.

She'd never yelled. She'd given me space when I asked, but was always there. She came and got me from Prom when I saw my date making out with someone else. She hadn't asked, she'd just held my hand in the car.

It hadn't been suffocating. It had been love; and I'd been too stupid to see it. Just like with Brooke. I'd kept waiting for the bad to happen, the sensation of being trapped. It didn't, yet I couldn't process the emotion. Why? Because I wasn't used to it. Being abandoned by my parents had done so much damage.

"Adrian ... you said you loved me."

"Yeah," I whisper. "I still do. And I love Ben too. I liked ... being his hero. Making him laugh. I liked hanging out with him and seeing him make progress with math and reading. For the first time in my life, I felt ...."

My leg bounces and I struggle for words. How can I explain something I barely fucking understand. "Fuck, why is this so hard? I can sell a bad deal without a second thought, but this ... this shouldn't be tripping me up."

"Can you ... will you try?"

"I felt seen and appreciated. Not for my wallet or business sense or my looks. Just who I am. No ulterior motive. You never asked me to take you to a five star restaurant. Never asked for jewelry or a shopping spree. Ben was just as happy playing in the backyard or in the living room as he was at that gaming arcade."

"Well ... yeah."

"It's new. I kept waiting for shit to hit the fan. For you to start wanting more. For me to fuck up. It got under my skin. Then you told me you were pregnant."

"Yeah. That." Her voice goes hollow.

I finally look at her. "I got drunk that night."

"What? Why? It was that terrible to hear?"

"I don't know. I talked with an old friend who has kids and it helped, but drinking got the best of me." I chuckle. "I actually bought an instruction manual to build a crib. I almost bought you balloons and a cake."

A small smile plays on her lips. "That's ridiculous."

"Drunk mind, sober mouth ... and amazon cart, I guess." I shrug. "I'm not perfect. This won't be easy, but I will do whatever it takes to earn your trust back."

"And I'm supposed to let you?"

"No." I shake my head. "Challenge me. Make me talk like this. If I pull away, call me out on it."

She rubs the desk. This is hard for her. I appreciate that. She swallows and strokes the card. "I don't know, Adrian. This isn't just about me."

"Ben doesn't have to know a thing until you're sure."

"As if he won't notice."

"He's uniquely observant," I agree.

"I have to think about it. Might take days. Maybe a week."

"I'll wait. And I'll show you how consistent I can be. And patient."

"Again, why?"

"I love you. That's reason enough."

Turning from the ghost of a smile on her face, I leave her office and head to mine. I work hard. Sal tells me he has enough funds to rebuild and I show up to help. I still make sure to see Brooke every morning. I bring her breakfast, since she likes muffins. I even go to the bakery she and Ben always rave about to get her favorite treats.

Brooke opens up a little, telling me little bits and pieces about her day. Although she doesn't rush me away, there's no trace of the relationship we once had.

Friday, I cut my office time short, canceling my meetings to spend all day with Sal. We work with some other volunteers to push hardwood into place and slap on drywall. He has the whole community backing him.

His daughter comes up to me as I take off my shirt and wipe my face. "I'm surprised to see you here, Mr. Thorpe. Especially without cameras."

"Sal is a good man. He deserves this," I reply. "Plus, how can the community handle not having his food?"

She smiles slightly. "Thank you. And thank you for that big donation. It really helped."

I nod and keep working until I hear a familiar laugh. Turning around, I see Brooke talking to Sal, handing him a bottle of water from her cooler. She passes them others, then gets to me.

When I turn and take it, she looks me over, lust flaring in her eyes. "Adrian."

"Brooke." I down the water, not realizing how thirsty I was. "Thank you."

"I can't believe you're actually here."

"I can do more than sign contracts and negotiate." I motion to the wall. "It's not exactly even though."

She smiles, then shows me a better way to do drywall. When she's done, she has pieces clinging to her face and hair. I brush her face clear of it and she lets me, standing there watching me with those deep brown eyes. Her lips tremble and she swallows hard.

"You're an amazing woman and you still wonder why I'd fight to have you?"

"Adrian, we're ..."

"I know right where we are, Kitten. Have I ever been good at keeping my hands to myself around you?"

She smiles slightly. "No."

My smile answers hers. "Are you staying to help or heading back to spend time with Ben?"

"He went to camp today. I don't know what to do with myself."

"Stay." I hear the desperation in my voice, but I don't care. "Let's help Sal."

And she does. We end up playing around, teasing each other. She smears my face with drywall, giggling as I gape at her. It's an easy day. By the time we're done, Sal has walls, a flower, and a ceiling. There's still plenty to do, but we've made more progress than anyone can say.

Sal hugs me and I don't fight him. I pat his back. "You're a good man, Sal."

"Thanks, Mr. Thorpe."

"Adrian." I say softly. "We're past the point of formality."

"Then you're going to eat here next time without a fork or knife."

I chuckle. "I look forward to it."

Heading out to the back, I rub myself down with my shirt. Brooke soon joins me, scratching at her nape. "You should clean up."

"And ruin this sexy handyman game?" I motion to myself.

Her eyes stroke over me and hunger ignites low in my belly. I curl my hand into a fist to avoid touching her. Because if I do, I won't be able to keep myself from kissing her. I'll start and won't be able to stop.

"I can't believe you spent all day here. Unpaid, just ... helping."

"I can be a good man. This little kitten I met reminded me of that." I reply with a grin.

Brooke hesitates, then closes the space between us, looking up at me. "I have a doctor's appointment coming up. Would you like to go?"

I blink at her in surprise. She's actually inviting me?

She swallows, staring down at her feet then back at me. "You don't have to. Really. I'm not pressuring, but I figured we could do that, get lunch or dinner maybe ... talk."

"Really talk?"

"Yes." She nods. "but only if—"

"Of course I want to, Brooke." I cup her dirty face in my hands. "I absolutely want to be there for you, for our little ..."

I hesitate. I haven't called it ours. She nods. "Tuesday."

I smile. "Tuesday."

God, I can't wait.

⁂

SINCE BROOKE'S NOT in the office on weekends, I text her, asking how she is, how pregnancy is, what I should be looking up. At first she's hesitant, but she opens up, slowly and surely. On Sunday, I go to see Lydia and George ... my real Mom and Dad. I update them on what's going on with me Brooke and we have dinner together. It's pleasant. For the first time, I don't have the urge to leave.

I think Brooke would like them.

George immediately offers to build the crib, saying he needs a challenge and I ask if I can help. Both of them light up and they can't stop asking about Brooke since she's clearly brought life back into me and they can't believe it.

I can only hope that they do get to meet her, as more than the mother of my child. I cross my fingers behind my back and hold my breath for Tuesday.

# Chapter 31

### Brooke

I didn't expect Adrian to pick me up for the doctor's appointment as he promised, despite his determination this last week, how hard he's been working to get time with me without any promise of sex or even kindness.

But he's here, wearing jeans and a button-up shirt pushed up to his elbows. It's casual for him. He opens the car door for me and has me sit, then hesitates. "Stupid question, is a seatbelt safe?"

I can't help it, I laugh. "Yes. It's okay."

Plus I trust him not to get into an accident. It's not much, but it's something, right?

We arrive at the doctor's office, and I make Adrian wait to come in until I'm in the gown and laying back with my feet in the stirrups. He glares at them, says they look uncomfortable as fuck, but he stands with me and holds my hand.

Our baby's healthy. It shows up on the monitor, heart beating wildly. Adrian drops to his seat. He swallows hard and squeezes my hand. I look over at him and see awe on his face. No trace of fear, no pale lips, no sweating, just wonder.

"Holy shit. You're actually ... growing a baby inside you."

I nod. "That's how it works."

"Congratulations." The doctor interrupts out moment. "Your baby's healthy and strong. You won't need to come in for a while unless you start having issues, Brooke. Everything is going well."

"It's really ..." Adrian licks his bottom lip. "Wow."

The doctor smiles. "First one?"

"For him," I tease.

The doctor chuckles, then both men clear out so I can get dressed. Adrian clears his throat as we walk out. "I have a surprise for you."

"What?"

He squeezes my hand, lacing our fingers together. "You haven't decided where we stand, but I hope this means I get to be a part of the baby's life."

"It does," I whisper.

I've been on the fence. He's been so diligent, so good. The tabloids are upset that he's behaving and Liz keeps telling me how much time he spends looking up information about babies, how he keeps trying to ask her how to make things right with me, not get me back, but make things right.

It keeps pulling at my heart.

As we sit in the car, I grab his hand before he can put it in gear. "You really weren't leaving, were you?"

"No," he says, staring at the steering wheel. I've learned it's hard for him to look at me when he's being vulnerable. "I wanted you to know where my head was. I'm still not ready for anything and I fear I'm going to fuck things up and not even realize it, but I want to try. I want to be here, Brooke. If friendship is all I can get, I'll understand. You've been hurt too much and I kept thinking ..."

I don't interrupt him this time.

"I kept thinking that honesty was the best. After your ex-husband, with all my issues, I didn't want to be unclear. I wanted to set the right expectations, but it was stupid. I should have told you right away that I'd planned on staying and then spoken with you in person about the rest."

I unbuckle my seat belt, drawing his attention, pulling his chin towards me, kissing him softly. "I didn't want you to leave. I thought you were, Adrian. You kept telling me how unready you were –

all the things you never do, the things you've never wanted and I assumed and I'm sorry."

He kisses me again, stroking my cheek as his tongue fills my mouth. I groan and stop fighting. I want him. I want this him, the one who's willing to talk, to be vulnerable, to level with me.

His fingers thread through my hair and he drags me closer, breathing me in as he claims my mouth over and over, searing my skin, making my heart burst, nearly making me cry because I'm so damn emotional.

When he draws back, he rests his forehead against mine. "I still have to fix things with Ben."

"Yes, you do."

"But you ... I can keep fixing things with you right now. Starting with a surprise lunch."

"It's not a surprise. You told me we were doing it."

He smiles slightly. "I'm introducing you to my parents. Lydia ... mom. She's excited to meet you. My dad has already started working on a crib."

"Adrian," I whisper, blown away. "You've ... you've talked about me, about the baby to your parents?"

"Yup. And Ben. They've been helpful. Encouraged me. I have you to thank for that. If you hadn't broken my heart, I wouldn't have been so open with my mom and I'd be missing out on this family time you keep hyping up."

I laugh, but still don't fully believe him until we're sitting at a restaurant with an older couple. The woman bounces in her seat and the man is as calm as Adrian, a gentleness about his face that seems at odd with how reserved he is.

"So you're the Brooke we've heard so much about!" The woman says. "I'm Lydia, Adrian's foster—"

"My mom," he interrupts, squeezing my hand under the table.

She beams. They talk eagerly about him when he was young and I swear, I can feel the love rolling off both of them. I tell them a few things, they ask about the baby and Ben. Adrian even answers questions about Ben without thinking about it.

I swoon all over again. At the end of the meal, both his parents hug me, and his father gives me a birdhouse painted with little animals. An elephant, a giraffe, a hippo, a monkey.

My eyes water and Lydia hugs me. "Adrian's trying so hard, Brooke. And I see why. I truly hope you can work things out."

I glance over at Adrian, deep in conversation with his father. For the sake of my heart, I hope so, too.

---

ADRIAN GETS ME TO MY door, beaming as he pulls me close. "Today was wonderful."

"It was," I reply. "Do you ... do you want to come in?"

"Are you serious?"

"Maybe."

"Brooke." He presses his forehead to mine. "If you invite me in, I won't be able to resist kissing you."

"Is that a bad thing?" I ask.

He groans. "Tell me, Kitten. I'm playing this day by day."

I take his hand and lead him to the house. Once we're inside, he pulls me to him gently and fits his mouth to mine. I stroke his sides and kiss him back. Our tongues slip and tangle together as he breathes life back into me. I clutch him tightly and his cock hardens against me. I can't stop my smile and that effectively ruins our kissing.

"Really?" I ask.

"I've been conditioned," he grumbles, adjusting himself. "And it's been a while. You know that."

I kiss his neck and over his shoulder. "You really love me?"

"I do."

A soft smile tugs my lips apart. I bury my face in his shirt.

"And I won't be mad if you don't say it back." He lifts my chin and kisses me softly. "We have time. No rushing."

"Yes, we do," I agree, but lead him towards the bedroom. Because I've craved him. I can't lie about that. I've missed his touch and I've missed having him inside me. "But I want to rush one thing."

"Brooke..." His warning tone comes with the side order of a steamy glare.

"It's called make up sex, Adrian. We're not back together until it happens."

A groan leaves his throat and he rushes me to the bedroom, making me laugh. He lays me down and slowly undresses me, kissing every inch of me slowly.

"Will this be like at your apartment? When you took your time?"

He grins a wicked smile. "Sounds like that's what you need, Kitten. A reminder of how good we are together in and out of bed."

"Maybe." I moan, catching his hand as he goes for my panties. "But if we're doing this, you're spending the night."

"That's not a deal." He kisses across my jaw. "Considering I want it. You're spoiling me."

And that seals it. I lose myself in Adrian, in the pleasure and warmth. His mouth, his fingers, the way he loves me slowly, and he's definitely loving me and not fucking me. I feel every stroke of him as he buries himself in me.

"Adrian, please," I whimper.

"Tell me what you need, Kitten." He kisses my throat as he rolls his hips again, thrusting deep inside me. "I'll give you the world."

My back arches and I drag my fingers down his back. He groans. "I love when you touch me."

I kiss the inside of his shoulder, biting softly. "Give me all of you. Don't hold back."

He takes a fistful of my hair and kisses me hard and hungry. Devouring my mouth in an onslaught of kisses that leave me breathless, hungry for more, and totally satisfied at the same time. Ecstasy fills my body, spreading with every heartbeat as my toes curl in the sheets.

"Just like that," I pant.

He increases the pace, faster, harder, deeper, and I can barely hold on. "Adrian!"

"Come for me." he demands. "Please, Brooke. Before I do."

That little hint of a beg pushes me over the edge. I come hard, and drag him with me. His whole body trembles and shakes as he collapses on me. His head rests on my chest as we pant and I stroke him slowly.

After a few minutes, Adrian lays on his side, stroking my hair and my cheek. "Be my girlfriend, Brooke."

"You want ... you're giving me a title?"

"I'm asking you to accept it." He kisses my nose. "I promise dates every week. Every other week, we'll have one without Ben. I'll come over for dinner at least twice a week, if that's okay. I'll babysit whenever you want girl's night. I'll cut it down to fifty-five hours a week."

"You'll sleep over?" I ask.

He nods and kisses me again. "I'll prove it tonight."

"We can try that. I'll be your ... your girlfriend," I agree.

He beams and we end up going another round, so intense and soul-stealing that I don't have a hope of untangling myself from him this time. Stupid, ill-advised, whatever it is. I can't let go of him. He's mine. He has to be.

But I don't quite believe it, even as I'm falling asleep.

Only when I wake up and see Adrian still asleep, wrapped around me as he snores softly does it kick in. We're dating. We're having a baby together. I brush his hair from his face and his breathing changes. He hums in his throat and adjusts, squeezing me before smiling sleepily.

"Good morning," I whisper.

He kisses my shoulder and nuzzles my neck. "Good morning, kitten. We have something important to do today."

"What's that?"

"Start advertising for Sal again," he replies. "And I'm making dinner tonight."

I laugh and stroke his cheek. "Full boyfriend mode?"

"Hell yes. And once Ben gets back, we should plan a party for him. A welcome back."

I arch an eyebrow. "So you can prove to Stacy and my parents that you're in this?"

He shrugs. "I'll do that in time. But I think he'd like the surprise. I would have."

My heart melts all over again and we end up both being late to work because I can't keep my hands or my mouth to myself.

## Chapter 32

### Adrian

On Thursday, I'm still beaming. I can't seem to wipe this smile off my face. Not that it's hurting business. My eyes drop to the screen of my laptop, the alarm signaling an upcoming meeting I've been looking forward to all day. A knock sounds on my door before Liz enters, her face lighting up as she studies my face.

"She took you back, didn't she?"

"Yes, she did. And I have you to thank for that."

"Don't thank me. Just don't mess this up," she says seriously.

"I promise, I'll do my best," I reply.

Liz nods and crosses her legs, her face all business now. "Why are we meeting, Mr. Thorpe?"

I clear my throat. "Miss Masters, I fear that I've failed you in our last few years together."

She arches an eyebrow.

"I've constantly minimized your talents and abilities. I won't be doing that anymore."

"Meaning what?"

"I realized I don't have a district manager. Seems to be why I'm always so busy as the CEO. Honestly, my people skills aren't wonderful and it's a true miracle that I've managed to get contracts."

"I see. I can start the hiring process and—"

"I'm offering you the job," I interrupt. "It comes with a large increase in wages, since you'll be salary. Of course, you may have to work a weekend a month or so, but You will have your own assistant and will be overseeing many of the contracts and large clients we've acquired. I will maintain a few, such as Sal, but I believe you're the perfect person for the job."

Her tablet falls off her lap as she gapes at me. "You're ... you're promoting me?"

"I am."

"Because I'm good at my job?"

"Because you've always done more than your job description and I'm wasting your talents. I won't tolerate keeping an ace in my hands when it can do more on the table." I fold my fingers together. "Are you up for the job?"

"Yes!" She beams. "Yes! Thank you!"

My cell phone rings as she bounces out my office, no doubt to give her boyfriend the good news. I stare at my phone for a long time, not expecting this call. "Ben?"

"Adrian, you picked up," he says, obviously surprised. "I um ... I don't want to be at camp anymore."

"What's wrong? Are kids being mean to you?" I demand.

"I miss home. There's only been two days, but I ... I miss mom." He says. "I'm all sunburned and I'm itchy all over. I miss my bed and Mom's cooking."

"Okay. Send me the address."

"Don't tell Mom right away, okay?" he asks. "You aren't talking to her, but ..."

"Well I have a surprise for you, kiddo."

"Really?"

"Yup. I'll be there soon."

".... Do you promise? Pinky swear promise?"

"Of course, Ben. If you want to come home, you're coming home." I swear. "And it's our secret ... until we see your Mom."

"Thanks, Adrian."

I grab my keys, stopping by Liz's desk on the way out. "I have to go. Can you handle the rest of the day?"

She nods. "Emergency?"

"Ben needs me. I'm on my way to pick him up."

She smirks. "You are so fucking whipped."

I lift my brows at her. "And I am still your boss."

Her expression sobers. "Of course, Mr. Thorpe. I can absolutely handle the rest of the day and anything that comes up."

It's an hour and a half drive to get Ben, but as soon as I pull up, he runs to the car. He hugs me tightly, his fingers knotting in my sides. I pat the top of his head. "What's up?"

He gets in the car and I join him. He swallows. "I miss home. I've wanted to come home since Monday. It's too long."

I hand him a pair of sunglasses I'd picked up on the way. "Well, I hope you don't mind some time with me. I'm thinking we get ice cream. We can play some games. We can-"

"Are you going to leave again?" he asks with a frown.

I sigh inwardly. Of course Ben isn't a kid who can be bought off. He won't forget. I shake my head slowly. "No. I'm not leaving again. I love your mom. I love you."

"And the baby."

"And the baby," I agree. "I love you all and I want to be with you. Is that okay?"

He considers that for a full half hour before finally nodding at me. "It's good. Mom's been sad."

"Has she?"

"Very sad. She tries not to let me see it. She stopped cooking. Didn't want to see Aunt Stacy very much."

"What about you?"

"I missed playing swords and video games with you," he says. "But if you leave again, I won't be nice."

"Of course not."

"I have to protect my mom from mean people. If you're mean, I'll fight you. I know lots of karate now."

"I bet you'd kick my ass," I say.

He points at me. "You get soap in your mouth for that."

"Let's not tell Mom." I wince at the idea of having soap in my mouth.

"Ice cream and skee ball." Ben barters. "Then I won't tell Mom."

"Deal. And you have to help me win her something from that claw machine. I've seen how good you are at it." He's scarily good.

And that's what we do. We get ice cream, spend two hours playing games together. Ben eagerly teaches me some of the new ones and we manage to get him in the top three on ski ball. We try to get Brooke a cute stuffed whale, but neither of us can manage to free it.

Ben huffs, then his face lightens with excitement. "I know what to do for Mom!"

"What?"

He leads me to a shop in town and he shows me a necklace. It's simple, with a sapphire set in diamonds. Ben points at it. "Mom looks at it whenever we come in here. Girls like jewelry, don't they?"

"They do." And I haven't properly lavished affection on my girlfriend. "Are you sure she'll like it?"

"Yeah. And we can get her daisies. She loves daisies. And …"

The list goes on. I buy the necklace, not hesitating even when I find out the price. Then we get her daisies, picking them from some yards and running before we can get caught. We get her a copy of her favorite movie, pick up a full dinner, some beer and soda, and finally, I buy a gift card to Sal's for both of them.

Ben stuffs it all in a gift bag, with the tissue paper on top. He holds the flowers carefully and adjusts the glitter hand cannons we got. I also manage to slip the man-eater video game into the bag for Ben because he deserves it.

When we pull into the house, I see her car, another car, and a few texts on my phone. She's worried about Ben, hasn't heard from him today, wants to know if I'm coming over.

I text her back, saying I'll be there soon, that I've been out of the office all day.

I take the flowers and leave the bag with Ben, then we get our cannons ready. He struggles to hold everything as he slowly unlocks the door. We sneak in and I hear Brooke talking to someone in the kitchen.

"Brooke!" I call.

"Adrian?" she shouts back, surprise in her voice.

When she rounds the corner, right before she can take us in, I yell "now!" and Ben pops his glitter cannon like I do. Brooke gasps and jumps. "What is ... Ben? Why aren't you at camp?"

He runs to her and hugs her tightly. Brooke looks up at me and I offer her the daisies as a brown-skinned woman comes out of the kitchen to look at us with a raised eyebrow.

"I didn't want to be there anymore, so I called Adrian," Ben says sheepishly. "You're busy and I didn't know if you'd come get me."

"Of course I would have," Brooke says. "Are you okay? You're all red and you have bites all over you!"

"Too much outside time." He wrinkles his nose. "Adrian and I got ice cream and played at the arcade. We couldn't win you a stuffed animal, so we got you presents instead."

Brooke shoots me a questioning stare and I shrug. "It was his idea."

She shakes her head and leads us into the kitchen as the woman looks me over. "Heartbreaker back for another round?"

"And you are?" I ask.

She crosses her arms on her chest, glaring at me. "The one who'll kick your ass if you hurt her again."

Brooke sighs. "Stacy—"

"I'm here to stay," I reply. "I'm not going to make the same mistake again."

"Yeah, well ... I have my eyes on you, old man."

"Fair enough." I offer her my hand. "Adrian."

"Oh I know." But she shakes my hand. "I'm Stacy, Brooke's best friend. Stand in daddy to that baby."

"Unnecessary, but appreciated." I say, trying to control my jealousy. "I'm not going anywhere."

She doesn't seem to buy it, but we turn our attention to Brooke as she pulls the gifts from the bag. She hands Ben the video game and he bounces on his toes. "No way! I wanted this one."

"Good. I figured you'd like getting to be a shark," I say with an easy grin.

Brooke sees the gift card, the food we got for dinner so she doesn't have to cook, her favorite movie, the root beer – which is her favorite – then finally the box with the jewelry. I scratch the back of my neck as her widens at me.

"For full disclosure, that wasn't my idea," I say.

Ben beams. "You always stare at it when we pass the store, Mommy."

She looks between us with misty eyes and opens it, putting a hand to her chest. "Oh my gosh."

Stacy grins and gives me a thumbs up. "About time you put your bank account to work."

"Stacy!" Brooke hisses. She fans her face. "Dinner and a movie and ... wow."

I walk over and kiss her softly, not caring if Ben sees, not caring if Stacy sees. She doesn't push me away either. She strokes through my hair. "Thank you, Adrian. This is wonderful."

"Had to make up for borrowing Ben." I wink.

My eyes lock with Stacy's as I clasp the necklace around Brooke's neck. She keeps giving me hesitant glances, like she doesn't want to like me, but when Ben makes a mess after dinner and I get up to help him clean it, I see her shoulders drop a little.

Ben and I play the video game while Stacy and Brooke chat outside. After Stacy leaves, Brooke comes in, sees that Ben's fading fast, and gets him through a shower. We cover him in anti-itch cream, which he constantly tries to rub on me too. I finally surrender my ankles, with plenty of bites from our Daisy adventure.

Then he's in bed and asleep after I read to him.

Brooke sits with me on the couch as I put the movie on. She leans against my side and I see her stroking the necklace.

"How am I doing at this whole boyfriend thing?" I ask.

She laughs. "Who would have known you'd be this good at it?"

I kiss her softly and rub down her back. "I'm going to keep getting better at it, Brooke. I'm not settling for 'good enough'. I'm going to earn you."

She kisses me softly, then again, and again. I draw back. "No way, kitten. We're watching this movie. We watched my favorite, we're watching your favorite. Then you can have me all to yourself."

"And you'll stay?"

"As long as you want me, I'm here," I assure.

Her eyes sparkle for me and she pounces. "We can watch the movie later."

She convinces me by feeding me kisses until we've exhausted ourselves and end up back on the couch. I sit there in my slacks as she wears my shirt. She rubs my chest as we watch her movie.

This is definitely the kind of life I can get used to.

I kiss the top of her head and hug her tightly.

"I love you, Adrian."

I shiver and squeeze her tighter. "I love you so much, Brooke."

"And you're not running away."

"Nope." I adjust her in my arms so I can kiss her. "I know where I want to be."

# Epilogue

### Brooke
*1.5 Years later*

Emily starts crying again and I hurry to get her before she can start screaming. Ben beats me, taking her hands. "Emmy, it's okay."

But she keeps crying. I pick her up and kiss Ben's head. "Thank you, Ben."

"Why's she upset?"

I adjust her and she paws at my shirt. "She's hungry."

"Oh. I can get the bottle." He runs to the kitchen, making her bottle like I taught him. We get her fed and bathed just as Adrian gets home. Ben runs to him. "Dad!"

It took him a year to start calling Adrian that, and Adrian lights up every time. He picks Ben up, spins him around and sets him down while rubbing his back. "I think you're getting too big for that."

"I'm going to be stronger than you soon!"

"Not too soon, I hope." Adrian ruffles his wild hair. "Tell me all about school."

While Ben talks his ear off, Adrian kisses my temple and rubs Emily's cheek. Once Ben gets to right now, Adrian nods. Adrian tells him all about his day, including me and I sigh. "It's been so much easier since we've merged and I can work from home."

"I'm glad." He rubs my shoulder. "Did Emily give you any trouble today?"

Emily fusses, as if she knows she's being talked about and pushes against me. She's been a daddy's girl since day one. She has his messy dark hair and my dark eyes. She reaches for him "Da!"

"Come here, princess." He lifts her up and helps her to stand on his lap. Ben watches anxiously, ready to catch her. "How was your day, huh? Drooling on everything? Yelling? Playing games with Ben?"

She babbles at him and he nods. "That's a ton to do. No wonder you're tired."

"She's getting fast," Ben says excitedly. "And she likes to play cars with me ... when she's not putting them in her mouth."

"Did you play Legos today?"

I fall for him all over again seeing him with our kids. And they're definitely *ours*. He's so patient with them, so good with all of us. I'm getting really close to believing he's not going anywhere.

Ben goes to play with his video game and Adrian kisses me fully, cupping my face between his hands and tangling his tongue with mine hungrily. "You're made of magic, Brooke. Handling the kids and work."

"It's a challenge sometimes," I admit.

"Well, you're only human," he teases. "Want me to order dinner?"

"And help with everything for her first birthday party. Are your parents coming?"

"Grandma Lydia?" Ben pops up. "And Grandpa George?"

"Yup." Adrian grins. "They wouldn't miss it for the world. Even with volcanos and dinosaurs, they'd be here."

Our parents became fast friends. They actually went on a cruise all together. Between all this relationship building, our businesses becoming one and expanding to the west coast, celebrating Liz's engagement and seeing Stacy with Logan, life has been wild. Not to mention having a baby who's eager to walk and be involved.

She's as ambitious as her father.

But even with all that going on, our life jumping forward at light speed, Adrian has never forgotten about me. He kisses me every single morning before he leaves. He comes home every night. We live in my house and makes sure to take plenty of pictures of us to decorate the house with. We have fun every weekend, sometimes at the house, sometimes off on adventures I never could have afforded alone.

He's made everything better. In ways I didn't expect. Ben is excelling in school like never before. He's confident and determined to be a good big brother. He wants to be an astronaut now and is committed to putting in the work to get there.

And I've never felt so loved. Adrian says it at least once a day, but he also shows it. Like right now, even while talking to Ben, he keeps touching me gently. He orders us dinner so I don't have to worry about cooking.

When Emily starts getting fussy, he changes her without any kind of worry or complaint. Once we put the kids to bed, Adrian joins me in the laundry room and nuzzles my neck. "Hi, beautiful."

"Ugh. I'm so frumpy." I motion to my oversized shirt and leggings.

"Sexiest woman I've ever seen." He swats my bottom. "Should I start doing that every time your ass distracts me."

I roll my eyes, but he turns on the radio and pulls me into the kitchen, dancing with me. "Emily's party is tomorrow, but I have a gift for you."

"Adrian, I don't need gifts. You already spoil me and our kids plenty."

"I'm competitive," he says simply. "I'm going to be the best man you've ever been with."

I roll my eyes and slide my arms around his neck. "You already are. I love you so much. Every day."

"One, I think we should get a pool. There's so much back yard and they'd love swimming," he says. "Two, let's do a check in."

"Adrian." I shake my head. "We don't need to check in."

"Please, humor me, kitten." He kisses the hollow under my ear, something that's not fair at all because he knows what it does to me, every time, without fail. "How are you with our relationship?"

"Happy," I breathe, continuing the slow dance with him. "So happy, Adrian. I love living together. You're such a good father, so supportive with them, so good with them. And you ... we're so good together."

"We haven't had a spat in a month."

"Well you learned where to put the diapers so, we're good there." He chuckles.

"And I learned it's better to talk to you about what I'm feeling instead of pushing it down and trying to stay happy." I meet his eyes.

"Never hide anything from me, Brooke. I want it all. All of you, forever."

"Forever, huh? I think that's a different negotiation, Mr. Thorpe."

"Well, it's kind of what I want to talk to you about." He slowly drops to his knee and I gasp, pressing my palm to my chest. "I love you, Brooke. I can't imagine not having you or our children in my life. You're the future I want, one who can love me, break me, rile me up, but is worth every hiccup. I want forever. Will you marry me?"

He opens the box, showing a sapphire ring set in a circle of diamonds. It matches the necklace he got me way back when. He swallows. "It's probably too soon, but I know what I want and I'm ambitious, can be impulsive ... I'm sure, Brooke. I want to be yours forever. I'll take your last name, I'll take anything you'll give."

I sink to my knees and swallow hard. "Yes, Adrian. No negotiation, just yes."

"No negotiation?" He shakes his head. "That's a first."

"I want you. Just you. Like this." I swallow. "Stop making me cry, damn it!"

He laughs and slides the ring onto my finger. He kisses me hungrily, soothing every fear, soothing every concern, all of it. Because we're good at this. I know we are. We can make it work.

"Forever means forever right? Not five years?"

"Until the day I die," he whispers, kissing my cheek. "I'm not Greg. I don't half-ass things. I know what I'm getting into. Don't forget how much of your prickly side I saw. I saw you angry, upset, happy, worried, pregnant, in labor. I'm here for it all."

A shiver teases my spine and I kiss him again. Confetti comes down over us and Adrian grins. "You don't think I did this without asking permission, did you?"

Ben comes over and hugs Adrian. I wrap my arms around them both. Adrian looks to Ben. "I have a question for you too, kiddo."

"What?" I ask at the same time Ben does.

"You don't have to say yes. But I know that Greg gave up custody. That means ..." he reaches into his pocket and pulls out a piece of paper. He unfolds it. "It means I can adopt you. If you want me to."

Ben looks at it my smile cramps my cheeks. "Do you know what that means, Ben?"

He shakes his head. "I don't need to be adopted. I'm not an orphan."

I expect Adrian to get frustrated, but he takes one of Ben's hands. "You know my parents? They adopted me when I was sixteen because my parents gave me up. Your mom never let you go. All this paper would do would mean that I'm your dad legally."

Ben's face is still screwed up. "But you're already my dad."

Adrian's face goes red and he hugs Ben tightly. "I know, Ben. I love you."

"I love you too." Ben squeezes him and I'm back to crying.

Knowing Adrian, he's already halfway to getting the paperwork done, because he wants to be Ben's dad in every way possible. By Emily's first birthday party, we have more to celebrate than ever. We announce the news to Stacy, Liz and my parents, with Ben keep flashing his copy of the adoption paper, as proud as Adrian is. Lydia and George soon arrive, and they are also elated when we share the news.

Adrian adjusts Emily in the harness that holds her to his big chest. He pinches her fat feet, making her squeal with joy. She kicks and he chuckles. "Are you ready for a sugar high, princess?"

"Cake!" Ben agrees. He bounces. "Emmy, we're going to have so many sweets and new toys to play with together."

She babbles back and Ben nods, like he understands every word. "I'm excited too."

This is happiness. Two healthy kids, a man who truly loves me, my entire family under one roof. I smile at Adrian and Stacy in conversation, both totally relaxed. My best friend and boyfriend are getting along. I'm truly contented. I can't ask for anything more.

Emily takes giant handfuls of cake and stuffs them in her mouth, then gets upset because she's sticky. After cleaning her up, I see Adrian talking to his mom as he drinks a beer with Ben tucked by his side. They have matching sunglasses and everything. My heart swoons, and I can't keep the smile from my face.

My dad rubs my shoulder, stealing my attention. "I know a thing or two, don't I, Princess?"

I smile. "You sure do. Thank you, Daddy."

He hugs me and steals my daughter. "And you're just pure sweetness, aren't you?"

Emily giggles and enjoys every second of the attention. I take her hand as her fingers wrap around one of mine. "She's going to be hopelessly spoiled."

"Loved," Dad corrects. "Just like you and Ben. And it's what you deserve."

He motions over to Adrian looking around and stealing some of Emily's cake for Ben. They treat it like it's top secret. I bite my lip. "I got really lucky, Dad. Who would have thought we'd work out?"

"That's life." He sets Emily in my arms. "Now go get your future husband."

I walk over to Adrian and kiss him full on the mouth, frosting and all. He beams at me, no trace of the grumpy workaholic I met way back when.

"How soon can we get married?" I whisper against his mouth.

"Um, if we elope or something, three days," he says softly.

"Not soon enough," I reply. "Because I need to call you my husband now."

He kisses me hungrily. Definitely none of that businessman always worried about perception, looks, or deals. Just the man I love giving me everything I've ever wanted and more. I can't wait for forever.

***

*Pssst* ... Do you enjoy reading full length novels? If yes, then I have some great *'insiders' info'* just for you, but keep this on the hush. This deal is only for readers who have at least read one of my books to the end, ok? Did you know you can have 8 full-length novels plus an extra steamy bonus story from IZZIE VEE[1], for just **$2.99** or *download it for free* if you are a Kindle Unlimited or Prime Member? This amazing deal is *over 2,100 pages*. Get this amazing deal below ^_^ ...

---

1. https://www.amazon.com/s?k=izzie+vee&i=digital-text&crid=31LQJTEQYT2EE&sprefix=izzie+vee%2Cdigital-text%2C121&ref=nb_sb_noss

[CLICK HERE TO GET THE DEAL](https://www.amazon.com/dp/B0B1YTNCKQ)
**A HOT, STEAMY COLLECTION OF AGE-GAP ROMANCE NOVELS.**
List of novels inside are:
Heating Up the Kitchen - a reverse harem romance
Just Can't Behave - a forbidden, age-gap romance
Protection Details - a bodyguard, forbidden, age-gap romance
Getting Through the Seasons - a stepbrother's best friend, enemies to lovers
Getting Through the Seasons 2
Getting Through the Seasons 3
A Dose of Sunshine - a rockstar, enemies to lovers romance
Mr. Grumpy's Fake Ex-wife - a boss, stalker, enemies to lovers romance

A Bonus Novella - My Roommate's Daddy - an instalove, OTT, age-gap romance
All are standalones, contain no cheating and have happy-ever-after endings ♡
Don't miss out on this fantastic offer, grab your copy today.
That's a completed 3 books series, 5 full length novels and a novella inside. **CLICK HERE**[4] to download and enjoy!
Let's connect.
Get this book for **FREE**[5] when you sign up for our newsletter.
WICKEDLY STEAMY & FILTHY!

[CLICK HERE TO GET FOR FREE](#)[7]

---

4. https://www.amazon.com/dp/B0B1YTNCKQ

5. https://dl.bookfunnel.com/c4j8urik87

6. https://dl.bookfunnel.com/c4j8urik87

7. https://dl.bookfunnel.com/c4j8urik87

## SAMPLE

I thought my big, over-protective stepbrother was the biggest prick ever,
Until Thanksgiving, when he brought home an even cockier devil, Sawyer,
A tattooed rebel with jawlines of steel and dark piercing eyes glinting with danger.
I can tell he's the type to fight in public brawls, someone who would protect me if I'm his,
But I'm not his type, I am too young, too inexperienced, no experience.
He has every intention of being the wicked menace to his best friend's little sister,
Hell-bent on driving me up the wall, taunting me, teasing me, torturing me, leaving me in puddles,
Yes, leaving me in puddles has become a sick little game to him,
Loving to watch me squirm in need,
Knowing damn well he'll never cross the forbidden line between us,
And my stepbrother will never let him either,
He knows Sawyer only uses shy, nerdy girls like me for a one-night stands, I know it too,
Then why do I get so weak to his tease, his touch,
I vow to myself that I will never give in to him,
My V-card will be given to a gentleman who deserves it, not a bad-ass bad boy like Sawyer,
But then I made a mistake, our lips touched ... **DOWNLOAD FOR FREE HERE**[8].

---

8. *https://dl.bookfunnel.com/c4j8urik87*

Made in United States
Orlando, FL
24 January 2023